Cantando
SINGING SOFTLY
Bajito

Cantando
SINGING SOFTLY
Bajito

A NOVEL BY
Carmen de Monteflores

spinsters | *aunt lute*

SAN FRANCISCO

Cover and Text Design: ~~~~~~~~~~ gn Studio
Cover Illustration: Debra DeBondt
Typesetting: Moire Martin and Comp-Type, Inc., Fort Bragg, CA
Production: Eileen Anderson   Laura Jiménez
               Martha Davis   Cindy Lamb
               Debra DeBondt   Aurora Levins Morales
               Ellen Doudna   Diana Vélez
               Rosana Francescato   Kathleen Wilkinson

This project was supported by a grant from the National Endowment for
the Arts.

This book was funded in part by the California Arts Council, a state
agency.

Printed in the U.S.A.

Library of Congress Cataloging-in-Publication Data
de Monteflores, Carmen
     Singing Softly = Cantando bajito/Carmen de Monteflores.
     First edition
     p.   cm.
     ISBN 0-933216-62-9
     1. Puerto Rico—United States—History—Fiction. I. Title.
II. Title: Cantando bajito
PS3563.05395S66   1989
813'.54—dc19   89-4125
                                                        CIP

Acknowledgements

To give thanks for the completion of this book is an overwhelming task. I feel deeply thankful for having had the opportunity to write it and know that many others who have as much need to speak and be heard and as much ability with words have not been as fortunate. Most of all this book is a tribute to them.

Without the presence in our community of people such as Sherry Thomas and Joan Pinkvoss, publishers of Spinsters/Aunt Lute, who have great vision, courage and commitment, and who are willing to take risks where mainstream publishers turn their backs, books such as the present one would not be possible. I am very indebted to them and their intelligent and hard-working staff: Debra DeBondt for wonderful photos, a well worked-out schedule and striking promotional materials; Martha Davis for her incredibly thorough and perceptive English copy-editing; Pam Wilson for a handsome cover design and a creative solution to the problem of a two-language title; Lorraine Grassano for bringing the manuscript to Joan and Sherry's attention; to Diana Vélez, Spanish copy-editor, for her language skills, her detailed editing and her support of Puerto Rican women writers; and to everyone at the press who has contributed their time and creativity to the production of this book.

To all of those who in significant, yet not always obvious ways, with generous spirit have helped me believe I could write; who nourished in me the notion that making art is one of the highest expressions of being and always a courageous act; seekers of meaning, companions in art: my thanks. To Dorothy Wall for a careful and enthusiastic reading of the early manuscript. To Aurora Levins Morales for proofreading the Spanish dialogue and for her interest in the book. To my Writer's Group: Sharon Aurora, Margot Geiger, Gail Golden, Ida VSW Red, and Kit Mellinger too, godmothers to this novel. To Jean Bolen and Betty Meador, guides of the soul. To my aunts for their reminiscences, for introducing me to literature, for their affection and most of all for being my models. To Fillo, for shared books and intellectual curiosity. To my children, with whom I have a "common language" of art: Nena, poet; Nino, songwriter; Philip, composer; María, writer and actor; Andrea, artist and writer; and Esther who is at this point pure creativity. To my father for paints, brushes, books, musicals and theater. To my mother for colors, flowers, movies and shells at the beach. And to both of them my special thanks for a garden to dream in.

And finally, to the four women who have shown me the way: to Susan Griffin, my teacher, for her wisdom, her sense of justice and integrity, her knowledge of the ways of the word, her warmth, generosity and sustaining support, as well as the challenges she presented me with: to look deeper into myself for the voices that needed to be heard, and to speak the truth. To Joan Pinkvoss, my editor and new friend, for excitement about the manuscript, her respectful yet precise comments; for her help in deepening my understanding of the book and its structure; for her politics, her fairness and her tireless efforts at finding solutions to complex problems. To Laurie, my life companion, who believes in me and believes in the magic of words; who inspires and nourishes me with her humor, her encouragement and her fierce loyalty; without whose intelligence the book would not have had a title and without whose love the book would not have had a soul. And to my grandmother, Provi, for her love of stories, her unwavering belief in learning, and for everything that this book means to me. With respect and gratitude.

Berkeley, California
February, 1989

To mami and abuelita:
here is a piece of the land we had lost,
and to Laurie,
who helps me discover where I belong.

BOOK ONE

□

☐ Bocarío. The house at the mouth of the river. Half-hidden behind bougainvillea and canarios. Like a secret; like conversations on the veranda whispered over the sewing and lemonade. Shaded by coconut palms, bearing the silence of the river that flows from inland, from the rain forest. But also at the mercy of the immense, as if it were an island. Feeling the inescapable force of the ocean, the pounding of the surf, the insistence of wind. Trying to create home, gentility. But when the rains come the horizon feels like absence and the damp heat becomes a prison.

I come upon it as though I were a spy. Few ever come here. Only those who know the way can approach it: ox-drawn carts with provisions, a figure alone on a horse, someone on foot seeking shelter.

I hear the house voices in the soft language of my childhood.

"¡Luisa!" I hear abuelita Pilar, my *grandmother*, calling. "¿Dónde ehtá esa muchacha?" *Where's that girl!*

Abuelita comes out on the veranda. Her white figure moving quickly to the wood railing. She leans forward to look towards the garden, then away towards the river. Soon she goes back inside calling a servant.

"¡Rosa! ¿Sabeh dónde ehtá Luisa? Hace rato que no la veo." *Rosa! Do you know where Luisa is! I haven't seen her for a while.*

Through the tall windows at the side of the house I see Pilar straining to find Luisa, but the old trees at the edge of the river block her view. She can see only the water between the tree trunks: dark, muddy, rushing towards the ocean.

Abuelita Pilar stands at the window silently, her serious eyes scanning the landscape. The mid-afternoon sun makes the trees very still. Their huge shadows extend halfway between the river and the house. Nothing moves except the river. Behind her, she hears at a distance the steady sound of the ocean.

She cannot stand there long. It is too quiet. The other children went to the village with a servant to get some fruit and candy. They seemed restless and bored, so she sent them on an errand. Luisa didn't get to go. She wasn't supposed to go out. She said she would rather stay with Pilar anyway, but Pilar didn't believe her this time.

"Eh tehtaruda," Pilar says to herself. *She's stubborn.*

Pilar worries about Luisa, her next-to-oldest daughter. She's afraid when Luisa walks on the beach by herself looking for shells and crabs. Often Pilar has to send someone out to look for her.

She hopes Luisa isn't out there now. Juan has forbidden her to go out of the house until he comes back from his trip. It's upsetting that Juan is often angry at Luisa. He thinks Luisa is not like his other daughters.

I see Pilar leave the window as I walk past the garden and through the tall grass towards the river.

I imagine myself here because I need to understand why I left the island. And why I didn't return.

I am old enough to be a grandmother. My own children have gone. Where I live now I am still learning the names of new plants. I want to have a garden there some day.

When I sit in my yard, as I used to at home, I look up at the sky and watch the tops of trees move as if I had come upon something I was seeing for the first time. I imagine Bocarío, the house between the river and the ocean, where abuelita Pilar lived as a woman of thirty-one, already with four children. I imagine a clearing next to the coconut palms, the house between sun and shade, a garden with roses, and beyond, the thick grass pushing its way everywhere that its roots feel the soft loam of the river's edge.

I find myself walking through the dense growth with some difficulty, but soon I am in the shadow of the big trees. The breeze mixes together the smell of river and ocean.

I walk slowly towards the water. Solemnly. Feeling silence and a rush of images all at once.

Suddenly I hear Pilar's voice calling again.

"¡Luisa!"

Then I notice an object moving fast down the river. I realize there is someone on it. The person is not on a boat. Maybe it is a log.

There is a child in a hollow tree trunk.

Other voices approach from the house. Pilar and other children and adults. They sound alarmed.

"¿Qué le habrá pasa'o?" someone says. *What happen to her!*

"¡Allí ehtá! ¡Mírala, agarrándose al tronco!" *There she is! Look at her! She's hanging on to the log!* one of the children screams.

"¡Luisa!" someone calls.

"¡Buhca a Santiago!" *Get Santiago!* Pilar says to one of the servants.

The servant returns quickly with a tall black man. He strips to the waist and dives into the water.

The child in the tree trunk is moving rapidly towards the mouth of the river where the ocean makes big whirlpools near the rocks.

Pilar calls out, "¡Esa nena ehtá loca! ¿Cómo puede haber hecho eso?" *That girl's crazy! How could she have done this!*

The children reach out with their bodies and their voices to the figure in the water.

"¡Avanza! ¡Apúrate, Santiago!" *Go ahead! Hurry up, Santiago!* they urge.

If the tree trunk hits the mouth of the river they will both be in danger of being smashed against the rocks.

Pilar stands at the edge of the water surrounded by two servants and several girl children, who call at first then stand quietly around their mother. She is immobile, only the lace around her neck quivers, like a white wing that needs to take flight. She is slender and tall, with an easy grace, like a palm. Her eyes are thoughtful, even in fear.

As Santiago approaches the fast-moving figure at the mouth of the river, Pilar reaches for a small hand at her side and holds tightly to it. Santiago grabs the child in the water. She resists at first, then she lets herself be carried towards the shore. Everyone watches silently while Santiago slowly steals the child from the current.

I can see the girl's eyes. They are like those of a wild creature that has been trapped. She keeps coughing and spitting water. When they reach the bank she can't stand up. Santiago picks her up and brings her to rest at Pilar's feet.

Pilar takes Luisa in her arms. She is a big girl, but her strong limbs yield to her mother's embrace. For a moment she seems like a child waking from a bad dream, needing soothing strokes on her forehead, kisses on her cheeks. But it's real, her hair is matted with mud and leaves and she has spit dripping out of her mouth. Pilar holds on to Luisa tightly and her white dress becomes streaked with the silt of the river and the drool from Luisa's mouth.

Santiago says, "Tie' que vomital el agua." *She got to throw up the water.*

He makes Luisa bend forward and slaps her back a few times until she vomits the water. The spit leaves wet spots on the ground.

"Vamoh a llevarla a la casa," Pilar says. *Let's take her to the house.*

Santiago picks up Luisa again and the whole group moves slowly towards the big house.

I stand next to the river looking up at the sky. There are a few bright clouds against deep blue. The voices fade.

The sun shines on the river. It is smooth and green now, as if nothing had happened. The light creates a kind of silence.

I walk along the bank of the river for a while. Towards the ocean. The tangled grass and the tree trunks carried to the shore by the current keep me from going further, so I walk around them until I reach the sand. I sit there for a while looking at the ocean waves. Feeling the wind. Then I lie down.

Pilar stood at the door of her room which opened to the veranda at the back of the house. She looked at the grey ocean and sky. At the dark pines outlining the shore. They seemed farther away today, like a picture she had seen somewhere.

She stood still in her white dress with the stains of silt from the river. The breeze moved a strand of black hair which had come loose from the bun at the back of her head. She leaned on the wood jamb.

Juan was gone again. Had been away for three months already.

She couldn't hold on to time. It slipped away. Into waiting; into being needed by the children.

Luisa. Luisa. Why did this have to happen? She should have known better. Fourteen already and still didn't have enough sense to stay out of the river.

Pilar sighed, wishing she could be fourteen again. Then she remembered Seña Alba. Pilar hadn't seen her since Elena's funeral, four months ago. The thought got caught in a tangle of memories. She felt as if she were holding her breath against pain.

Pilar pushed away the sad images. She only wanted to remember the happy times, when she used to go for walks with Seña Alba at the beach. Seña Alba told her stories. And she looked at everything. Pilar didn't know anyone else who looked at things like Seña Alba did. Natural things. She didn't waste too much time looking at man-made things. Thought they were mostly ugly. She liked to look at the ocean, the coconut trees, the moon, even the sugar cane fields.

Pilar didn't understand at first, way back before she even knew Juan, what there was to look at in a sugar cane field. It all looked the same to her. Acres and acres of it. Growing tall and the men sweating, cursing and singing while cutting it. Nothing to look at.

Now flowers, that was something else. Not the ones that grew in the fields, but the ones with many colors behind the fence of the mill owner's house. Who would have thought there were so many different kinds of pink and red?

Her oldest sister, Patria, didn't care much for flowers. Even made fun of Pilar about it. But Patria let Pilar come with her sometimes to look at the flowers near the patrón's house because Patria wanted to catch the eye of the stable boy. He was about Patria's age, brown like a coconut and with big muscles on his arms. Pilar got to look at the flowers while Patria looked at the boy.

Pilar promised herself then, when she was still very young, that if she ever could, she would have flowers like that. Even a few. She would save money. Didn't know how, but she would. Pilar made promises to herself. And she knew that when she promised something, she always kept her promise. She didn't even care if her sisters made fun of her about it.

Seña Alba didn't make fun of her. That's one of the first things Pilar noticed when she met her.

Patria got herself pregnant by the stable boy and was having a hard time of it. Everyone thought she was going to miscarry. And nobody was too sorry either.

"Tenemoh demasia' criaturah." *Too many children anyway,* Marta, Pilar's mother, said. "Y lo piol eh que no va habel quién se case con ella." *Worst part is nobody going to marry her.*

Patria was scared, and angry at the stable boy who wouldn't even talk to her after he found out she was pregnant. She started spotting and was sent to bed by her mother. Marta didn't want any more trouble. Had enough trouble herself having children.

Marta stood there with her brown hands on her hips. Her belly was round from many pregnancies and her breasts were low to her waist. She had suckled enough, she said. Each one had made her lose a tooth, so now she had to gum her chicharrón, the crisp *pork rind* that came from the pig cooked on a spit behind the village store. But, Marta said, it was God's will.

That was when Pilar was nine. She already knew that it was hard to figure out God's will even though everyone talked about it like it was simple and clear. Like the sun going up.

Pilar didn't tell anybody what she thought about it. And what she thought about a lot of other things. Not since that time when Marta hit her when she was six, the first time she could remember being slapped by her mother, because Pilar said it wasn't very good that God had sent a hurricane. That was the big one that had killed all the coffee plants, a lot of people and had wrecked people's homes.

Pilar cried herself to sleep holding her swollen face. After that night she didn't pray anymore, at least not to the God that made hurricanes. She thought there must be another God that made mangos and colors and that kept the people she loved from dying.

Standing at the door to the veranda, Pilar felt a sweet sadness coming into her. She remembered the first time she met Seña Alba. Had to thank Patria for that because if Patria hadn't been so sick she wouldn't have found Seña Alba.

Patria had been in bed for a few days spotting and crying. No one could help hearing her because it was a small house and Patria never hid her feelings. She was heard howling even a few houses down the muddy road. Neighbors would come in and ask about her. Bring a bunch of quenepas, or a mango.

Marta was worn out from looking after her other nine children and Pablo, Pilar's father, in a house with only three rooms. Made for mice, not people, she used to say.

One room was for Pablo, Marta and the smaller children. Another for the older girls: Patria, Asunción, Elena, Pilar and Azucena. Didn't make much sense to put the boys and the girls together, it always got them in trouble, Marta said. So the two older boys, Pepe and Quique, slept in the third room, which was also the living room, dining room and kitchen.

Everybody had been screaming at each other ever since Patria had to stay in bed, on one of several mats on the wooden floor.

It had been raining for days.

"Uno de loh pioleh. El agohto máh moja'o qu'e vihto en mi vi'a," Marta said. *One of the worst. Wettest August I seen in my life.*

Pilar thought they were always like this. But for Marta each one was the worst. Pilar thought maybe they piled up after you got older. Marta remembered the first time anything happened. And all the other times afterwards. And she was very good at remembering bad things like hurricanes, fires, deaths and difficult births.

"Nunca oí a naide grital tanto. Esa se va aboltal y se va moril de desangral si sigue llorando así," Marta said about Patria's crying.

I never hear nobody scream so much. That one's going to miscarry and bleed to death if she keep screaming.

A neighbor who was visiting, called Doña Bochinche by the children because she was the worst gossip in the village, asked why Marta didn't send for Seña Alba.

"¿Quién eh Seña Alba?" Marta asked. *Who's Seña Alba?*

"Una comadrona del Cebuco," Doña Bochinche said happily. She prided herself in knowing everything that happened in the village. "Salvó a la hija del patrón de un mal palto. Dicen pol ahí que la muchacha no salió encinta del mari'o sino de un negro[1] que era peón de la central, polque la criatura era prietesita y tenía el pelo malo." *A midwife from Cebuco. She save the patrón's daughter from a bad childbirth. They say the girl don't get pregnant by her husband. That she get the baby from a nigger that work at the sugar mill. Can tell. Child is sure dark and has kinky hair.*

She would have gone on but Marta interrupted her. She had already heard that story several times.

"Pero ¿y esa Seña Alba?" *But what about this Seña Alba?*

"Eh una negra bien prieta y jovencita, pero pa'ece que tie' unah manoh buenah. Dicen qu'eh bruja también." *Real black nigger and pretty young, but look like she's got good hands. They say she's a witch too.*

Marta crossed herself.

"¿Bruja? ¡Ay no, m'ija! Yo le tengo miedo a lah brujeríah. No quiero un nieto con seih dedoh en ca' mano y el labio palti'o." *A witch? Oh, no! I'm scared of spells. Don't want no grandchild with six fingers on each hand and a split lip.*

"¿Y dehde cuándo ehtáh tan blanquita?" Doña Bochinche said, putting her fists on her hips. "¿Prefiereh qu'ese dotol borrachón le meta lah manoh a Patria?" *You sure turning white. You rather the drunk doctor get his hands into Patria?*

She went on with a detailed description of what the white doctor would do to Patria with his hands. Pilar didn't want to hear so she went to stand by the back door. But the house was too small to get away. And it was raining outside.

Pilar sat in the rocking chair that faced the open door to the veranda, slowly unravelling her memories. The breeze from the ocean lulled her. Behind her closed eyes she could see the rows of flowers in the garden. A climbing rose, very pale like the inside of a shell. Hibiscus, hydrangea, geraniums. The tough native grass and the tangled mass of vines had to be pulled out first before the flowers could grow.

There were no flowers around the house where she grew up. There was only packed dirt. The house was up on stilts and the children played under it: dug holes with sticks and rolled small stones into them, threw clumps of dirt at each other and drew faces with charcoal bits on dried mango pits. There was a mango tree on one side and a breadfruit tree on the other, which most of the children learned to climb. Behind the house there were a few bushes and a huge field of sugar cane. A narrow dirt road passed in front of the house. In the rainy season it turned into mud which stuck to the feet. Along the road, there were other houses that the mill gave to the sugar cane cutters as part of their wages. The men walked down the road on their way to the fields or to the village to buy rum and bet on the cock fights. The women stayed home, for the most part. The children ran errands to the neighbors or to the village for the few provisions they could afford.

Pilar remembered the time her mother had been very sick. She had a bad infection. That was even before they knew about Seña Alba, and before Patria got pregnant.

They had to go a long way on the road to get the white doctor. Everybody always knew where to find him: sprawled out on a hammock between two palm trees in the back of his house. Drunk. His black woman fanning the flies off his face.

There was no one to go find him. Patria had disappeared and Pablo didn't like to be bothered with women's sickness. Besides, they weren't supposed to go get Pablo when he was in the middle of cutting the cane. And Asunción, she was next to oldest, said, "Yo no me siento bien tampoco. Elena, vete tú con Pilar a buhcal al dotol." *I don't feel good neither. Elena, you go find the doctor with Pilar.*

It didn't surprise Pilar. Asunción never wanted to do anything that was work.

Elena was the third oldest. Pilar always thought she was going to be blown away by the wind, but at least she wanted to help. She took Pilar by the hand. Wasn't more than a year older than Pilar.

Tito wanted to come along too. He was the youngest of the boys, five or six at the time. Always wanted to be older.

"Yo lah cuido," he said. *I look after you.*

Asunción laughed at him.

"Mira'l mocoso. Ya se cree qu'eh hombre." *Snot-nose kid. Think he's a man.*

They found the doctor asleep in his hammock. Pilar had never been that close to someone who was drunk. Smelled of rum. "Graciah a Dioh que Pablo no bebe." *Thank God Pablo don't drink,* Marta said often.

The doctor's woman looked at them.

"¿Qué quieren?" *What you want?*

"Mi mamá s'ehtá muriendo." *Mamá's dying,* Pilar blurted out.

The doctor opened his bloodshot eyes.

Pilar knew that look. It didn't matter whether she was alone or with her mother and sisters. There was no stopping that look. It got under her clothes.

Pilar was scared. She was glad Elena and Tito were there, even though Elena looked like she was going to faint, and Tito had hidden behind Pilar.

The black woman didn't look friendly.

"Mi mamá s'ehtá muriendo." *Mamá's dying,* Pilar repeated. She was so scared! But she had to make sure he heard.

The doctor's smile was wet with drool. He pushed himself upright. Pilar moved back. She was sure he was going to fall down on them.

"¡Negra, tráime un vaso de agua!" he shouted. *Nigger woman! Bring me a glass of water!*

When she left, he reached for Pilar's hand.

"¿Qué me das si vengo?" he said. *What will you give me if I come?*

She stood very still.

"No tenemoh dinero," she answered. *We don't have money.*

"Eso no es lo que quiero de tí, niña," he said. *That's not what I want from you, girl.*

Pilar was terrified.

"¡Cállate!" Marta finally said to Doña Bochinche. "Ehtah mucha-chah van a oil to'." *Shut up! These girls going to hear everything.*

"Patria ya sabe de to' eso, sin que tú se lo digah," Doña Bochinche laughed maliciously. "El negrito del ehtablo ya le metió la mano." *Patria already know about all that without your telling her. The black kid at that stable done it to her already.*

"¡Yo no sé como te aguanto! ¡Bochinchera!" *Don't know how I put up with you! Old gossip!*

Underneath her anger Marta felt ashamed. She turned away, towards the bucket where she washed dishes.

Pilar went to her mother and put her arm around her. Doña Bochinche laughed loudly and Patria screamed in the next room.

"Manda buhcal a Seña Alba, mamá. Patria ehtá bien mala. Yo no quiero que se muera." *Send for Seña Alba, mamá. Patria's very sick. I don't want her to die.*

Pilar had tears in her eyes. Marta softened a little when she saw Pilar's face. She sat down on the bench by the kitchen table holding her head.

"Eh la volunta' de Dioh." *It's God's will,* Marta muttered.

Doña Bochinche laughed and Patria sobbed.

"Llama a Seña Alba, mamá," Pilar insisted. *Call Seña Alba, mamá.*

"Deja que le hable a Pablo cuando él venga," Marta said. *I talk to Pablo when he come home.*

Doña Bochinche laughed even more loudly.

"Ese pendejo nunca decide na'. Tú sabeh quien tie' loh pantaloneh en ehta familia." *That asshole never decide anything. You know who got the pants in this family.*

Marta started crying.

Pilar couldn't contain herself.

"¡No le hableh así a mamá! ¡Sal de aquí, vieja bochinchera!" *Don't talk that way to mamá! Get out of here, you old gossip!* she screamed at Doña Bochinche.

The younger children were watching from the doorway of Marta's room.

"¡Sálte de aquí!" *Get out!* Pilar screamed again, getting closer to Doña Bochinche, who seemed a little startled.

Doña Bochinche stood up.

"Ni le hah enseña'o rehpeto a ehtah criaturah, Marta. Ehta

Pilar eh una fiera. No sé a quien ha salí'o. Dioh sabe con quien t'embarrahte pa' sacal ehte animal." *You don't even teach respect to these children, Marta. This Pilar, she's wild. Don't know who she take after. God only know who knocked you up with this animal.*

She laughed and left, walking barefooted in the mud. Marta was still crying.

Pilar hugged her mother.

"Llama a Seña Alba," she kept repeating. *Call Seña Alba.*

"¡Barlovento! ¡Barlovento!
¡Amarra el perro
y suelta el viento!"
Barlovento! Barlovento!
Tie the dog
and let the wind loose!

I hear the call to the wind abuelita taught me. It comes up in me suddenly, loosening memories. Language of the soul.

Wind of the islands. Rain season. Hurricane season.

A tree trunk rolls down the wet sand. And back up. And down. I sit near the water looking for shells.

When I was young and abuelita called me Meli, I tore my shirt climbing trees reaching for a mango, or looking for a kite tangled in the branches. I crawled behind bushes and put dirt in my mouth; caught a ray of sun in a mirror; opened my eyes underwater; and went to sleep watching the moon on the coconut palms. I was afraid of spiders, salamanders and the black moth which announced when somebody was going to die.

Meli, this child in me, guides me back to abuelita, to the heartsounds of my past which dwell in exile, my body still longing for the color of an afternoon near the sea. Meli speaks to me with images, stories, memories. We go to places and times I had almost forgotten. She loves to see new things. I still dwell on old ones.

"Vamoh a la casa. Va a llover." *Let's go to the house. It's going to rain,* I hear Meli say, putting her hand in mine.

When I take Meli's hand, I walk into a world made real by longing. With her I recreate my closeness to abuelita. My veined hand becomes hers; Meli's small one is my own, reaching across time to hold, recognize, find home.

She leads me back up the beach path to the house. The door to the veranda is open. Through it I can see Pilar sitting on a rocking chair looking at the ocean.

Pilar wished she could talk to Seña Alba about what had happened that day; about Luisa being dragged out of the river. Images of the near-drowning kept repeating themselves in Pilar's head.

She hated to admit it because she was still angry, but she missed Seña Alba.

Seña Alba usually squatted by the door with the shutters that opened to the veranda. She never liked to sit on chairs. And they always talked in Pilar's room. The servants and the children were too curious. Didn't leave them alone. They wanted to hear Seña Alba tell stories.

That day Pilar felt a deep longing for her. She was the only person Pilar ever talked to about anything that was important to her. Pilar talked to her even now, when Seña Alba wasn't there. Pilar had fallen into the habit of doing that in the past months when she felt lonely.

"¿Le vah a contal a Juan que Luisa se metió en el río?" *You going to tell Juan that Luisa got into the river?* Pilar heard Seña Alba ask.

Pilar shook her head and looked away.

"L'ehtáh tan agradecí'a a Juan pol dalte ehta casa que no le pue'h hablal de ná'," Seña Alba said. *You so grateful to Juan for this house you can't talk to him about anything.*

Pilar defended him.

"Eh bueno, pero eh hombre y loh hombreh tienen ideah fijah sobre lah mujereh. No se leh puede hablar de algunah cosah." *He's good but he's a man, and men have fixed ideas about women. There are things you can't talk to them about,* Pilar said.

Seña Alba ignored her and went on.

"No le pue'h decil qu'ehtáh trihte siempre qu'él no ehtá aquí. Y qu'ehtáh trihte polque tie' otrah mujereh." *You can't tell him you're always sad when he's not here. And that you're sad because he has other women.*

Seña Alba was the only person who dared talk to Pilar about Juan's other women.

"Tú sabeh que a mí no me guhta hablar d'eso," Pilar said. *You know I don't like to talk about that.*

"Pol eso te lo digo. Pa' que no vivah en lah nubeh. Ehto te come pol dentro m'ija. Ca' veh que vengo t'encuentro sentá' aquí mirando al mal. Ehperándolo," Seña Alba insisted. *That's why I tell you. Don't want you to live in the clouds. Eats you up, child. Each time I come, I find you sitting there looking at the sea. Waiting for him.*

"No eh verdad," Pilar protested. "Cuando tú vieneh eh que me siento. No sé qué eh lo que me tiene tan ocupada. Loh maloh ratoh," she added. "El suhto que me dió Luisa ehta tarde cuando la encontramoh flotando en camino al mar." *It's not true. I get to sit down when you come. Don't know what keeps me so busy. All these troubles. The scare Luisa gave me this afternoon when we found her floating towards the ocean.*

"Eh como tú. Me acueldo del día que m'encontrahte en la playa." *She's like you. Reminds me of the day you find me at the beach.*

In her mind Pilar could see Seña Alba's eyes. They were bright. Almost tearful. Pilar turned away from the image.

She caught a glimpse of her own black laced shoes. Remembered Seña Alba's bare feet on the varnished wood of the floor.

She looked around her room: at the embroidered bedspread, the four-poster bed, the chests of drawers. The big mirror. Things Juan had brought for her.

Pilar thought of Seña Alba who had so little. Of Marta and Pablo, and of Patria, who had seven children already from different men. The last one beat her. Pilar had to send for Candelario to throw Patria's man out. Candelario was a giant of a black man. He was the man cutters bet on when they wrestled behind the mill.

Patria had screamed at Pilar that time. Called her names. Pilar had no right to get rid of her man. None of her business if he drank a little.

Patria sobbed daily and her bleeding got worse that first time she was pregnant. Pilar had asked her mother for several days to send for Seña Alba. Had asked her father too. But Pablo said it was up to Marta.

"Esas son cosas de mujeres. Yo no sé de eso," he said. *Those are women's things. None of my business.*

They kept having to wash rags to put between Patria's legs. They hardly got dry in the rainy, damp weather before they had to be pulled down from the line near the open coals.

The house was damp, hot and somehow full of tears, Pilar thought. Like the whole world was crying and everything was damp with tears.

Pilar couldn't stand it anymore. After about the fourth day of begging her mother to call Seña Alba, there was a short break in the rain. Pilar went to a neighbor, Tía Micaela. She always helped when there was trouble at the house.

Pilar asked her whether she knew Seña Alba, and would she know where to find the midwife.

"Sí, oigo hablal d'ella. Dicen qu'eh bruja. Pero la gente la reh-peta también. Hahta loh blancoh. Naide sabe dónde vive. La ven caminal pol la playa. Yo voy a il al pueblo mañana y pue'o pregun-tal pol ella, m'ija. Y mira, dále ese coco a tu mamá. Díle que le dé la leche a Patria." *Yes, I hear people talk about her. They say she's a witch. But people respect her. Even whites. Nobody know where she live. They see her walking at the beach. I'm going to the village tomorrow and I ask about her. And give your mother this coconut. Tell her to give Patria the milk.*

"Graciah, Tía Micaela. Un día te voy a hacel un favol," Pilar called out as she ran happily out the door. "Y no le digah na' a mamá." *Thanks, Tía Micaela. Some day I do you a favor. And don't say anything to mamá.*

Tía Micaela tried to find Seña Alba. Pilar waited for days, but when it got to be a week Pilar knew she had to do something. She woke up many times in the night and listened to Patria's breathing. She was afraid Patria was going to die.

Pilar knew she had to get out of the house, rain or no rain, and find Seña Alba. It didn't matter that she didn't know where to look. And it didn't matter that she wasn't supposed to go places by herself.

She went out early, after Pablo had left for the sugar cane fields and her mother was busy washing clothes over a bucket. She was scared. She had never done this. Never gone very far from the house by herself. Didn't say anything to the other children either. Didn't want them to talk. She figured they would be busy. Pilar spent a lot of time by herself anyway, on the back steps under the roof overhang. It was a little damp there but she could sit, talk to herself and get away from the screaming in the house. So maybe they wouldn't miss her.

She made up her mind she would try to go to the beach, but not on the muddy road where she could be seen. She thought it would be better to cut through the bushes and go around the sugar cane fields.

Pilar had been walking for a while when she heard men's voices. She lay down under some branches until they walked by. Thought they were going to hear her heart pounding against the wet ground. She was so scared. And her dress got all muddy. But she figured the rain would wash the mud away.

It was kind of pretty when she forgot to be scared. Sugar cane branches dripping with rain and little rivers everywhere on the red clay. The rain felt good on her hot face and her scratched arms.

There were some houses ahead, near the beach. On high stilts. With palm fronds for roofs. They must leak, she thought. At least her house had a zinc roof and it was pretty dry inside. She had heard that those palm roofs had bugs in them too. She didn't like alacranes. Pilar was scared again. She began looking everywhere near her bare feet for the *scorpions*. Maybe they didn't come out when it was raining so hard. The good thing about rain was nobody was out except the men cutting the cane, but she wasn't going to walk near the places they were cutting.

Maybe Seña Alba wasn't out either. But something told Pilar Seña Alba liked being alone too. Must be why she didn't tell anybody where she lived. Pilar liked that. She liked this Seña Alba already. She seemed to know things.

Pilar watched the houses for a while from the edge of the sugar cane field. She made sure there was no one coming out. She was afraid someone would see her when she walked under the coconut trees on the bare sandy dirt near the beach. There were few bushes.

She waited until the rain came down heaviest. Felt as if it would hide her somehow. Then she ran from one palm trunk to another, hiding behind each one. As far away from the houses as she could, until she got to the edge of the beach where the uva de playa, the *beach grape* bushes were. She could lie behind them.

From there she could look over the beach. It was rocky, with big white splashes of surf. A little scary. She remembered all the drownings there that summer.

"Mucho piol que otroh añoh," Marta said. *Worse than other years.*

Young boys dared each other to climb on the slippery rocks. Some of them didn't make it.

Pilar was glad she didn't have to climb on the rocks. There was a strip of sand between the bushes and the rocks she could walk on. And if she had to climb over the rocks, she would stay as far away as possible from the edge of the ocean.

There were no fishermen there that day. She thanked the rain for keeping everyone away. But what if Seña Alba wasn't there either?

At least she was far enough away from the houses so nobody could see her. It was scary to be so alone, though, with the big sound of the ocean.

Scary and happy at the same time. Pilar remembered the feeling of that day. She wanted to recapture it. Being away from the four walls of her parents' house, away from Patria's crying, away from Marta's complaints, away from all the voices of all the children in the house, away from the smell of food and sweat and blood.

There was something about getting away from the house and being out there at the ocean. Pilar hadn't had a name for it. Whatever it was it had made her fear go away. Standing between the grey sky and the roaring ocean. Soaking from the rain. Alone.

"¡Mamá!" She heard Luisa's voice. It pulled Pilar out of her memories. But Pilar didn't want to tear herself away from those images yet.

"¡Mamá!" Luisa was knocking at the hallway door insistently.

"Un momento. Voy enseguida." *Just a moment! I'm coming,* Pilar called out.

She was almost resentful of the interruption. She sighed and looked again at the ocean before getting up from her rocking chair and walking to the bedroom door. She remembered that there were no doors in her mother's house.

She opened the door to Luisa, who looked awkward in her dress. Luisa's hair was short and, Pilar noticed, not combed well enough.

"Dime," Pilar said. *What is it?*

She wasn't sure whether Luisa was embarrassed or angry.

"Perdona que te diera un mal rato," Luisa said, looking down. *I'm sorry I gave you a scare.*

Pilar smoothed out the hair on her daughter's forehead.

"¿Ehtáh bien?" *Do you feel all right?*

Luisa moved away slightly. She stood uneasily. This happened often between them now. Luisa didn't seem to want to be touched by Pilar.

Pilar pulled her hand away.

"Sí," Luisa said. "Ehtoy bien." *Yes, I'm fine.*

"Me dihte un suhto," Pilar said. *You really scared me.*

"Perdóname." *Forgive me,* Luisa said, looking away.

"Ehtáh perdonada. Pero, no lo hagah denuevo. Y no le voy a decir nada a Juan." *You're forgiven, but don't do it again. And I won't say anything to Juan.*

Luisa smiled gratefully but uneasily.

Pilar wanted to ask what was the matter but she knew it was no use. It never worked. Luisa would say nothing and that would be the end of that. She would come around and be close when she was ready to.

Pilar was upset. She didn't understand Luisa's silent stubbornness. And she was afraid that some day Luisa would be hurt by it.

"Me voy a ir a coser. Le dije a Mercedes que la iba a ayudar." *I'm going to sew. I told Mercedes I would help her,* Luisa said quickly and left.

Pilar was sure that Mercedes, Luisa's oldest sister, had told Luisa to come and apologize to Pilar. Luisa wouldn't have done it all by herself. She would have felt bad but wouldn't have said anything.

"¿Porqué eh así conmigo esa criatura? ¿Porqué? ¿Porqué?" Pilar kept asking herself. *Why is this child like that with me? Why? Why?*

Pilar felt that Luisa pushed her away with her stubbornness. Her head began to hurt as she sat again by the open door to the veranda. Slowly she slipped back into the past.

Suddenly Pilar felt someone's presence. That's how she always remembered it. She was at the beach and all of a sudden she was not alone. She turned around to look and there was a very black woman behind her, smaller than herself, in dark clothes which stuck to her thin body in the rain. Like a wet lagartijo, *a tree lizard.* Most of all Pilar noticed her eyes. They didn't miss anything. They got way inside you. Made her feel safe.

Pilar knew instantly that it was Seña Alba.

"¿M'ehtáh buhcando?" Seña Alba asked. *You looking for me?*

"¿Cómo lo sabíah?" Pilar asked. *How you know?*

"Nadie anda pol ahí en un día así sin necesida'. Y nunca m'encuentro niñah caminando solah pol la playa. Ademáh que me dijeron que tu helmana ehtaba enfelma," Seña Alba responded. *Nobody's out on a day like this when they don't have to. And I never find girls out at the beach by themselves. Besides, somebody say your sister's sick.*

Pilar kept being more and more surprised at how much Seña Alba knew.

"Ereh bien brava de salil pa' fuera hoy. Debeh querel mucho a tu helmana," Seña Alba added. *You're very brave to go out today. I guess you love your sister a lot.*

Pilar's eyes were tearful. Seña Alba didn't laugh at her and didn't scold her.

"Vine pol mi mamá," she blurted out. "Ella ehtá cansá' de cuidal a Patria. Yo quería ayuda'la." *I came because of mamá. She's tired of looking after Patria. I wanted to help her.*

"Ehtá bien. Yo vengo a tu casa," Seña Alba said. *That's good. I come to your house.*

She took Pilar's hand and they walked along the ocean in the rain on the way back to Marta's house.

On her way home Pilar wanted to run and walk slowly. All at once. She was afraid her mother would be angry, but most of all she was happy that Marta wouldn't have to worry about Patria anymore.

Seña Alba walked up the front steps first. She stopped at the threshold to wipe the mud off her feet with the rags Marta always left there. Then she went in.

Pilar sat at the top of the steps wiping her feet too. She took a little longer than she needed. She didn't want to face her mother because she had gone out without permission. But out of the corner of her eye she was watching Seña Alba.

"Yo soy Alba. ¿Dónde ehtá la enfelma?" she said without explaining anything. *I'm Alba. Where's the sick woman?*

Marta looked up from her washing bucket. She seemed startled at first but then her face brightened. Without responding to Seña Alba, she moved quickly to the door of the room where Patria was lying.

"¡Patria! ¡Patria! ¡Ehto eh un milagro! ¡Dioh noh oyó! ¡Noh ha manda'o la comadrona!" she said. *Patria! Patria! It's a miracle! God hear us! He send us the midwife!*

Marta was practically shaking Patria who after many days of crying and bleeding had become pale and weak.

Pilar walked in and stood in the middle of the room near Seña Alba. She was glad that her mother thought God made Seña Alba come. And she hoped Marta would forget Pilar's part in this.

But a deeper feeling grew in her. Pilar was disappointed that she had to come back to the house.

The breeze from the ocean made Pilar long to be out there at the beach holding Seña Alba's hand and not being afraid of anything.

From her bedroom at Bocarío, Pilar could see the neat gravel path to the beach. The grass grew thick around it. Underneath the grass the ground was red clay. Pilar hated it. When she was a child it would stick to her feet in big clumps. She didn't have shoes she could take off and leave outside the door. She had to sit down, in the rain, and scrape the mud off on the wooden steps. Scrape it off real well, then wipe what was left with a rag. Her mother would see her footprints on the floor if she didn't.

"Vamoh a sel negroh limpioh aunque seamoh pobreh," Marta used to say. *We going to be clean black folks. No matter if we're poor!*

For a moment Pilar hated herself. Hated having to be in this house. Having to wait. She felt as if she couldn't breathe. She had to get up and open the door to the veranda wider.

Something tough in her ripped open. An old scar opened up. Pilar saw her mother caught in an unmoving gesture, bent over the bucket, washing clothes. Pilar felt trapped in her black laced shoes.

Seña Alba cured Patria.

Pilar remembered how Seña Alba had looked Patria over, burnt herbs, pressed her belly in a couple of places and given her a remedio, a *remedy.* All the children, including Pilar, stood by the door watching. Marta kept telling them to go do something in the other room. They moved back a little but didn't really leave. Marta was too relieved and too curious herself to remember the children. A great weight had been taken off her.

"Esa negra sabe lo qu'ehtá haciendo," Pilar overheard her telling Pablo later. *That nigger woman know what she doing.*

Pablo sat on the front steps with his straw hat shading his lined face. His chest and arms were so brown Pilar often forgot he was white. He spit tobacco on the dirt and shook his head.

"Cosas de mujeres." *Women's things,* he said.

Pilar knew that Pablo didn't want to hear any more when he said that. She also knew that it made Marta feel bad. Women's things was bleeding and crying.

When Marta had Patria, Pablo just sat there, like that, chewing his tobacco while Marta screamed. Didn't even go for a neighbor, Marta said.

Later, someone going down the road turned up when he heard the screams. Pablo told him, "Las mujeres son como los animales. Ya saben lo que tienen que hacer para parir." *Women are like animals. They know already what they need to do to have children.*

Except that Marta had never done it before. That's what she told Pilar one time. Patria had been her first. Marta said she felt like she was getting cut up with knives inside. It was a good thing she remembered the story the white priest had told about Eve. That Eve had to suffer in childbirth because of her sin, and that's why women were supposed to have pain. It was a good thing she remembered, she told Pilar. Made the pain easier when she knew there was a reason for it.

She had told that story to her daughters many times. About Eve. Marta wanted them to know what it was all about, the pain of childbirth. She wanted to make it easier for them too.

When Pilar was a child she didn't understand why it had to hurt so much. Having babies. Eve didn't seem to have done anything so bad.

She asked Seña Alba about it one time they walked at the beach.

Seña Alba didn't have much to say. She didn't meddle with white people's stories. She said some women have pain. Others don't. Had to do with how strong they were and how much they wanted the child.

"¿Y pa' qué son esah yerbah que quemahte?" Pilar asked. *And what are the herbs for? The ones you burn?*

She could ask Seña Alba questions because Seña Alba was not like Marta. She never said you're not supposed to ask that.

But sometimes Seña Alba didn't answer. She told a little story instead.

"¿Tú sabeh cómo lah pájarah no quieren a suh hijitoh dehpuéh que alguien loh toca?" *You know how birds don't want their babies anymore after someone touches them?*

Pilar hadn't really noticed. She never took nests down from trees and she didn't let the other children do it either. If she saw them. Didn't feel right.

Pilar just nodded at Seña Alba.

"Pa'ece que creen que ya no son suyoh. Huelen diferenteh. Yo creo qu'eh igual con la gente. Huelen diferenteh polque viven en casah. La tierra no loh conoce. Como si fueran ehtrañoh. Ella no loh ayuda. Y la gente se ha olvida'o de la tierra también." *Seem to think they don't belong to them anymore. Smell different. It's the same with people. They smell different from living in houses. The ground don't know them. Like they are strangers. She don't help them. And people forget the ground too.*

Pilar remembered when she was lying on the muddy ground in the rain when she was looking for Seña Alba. She thought she had heard her own heartbeat but maybe it was the heartbeat of the ground she heard. She decided she was going to listen to things more. She wondered whether trees had heartbeats too.

Pilar had never thought of the ground that way. Like it was a person. It was just something you walked on to get somewhere. Mostly it was very hard and you rolled round stones on it, or it was muddy. She had always liked trees though. To climb on, hang from, hide in and sit under in the shade when it was hot. And they had nice shapes. Besides, some trees had fruit. Like mangos. Everybody knew Pilar was crazy about mangos. It was the only thing she had ever stolen. But she didn't like to think about that. She didn't want to feel bad about it.

"Lah yelbah que quemo cuando alguien va paril," Seña Alba said, "son pa' hacel que lah mujereh huelan como la tierra. Entonceh ella lah cuida. Ella leh hace el palto máh fácil." *The herbs I burn when somebody going to have a baby is to make women smell like the ground. Then she help them. She make childbirth easier.*

Pilar remembered the smell of those herbs filling up the small room where Patria lay. A smell which got mixed with the smell of sweat, blood, wood fire, mold and earth. For a while, after Seña Alba first came, the house smelled of the fields and the trees. But it was soon gone. For years after that Pilar tried to scrub off the smells of Marta's house with Castile soap, powder and perfume.

When she remembered the perfume Juan had brought her, Pilar thought of their first house. In the hills. You could hardly see it behind the trees. That's all there was, the house, the trees and a little patch of ocean you could see at a great distance. The path wound around the hill just wide enough for a horse. And you found the house suddenly, at the turn of the path, like somebody put it there just for you. It was painted white inside and out, and the floors were so shiny you didn't want to walk on them. It wasn't big either. It just fit the two of them. For a while. Until Fernanda came to help out. But that was later.

There was so much she hadn't known when Juan took her there. Their first house. Both of them on his horse. His hard and clean body. Cool almost. Not like anything she had felt before. The closest thing she could think of was a smooth coconut palm. Going on his horse as fast as a bird flying. She was afraid to fall any minute and had to hang on to him tight.

She was shy at first. Hadn't known much about clothes and soaps. She hadn't known about furniture either. Except at church and at the Fiehta de Cruh, the *Feast of the Cross*, at Doña Teresa's, that first time she had been with Juan.

Marta had been suspicious of Juan from the beginning. And Seña Alba too. Seña Alba thought Juan was going to take advantage of Pilar. But Pilar didn't need to be reminded of what had happened to Patria. She wasn't going to be like that. No matter what. Besides, Juan was not like the other men who looked her over when she went to the village store.

Men at the village stared at Pilar, but not Juan. He worked at the store for his uncle. He ran things. His family owned all the businesses in the village.

Pilar was very shy when he was there. He treated her like a lady. Marta too. Juan told his clerk to give them extra portions of things. She remembered the time he tried to give them some material for dresses, and how angry Pablo had been.

Pilar was soothed by the movement of the rocking chair. There was an empty feeling in her belly when Juan was gone.

It was beginning to get dark. There was only a narrow band of light low in the sky. The ocean felt alive. Breathing.

She had been shy with Juan. And he had become more formal in the sixteen years they had been together.

"Juntoh y separadoh," Pilar thought. "Juntoh y separadoh. Nunca completamente juntoh." *Together and separate. Together and separate. Never completely together.*

Everyone thought she was beautiful, Pilar remembered.

Except Marta. She said Pilar thought too much and it did something to her face. Couldn't really say what. Made her too pale maybe, or too serious. No man was going to bother with a girl that sat around thinking all the time.

Pilar had overheard her mother say to Tía Micaela that Asunción was the real beauty in the family. Didn't think much of Patria's looks.

"Demasia'o prieta," she said of Patria. *Too dark.*

"Asunción eh colol café. Pilar eh demasia'o pálida. Salió al pai," Marta had said. *Asunción is coffee-colored. Pilar is too pale. Takes after her pa.*

Pilar would put mud on her face to make herself darker. Wanted to be the same color as her mother, or like Asunción. Café con leche. Like *coffee with milk.* Pilar knew that Marta thought that was the right color to be although she didn't say it out loud where the children could hear.

Pilar had been skinny and pale in spite of Marta's efforts to fatten her up. Until she was about twelve. It was about time she started bleeding, Marta said. Was getting worried. Not that it was so good to get pregnant, but who's going to want a girl that don't bleed?

Pilar didn't really want it. It was a lot of trouble. And smelled. She even said that to Seña Alba.

"Esa sangre huele mal." *That blood smell bad.*

Seña Alba said, "No hay animaleh ni matah que huelen mal. Bueno, a veceh huelen mal pa' protejelse. No, m'ija eh la gente que apehta polque siempre s'ehtán cubriendo. El cuelpo tie' que tenel aire." *There's no animal or plant that smell bad. Well, sometimes they smell bad to protect themselves. No, child, it's people that stink because they cover themselves all the time. Body need air.*

Then she laughed. "¿Tú sabeh una cosa? En lah casah de loh ricoh hay un cualto pa' hacel caca y pa' lavalse. ¡Ay! yo no sé polque tien' que cagal en la casa. Pol eso eh que deben tenel que lavalse tanto. La pehte de la caca se leh pega." *You know some-thing! Rich folks have a room in their houses to shit in and to wash. Lord! Don't know why they have to shit in the house. Must be why they have to wash so much. Smell of shit must stick to them.*

I smile remembering the stories of Seña Alba abuelita told me. As if watching a film, I see Meli lying on the window seat in the dining room at La Serena. Her head on abuelita's lap. Her braids draped over abuelita's print dress and her brown legs stretched out from under her white shorts. Those legs are getting longer every day, abuelita would say.

Beyond the milk glass panels of the windows Meli could see the leaves of the mango tree hanging above the driveway. Papi parked the car in the driveway under the tree when he came home from the city. La Serena was a suburb of the capital. There had been few houses around until the last two years. Meli wished it hadn't changed. She liked to pretend it was the country. Like in the stories abuelita told her del tiempo de antes, *of the old times.*

She didn't know whether the stories were true or not. She had never asked either. There was one about Seña Alba hiding in the bushes. Making caca. She heard someone coming. She tried to hurry up to do it before they came close, but the turd got stuck. Seña Alba started moaning. The people who heard it thought it was spirits. They crossed themselves and ran away. This started a rumor in the village that there was a moaning bush inhabited by spirits.

"Eh una mata bendita," people said in the village, "polque ahí hay una pehte terrible. Debe protegel contra la muelte." *It's a blessed bush, because it make a terrible stink. Must protect people from death.*

No one dared get too close because of the stink, and for many years people would swear that they could hear the moaning. And if you could hear the moaning, no one that was dear to you would die.

Abuelita said Seña Alba would roll on the floor laughing when she told the story. Abuelita didn't let Seña Alba tell that story to her own children. Juan wouldn't have liked it. In fact, abuelita hadn't told anyone before Meli.

Meli loved hearing stories. She got pictures in her head about the bush and the expressions on the faces of the people running away. She imagined Seña Alba squatting on the ground. Or rolling with laughter.

It was like a movie.

Meli thought about things in pictures. That was how she spoke too. She didn't hook one picture to another either; it wasn't like an album. The pictures were loose in her and they mixed in different ways, without logic. When she was drawn to an image it was just there, endlessly insistent. But sometimes this was frightening. Then she felt haunted.

Meli often wondered about what had happened to mami. To her mother. But she didn't talk to anybody about it.

There was a photo of mami she really liked. Meli had found it in a pile of photographs in the back of her closet. On the picture it said: "Luisa a los 18 años." The picture had that funny brown color of old photographs. Looked almost like a charcoal drawing. Like the drawings Meli was learning to make in her art class at school. She used stumps. Fat ones and skinny ones, to spread the charcoal powder. She made smooth shadows on the cheeks of faces, or on pictures of grapes. She couldn't make pictures of real things yet, just copies of old paintings. It was like magic to make something appear on the paper, like you could go around and see it from the other side. Even if it was just a drawing of a plaster-cast eye, or a nose.

Mami's photograph looked like those drawings. A face without a body. Very beautiful, with her deep-set eyes and strong cheekbones. But Meli would have liked to have a picture of mami come to life to see what she used to be like.

Mami didn't look like that anymore.

Meli looked through some of the other pictures, trying to find an answer. Mami and papi with their first baby, her brother. Mami at the place near the beach where she went to recover. They said she had terrible pneumonia. It was frightening to think that mami had that, but she didn't look sick in the pictures. Just kind of thin.

There were many photos of the house at La Serena too. Papi had wanted to show them to people. It was a big two-story house with a pitched roof, different from the cement block houses with metal grilles one saw everywhere. Meli liked that it was different. Papi must have been pleased with all the remodelling he had done, especially in the yard. The huge yard was Meli's domain, even before papi had the formal garden built, next to the house, with gravel walks and cement seats, hibiscus hedges, trellises and sections of lawn bordered by crotons. She knew every corner of it, especially the wilder back part, from the high branches of trees and the tops of the fences to behind the hedges. Meli even had a grand view of it all from her bedroom window upstairs near the flowers of the flamboyán trees, the *royal poincianas*, which turned red in the summer.

There were other photos. Of mami and papi on the big ship going to Spain. That was the year before Meli was born. They went to Spain to visit papi's mother. She had died not too long ago and Meli had to wear a black band around her arm. Kids at school asked her who had died. She said her grandmother in Spain. They were sorry, but Meli never even met her. The house was kind of quiet, that's all. Papi didn't turn on the radio for a few days, or read the paper on the front porch.

After the trip to Spain there weren't any pictures of mami. Mostly pictures of papi at parties he had to go to for his work.

Mami stopped going out with him.

One night when Meli went back to her room, Seña Alba was squatting under the clothes hanging in the closet. Looking at Meli. Gave Meli a start. But she wasn't afraid. She had imagined Seña Alba so many times anyway. Just like this.

Seña Alba's eyes sparkled.

"Ehtaba mirando ehtoh retratoh," Meli said. "¿Quiereh mirarloh conmigo?" *I was looking at these pictures. Do you want to look at them with me?*

Seña Alba nodded.

Meli put the pictures between them on the floor.

"Ehtoh son como ehpírituh que se te aparecen." *The pictures is like spirits haunting you,* Seña Alba said.

Meli didn't like the idea. She didn't feel like looking at them anymore. Didn't like to talk about spirits. But Seña Alba didn't notice. She was too busy scattering the pictures with her hands like a chicken picking at grains of corn.

Then she said, "Tu mai ehtá asuhtá' en to'h ehtoh retratoh." *Your ma is scared in all the pictures.*

Meli made herself look at them. Seña Alba was right. She had never noticed it before.

"Pero ¿de qué?" Meli asked Seña Alba. *But of what?*

It was hard for Meli to think about mami being scared. She didn't think mami was scared of anything. She hadn't seemed scared when abuelita got sick, or when papi had a car accident and was in the hospital. Or when there was a hurricane coming. Or even that time when there was an earthquake and the lamp swung from the ceiling. Mami wasn't afraid of scary movies either. Or of electricity. She fixed the outlets in the house. She wasn't afraid of geese, or dogs, or dogs giving birth to puppies in the downstairs closet. She wasn't worried about leaving the gas stove on, like abuelita was, or of somebody breaking into the house. She didn't worry about locking the house or anything.

But she was kind of afraid of people.

It was hard to think about that. Meli hadn't seen it that way. Mostly Meli thought mami didn't want to do things. Didn't want people at the house. Except family. And she said she didn't want to go out with papi because she didn't have the right clothes. But she did go out with Meli. To the movies and Meli's piano lesson. Went to her sisters' too.

"Le tiene miedo a la gente," Meli blurted out to Seña Alba. *She's afraid of people.*

She wouldn't have said that out loud to anyone except Seña Alba. Not even to abuelita. Abuelita criticized mami. It was hard for Meli to hear abuelita criticize mami, even though Meli herself wished she could make her mother go more places.

Meli wanted to know why mami was afraid of people.

Seña Alba didn't say anything.

Pilar remembered that when she was a child she thought Seña Alba lived in a cave by the ocean. She tried to imagine living in one. But she knew she was going to be too afraid to live like Seña Alba. Pilar was afraid especially of how men looked at her after she started bleeding and getting breasts. Even when she went to the village with Marta or Tía Micaela. No, she wouldn't be able to live like Seña Alba. Pilar had cried when she first said that to herself. It wasn't long after that that Pilar found the blood trickling down her thigh. She cried then too. Felt broken. And ashamed that she couldn't be brave like Seña Alba. Pilar was so ashamed she couldn't talk about it.

After she stopped crying with her face on the ground, under the bushes behind the house, Pilar thought that if she was going to live in a house, she wanted to live in a nice one with enough water to wash. And she would make sure she got herbs from Seña Alba too.

Pilar promised herself some other things after she became a woman. She decided she was not going to be like her mother, working all the time, getting angry and having nobody listening to her. And Pilar decided also that she would never, never marry a man like those who leered at her outside the village store. The ones who slept with putas, *whores,* women who wore dresses that showed their breasts and legs. Pilar had seen them at a distance.

Pilar remembered her mother saying, "La ropa eh pa' cubrilse. No somoh animaleh enseñando to'ah lah palteh privadah." *Clothes is for covering yourself. We're not animals showing the private parts.*

Then Marta would add under her breath, almost angrily, "Putah."

"¿Qué eh una puta?" Pilar asked Seña Alba. "Y ¿pol qué mamá tiene coraje con ellah?" *What's a whore? And why mamá's angry at them?*

Seña Alba was silent for a while.

"Son mujeleh que duelmen con hombreh. Elloh leh pagan pa' domil con elloh." *They're women that sleep with men. Men pay them to sleep with them.*

Pilar remembered the men who stood around the store drinking. It made her sick to think that a woman would want to sleep with them. Money or no money.

Seña Alba noticed that Pilar was making a face.

"¿Te dihguhta eso?" Seña Alba asked. *It make you sick?*

"Esoh borrachoh en el pueblo me enfelman," Pilar said. "Mamá dice que el diablo se metió en el ron. ¿Lah putah se acuehtan con esoh hombreh?" *The drunks in the village make me sick. Mamá say rum's got the devil in it. Whores sleep with those men?*

Seña Alba was silent for a long time. Pilar began to wonder whether she should have asked.

Seña Alba was frowning when she answered.

"Necesitan loh chavoh pa' comel." *They need the money to eat.*

She would eat dirt instead of getting in bed with one of those men, Pilar thought. Sleep in a cave. Maybe that's why Seña Alba slept outside. Pilar wondered whether Seña Alba slept with men. Not with drunk ones, Pilar was sure. But she didn't dare ask about that.

Pilar knew she didn't want to be like those women, but she didn't know what she was going to do. She wished she could be a midwife like Seña Alba, but she wasn't brave enough to go somewhere in the middle of the night, walking through the sugar cane fields to deliver a baby.

Pilar had said to Seña Alba that she didn't want to be like her mother and she didn't want to be like Patria, or like the putah. What could she do?

"Pue'h sel maehtra," Seña Alba had said. *You can be a teacher.*

"¿Maehtra?" *Teacher?*

She was surprised that Seña Alba would say that. Teacher. That was for the rich white people.

"Seña Alba, no me hagah burlah." *Seña Alba, don't make fun of me,* Pilar said.

They were sitting on a rock near the ocean. It was very hot. The sky was solid blue. Looked like the ceiling of the church. Pilar realized that day at the beach that the ceiling of the church had been painted blue to make it look like the sky. One time at the church she had spent the whole time looking at the ceiling. The color changed in places. She kept looking because she didn't know how they had made it so pretty and she couldn't figure out how come it looked different in different places. She had seen paint once in big cans at the store. Plain colors. Never saw this color in a can. Maybe it was special for churches. Or it was a miracle.

She didn't even remember why she was at the church. Oh, yes. How could she forget? They had brought a new statue of the Virgin from Spain. There was a big celebration. People came from all the villages around to see it when it was going to be blessed. The bishop was coming too.

Marta was fretting for weeks because she didn't know what the girls were going to wear. She kept saying she was sorry they didn't have shoes, and cried a lot at night. Pilar could hear her. She also heard Pablo say, "¡Cállate, mujer!" *Shut up, woman!*

Tía Micaela had finally put sense into Marta.

"Jesuh no tenía zapatoh tampoco," she said. *Jesus don't have shoes either.*

Tía Micaela had seen a picture of Jesus barefoot when she was growing up. Her mother had had this picture, which came from Spain. She would kneel in front of it every night. After her mother died, the picture got lost in one of the big hurricanes. Tía Micaela's eyes would get moist talking about it, then she would say, "¡Maldítoh huracaneh!" and cross herself. *Damn hurricanes!*

That settled it for Marta. If Jesus didn't wear shoes, it would be all right for the children to go to church without shoes. Marta herself had some torn-up shoes. Hand me downs. Pablo didn't know where they came from. If he had known it was charity, he would have thrown them away. She had told him they had come from Tía Micaela. Marta couldn't even remember when she got them. Never fit. But that didn't matter. She carried them to the edge of the village, washed her feet in the creek and then put them on.

Pablo wore his work boots. The only pair he had. Marta had wiped them extra well and even covered up some of the worst scratches with fat mixed with charred wood. Didn't smell so good, Pablo said. He was afraid the dogs would follow him, licking his boots. Didn't want everyone laughing at him. But he did admit they looked better.

Marta was pleased with herself.

All their good clothes, which they kept on a shelf high up in the room they slept in, were washed, dried in the sun to smell good and smoothed out with hot rocks wrapped in rags. Marta burnt her fingers several times in the process. Pilar didn't think the clothes looked all that different, but it made Marta feel better.

The day before the blessing of the statue of the Virgin, Marta washed each one of the children until their skin and scalp were red from scrubbing. That day they couldn't go out because she didn't want them to get dirty.

Marta and the older girls went several times to the creek to carry water home in cans to heat outside, in back of the house. Marta sent the boys to play at Tía Micaela's when she washed the older girls. The boys kept sneaking back to peek until Marta grabbed a branch off the flamboyán and whipped them. Patria was angry that she couldn't go out. She tried it, but she should have taken a lesson from the boys. She also got a whipping.

It was unusual that Marta was so sure of what she wanted. Pilar liked that her mother seemed happier than she had ever seen her, once the business of Jesus not wearing shoes was settled.

By the time Pablo came home at sundown, they were all clean and Marta had heated some water for him too. She would use it after he did.

Pilar noticed that Pablo looked at her mother differently that night. A look she had noticed sometimes before. She didn't remember when, but it was familiar somehow.

Patria told her how it was done. How a man and a woman lay together. That was even before Pilar got her period.

Pilar wanted to know and didn't want to know. She hadn't asked, but Patria told her anyway.

It was the day Marta had sent Patria on an errand to a neighbor. Patria knew that her mother usually lost track of time and that if she was late, she could always say to Marta, "¡Ay, mamá! ¡No te dah cuenta del tiempo!" *Mamá, you don't notice what time it is!*

Patria made Pilar swear she wouldn't tell.

Patria went to see the stable boy that day and Pilar sat by the fence on the side where she couldn't be seen from the road. On the ground next to the flowers.

Pilar remembered how she picked flowers when she was little. The ones that grew wild in back of the house or along the road. Brought them home, but they never looked the same when they were in the house. Died right away. So she stopped picking them. Would just sit near them where they grew. Just looking at them.

"Esa Pilar eh tonta." *That Pilar is dumb,* her mother used to say when she found Pilar sitting next to the flowers in back of the house. That's when Marta started worrying about Pilar thinking too much.

But Pilar wasn't thinking. It was not like saying things to herself. She did that too. Often. Had whole conversations inside her head. She wondered whether anybody else did that. But when she was a child, she mostly wasn't talking to herself or talking to the flowers, she was just looking at the colors.

So she lost track of time. Like Marta.

It had taken Patria a long time though. Pilar started getting worried that Marta might notice and give them a beating when they got home.

Then Patria showed up.

She looked different. Like she had been crying or running. Her face all red and sweaty. And dirt on her. Maybe she had fallen down.

"¿Qué te pasó?" Pilar asked anxiously. "Te tomó mucho tiempo. Mamá noh va matal." *What happen to you! You took too long. Mamá's going to kill us.*

"Vámonoh. Te cuento pol el camino." *Let's go. I'll tell you on the way,* Patria said.

Patria was walking so fast it was hard for Pilar to keep up with her and hear what Patria was saying at the same time.

Patria told her. In detail. About the hard pipí and how it hurt when it went inside her. And how she was afraid he was going to pee inside her. Didn't have time to wipe herself too well either. And it was sticky.

Pilar thought it sounded awful but Patria seemed excited. Almost happy.

Marta beat them both that day.

Marta probably wouldn't have, except Patria seemed to provoke her. Marta was cooking and screaming at the boys. They had got into a fight. Bumped into the kitchen table.

"¡Dioh mío! ¿Cuando Pablo va arreglal la pata d'esa mesa?" Marta exclaimed. *My God! When is Pablo going to fix the leg of that table?* The boys had just spilled the rice she had washed.

"¡Carájo! ¡Esa mesa se cae de mirala na' máh!" she cursed. *Goddammit! That table fall down from just looking at it!*

Pilar and Patria walked in when Marta was making the boys pick up the rice. She was standing there making sure every grain was picked up.

"¡Ehtoh sinvelgüenzah se cren que se pue' botal la comi'a!" *Those shameless runts think they can waste food!* Marta was in the middle of saying when Patria and Pilar appeared at the doorway.

"¿Qué pasó, mamá?" Pilar asked. *What happened, mamá?*

"Me acaban ehtoh condena'oh muchachoh," Marta responded wearily. *These damn boys are killing me.*

Marta sat down now that she had somebody to listen to her. "Uhtedeh no saben lo que eh bregal con esah criaturah." *You don't know what it's like to struggle with these children.*

Pilar felt safe now that her mother was getting started on how being a mother was hell. Blaming it all on Eve. Had no business eating those apples. Plenty of mangos around. Nobody's happy with their lot anyway. Look at how much they had to be thankful for. A roof over their heads. Food on the table, when those snot-nosed runts didn't waste it, that is. And a man in the house that didn't get drunk. Graciah a Dioh. *Thank God.*

Patria was standing by the doorway of the bedroom. She started laughing. Pilar thought Patria looked like she wanted to make Marta angry.

"Oye ¿y de qué te rieh tú?" Marta asked Patria. *Hey! What you laughing about?*

"De na'," Patria said with a little smile on her face. *About nothing.*

Pilar didn't like what was happening. She went to sit on the back steps. All she could see was the sugar cane field, but she could still feel a little breeze coming from the ocean. She always wished she could see the ocean from the house. Marta had never wanted a house near the ocean. Never know when a hurricane is coming. Can't sleep listening to the ocean either. Afraid it come in the night and wash the house away.

"¿Y pol qué leh cogió tanto tiempo?" Pilar heard Marta ask from inside the house. *And why you take so long?*

Patria laughed.

"Tú no te dah cuenta del tiempo," Patria said to her mother. *You don't notice time.*

"¿Pero tú te creeh que yo soy idiota? Tú y Pilar se fueron to'a la talde." *You think I'm stupid? You and Pilar are gone the whole afternoon.*

Pilar's stomach hurt.

"Tú no te dah cuenta del tiempo," Patria repeated, laughing. *You lose track of time.*

"¿Tú t'ehtáh riendo de mí? ¡Ay, Dioh mío! ¿Pol qué me hah manda'o ehtah criaturah? ¿Qué hice yo pa' merecel ehto?" *You laughing at me? Lord! Why you send me these creatures? What I do to deserve this?*

She started crying loudly.

Pilar couldn't stand it. She came in and put her arms around her mother.

"Mamá, peldónanoh," she said. *Mamá, forgive us.*

"¿Peldonálnoh pol qué? No hacemoh na'," Patria said, laughing. *Forgive us for what? We don't do anything.*

Pilar didn't know what to say.

Marta stood up suddenly and grabbed Patria by the arm.

"¡No le tie'h rehpeto a tu mai! ¡Te voy a enseñal rehpeto!" *You have no respect for your ma! I going to teach you respect!* Marta grabbed the branch leaning by the door and started swinging at Patria. Hitting her back and legs. Usually Patria would run away after Marta hit her the first time. Today she didn't resist.

"¿Y uhte'?" Marta turned towards Pilar. *And you?*

"¡No, mamá!" Pilar said. "¡Peldóname!" *No, mamá! Forgive me!*

"¿Peldonálte pol dalme un mal rato?" Marta screamed. *Forgive you for giving me trouble!*

It stung so bad.

Pilar wet a rag and put it on the welts on her legs. Marta must have known about what happened with Patria, Pilar thought. But didn't say anything. Pilar noticed, for days after, that her mother was upset. She was even more distracted than usual.

Pilar kept thinking about Patria. Pipís. Didn't want to think about it. Her face got warm when she did. So she hid in the bushes behind the house. Put her face on the damp ground to cool off her cheeks. But then the images came up again. Patria with dirt on her clothes and her eyes so bright, like she had been looking at coals for hours.

Pilar looked at herself one day.

Wanted to see where the pipí would go. Patria hadn't said. Only two places for it to go. Wouldn't go where the shit came out of. Would have to go where women bled.

But it was so little. How could a big pipí go in there?

She had seen one. It was the time Patria and Asunción and herself had gone on an errand for their mother, and they had seen a man with his pants open. Didn't seem to be peeing. It was like he was holding himself. His pipí was so big Pilar was startled. Looked like an animal. She couldn't take her eyes off of it.

Then her sisters started running and pulling her.

It must hurt, she figured.

Come to think of it, Patria had blood on her that day she had been with the stable boy. It must have hurt a lot.

Pilar thought about her own daughters as she closed the doors to the veranda and began to undress for bed. She caught a glimpse of herself in the mirror in her embroidered undershirt and long slip. Her curly hair held behind her head in a bun.

Still beautiful, everyone said, although she was thirty-one and had four children.

Pilar felt her belly get warm. Like bread that had just been baked, Juan had said. She remembered that Juan had loved how she felt in the morning. Sleepy and damp. How he looked at her.

She was hot all over her body now. She looked quickly at the door of her room. Hoped the children were asleep. She felt embarrassed to feel this way. Still.

Didn't talk to anyone about that. Not even Seña Alba. She wondered again whether Seña Alba was ever with a man. Pilar didn't think so. It didn't seem like Seña Alba needed anyone.

What could Pilar say anyway? Her body just seemed to do things on its own. Get warm and tingly. And all of a sudden she didn't notice much else.

She didn't know whether anyone else felt that way. Her body fired up, like the flamboyán in the summer when it got covered with red flowers. Maybe plants felt that way when they had flowers. Spread out. Open to the sun.

When she and Juan were together at first, she went around hugging trees. Lying on the ground. She even told Juan one night that she was sure she could feel the ground breathe.

He just laughed. Took her in his arms, carried her outside under the trees and put her carefully on the ground. Then he lay on her.

Pilar breathed deeply, remembering.

Nothing felt like it.

Pinned between his body and the ground. Safe. Like nothing could ever hurt her.

This was home. His heartbeat. Hers. The ground breathing. The leaves above moving.

And this explosion inside. As if she were in the middle of a flame.

It had been scary afterwards. The first time she felt that way. Didn't expect it. As if her body didn't belong to her. Doing something she didn't ask it to do. Felt like she had been to some other place.

It made her shy too. She didn't know whether she was supposed to feel that way. Didn't dare look at his face. Kept hers tucked in his shoulder.

When she finally looked at him his eyes looked like a child's. She wanted suddenly to hold his head to her breast. Give him her nipple which felt swollen and full.

Pilar looked at the rose petals which had fallen on top of the dresser. Their color reminded her of her nightgowns. The nightgowns Juan had brought from Spain, which she wore for him. They were a present he brought from his first long trip away from her. He had been gone two months that time. She hadn't known how she would be able to stand it. She was used to waking up with him every morning, with the sun coming in through the windows. It hurt her eyes to see the sky. And to see everything so green around her.

She had never noticed things being so bright before being with Juan. Seña Alba said it was because she was happy.

In those early days she felt filled up to the brim, like she couldn't hold any more happiness. Then there was more. Every day more. Birds playing hide-and-go-seek in the branches. The sun spilling on the polished floors. The house so still, as if it were listening to the breeze. And the leaves turning greener every morning. The day stretched out like it was never going to end.

She used to think maybe it was a sin.

Tía Micaela, who was the only one she knew who used to go to church as often as she could, had said you tell the priest things you had never told anyone else. And that's what a sin was. Things you couldn't talk to anyone about.

Pilar thought she must have plenty of those. There were a lot of things she couldn't talk about.

She couldn't talk about Seña Alba being gone. What could she say?

She looked at the spot near the door to the veranda where Seña Alba used to squat, roll the tobacco and blow the smoke out the door. It was after Seña Alba left that Pilar began to notice how alone she was. No one else came there. Except Juan.

Her life was about waiting.

Juan had started leaving after they had been together for almost a year at the other house. He had to do business in another town. It had taken Pilar a while to get used to watching for him at the window to come up the trail on his horse.

"¡Fernanda, ahí viene!"·she would call out. *Fernanda, here he comes!*

Fernanda was a big black woman Juan had hired to help out with the chores, but mostly to keep Pilar company. He didn't want her to be alone in the house.

Pilar hadn't liked it at first because she felt shyer with him when there was someone else around. She didn't want Fernanda talking to everyone about Juan and her.

Pilar knew how everybody talked. Her mother. Tía Micaela. Everyone talked about everybody else's business. Except Seña Alba. Seña Alba knew a lot about what was going on but she never gossiped.

Pilar remembered Seña Alba had said Juan had another woman.

It must be true.

All men did it. Pilar had hated to hear her mother say that. And Tía Micaela, and everyone. Even Seña Alba. But Seña Alba added that all women would do it too if men would let them, and that many women did but kept it to themselves.

Pilar knew she hadn't felt that way about any other man. Seña Alba must be talking about women like Patria. But Patria must not have felt like Pilar did with Juan in the early days. If she had, she wouldn't have wanted anyone else.

Men must be different from women that way. Can't help themselves, she thought. Like having to pee.

But how could Juan be with another woman like he had been with her?

Seña Alba was right that it was hard for Pilar to talk to Juan about how she felt about things.

She had been able to at first. A little. At the house on the hills. He was with her a lot. So she got over some of her shyness. Pilar remembered she had told him how much she liked flowers. The next day Juan had a man come and plant roses around the front of the house. And amapolas, *hibiscus*, azucenas, *tuberoses*, and lilies. Had to clear some of the branches of the trees too.

But she couldn't tell him that she was worried about Marta, Pablo and her little brothers and sisters. She didn't like to talk about it because she knew Juan was angry at Pablo.

Most of all, Pilar couldn't talk to Juan about his being gone. He was gone for a short time at first, but then he had to go to another part of the island on business, or to another country. Even to Spain. He was gone sometimes for months. Like this time.

Pilar pulled back the mosquito netting and sat at the edge of her bed. Still wasn't used to it, the netting. Too enclosed. When she had first slept on a bed, off the ground, she would hold Juan not just because she loved feeling him but because she was afraid of falling off. She never told him though. She didn't want to seem stupid.

"No sé polqué la gente duelme lejoh de la tierra. Se olvidan que somoh palte d'ella." *Don't know why people sleep so far from the ground. They forget we're part of her,* Seña Alba had said when Pilar told her about sleeping on the high four-poster bed. Seña Alba laughed about the mosquito netting too.

"Loh blancoh tie'n la piel demasia'o ablandá. Le tie'n miedo a to'," she added. *Whites got too soft skin. They're afraid of everything.*

Pilar didn't agree with Seña Alba that time. Didn't quite know why. Maybe it was because she was part white too, like her father. Like Juan.

"Juan no le tie' miedo a to'," Pilar said before even thinking about what she was saying. *Juan's not afraid of everything.*

Seña Alba looked at her carefully, but didn't say anything.

Pilar realized, looking back, that Seña Alba had stopped saying things about white people to her after that. Spoke only about people in general.

Maybe something began to change then. Pilar didn't have words to describe how she felt about Seña Alba. For a moment it was as if she didn't know her.

"Somoh diferenteh." *We're different,* she said to herself.

Pilar slipped into her nightgown. The one Juan liked most. She wore it when she missed him.

He always brought presents. She didn't want presents. Her dresser and wardrobe closet were full of them. She wanted him.

But she couldn't say anything. She was so happy to see him she forgot she had been sad. When he was home she forgot nearly everything else.

It must be her fault too that the children couldn't talk to him. She wanted him all to herself when he was there.

She had been selfish, she thought as she turned off the kerosene lamp and slipped under the mosquito netting.

BOOK TWO
□

☐ Pilar looked up at the tall man standing behind the counter. She felt caught in his fixed gaze. Couldn't hide from it. She scanned his face anxiously, looking for a smile, but couldn't find one behind his black moustache. His jaw was smooth; he was pale like an apparition. She had never seen a man like him. He was like the pictures at the church. Like he belonged with the saints and the angels; not a man to walk in the dust, or get scratched by bushes, or be in a knife fight. There was no dirt on his white shirt, or under his fingernails. Not at all like the cutters who were dark and rough like trunks of trees. He came from another world where being strong meant knowing what you wanted. And he looked at you steadily, as though once he wanted something he wouldn't let go until he got it.

Then she noticed his hair. It was brown but getting thin above the forehead. Her body felt warm and soft. Suddenly she wanted to reach out, touch him, look after him.

She blushed and turned away from the feeling and from his eyes to stare at her feet. They were bare and muddy on the floor of the store. The uneven planks had a knot that looked like a flying bird. She imagined it flying over the ocean.

That's how Pilar always remembered meeting Juan.

He kept looking at her like he wanted to know something. But he hadn't talked to her, at least she didn't think so. Maybe she didn't hear the question. It made her nervous to think he might have asked something and she hadn't heard.

She glanced at her mother instead. It was hard to bear his look. Marta was the same as always. It made Pilar feel a little easier. Marta was telling Juan what she needed from the store and was talking about the weather. If he had asked a question, Marta would have heard it.

Pilar kept looking at her mother. Noticed how her dress was not very clean and how dark she was next to him.

She wanted to hide. Didn't want him to see their muddy feet. Their clothes were old too. She didn't want to be there.

"Doña Marta," he was saying. His voice seemed so loud, like it was shaking the walls and was shaking her.

"Doña Marta, hay una Fiesta de Cruz en casa de mi tía. ¿Le gustaría venir y traer a las muchachas?" *Doña Marta, there's going to be a Feast of the Cross at my aunt's house. Would you like to come and bring your girls?*

Marta was startled. Pilar didn't know what was happening. She was still wondering whether there was an earthquake, but the floor didn't seem to be moving. She didn't dare look up. She didn't want to see the question in his eyes again.

"Don Juan, no sé qué decil. Se le agradece mucho, pero somoh pobreh. No tenemoh na' que ponelnoh pa' il a fiehtah de ricoh," Marta said. *Don Juan, I don't know what to say. We thank you but we're poor, don't have nothing to put on to go to rich folks' parties.*

"Mire, Doña Marta, ahí le voy a dar una tela. Y en cuanto a las muchachas, son tan bonitas como las flores, no necesitan vestirse como si fueran a la corte de España," he laughed. *Look, Doña Marta, I'm going to give you some fabric for a dress. As far as the girls go, they are as pretty as flowers, they don't need to dress as if they were going to the court of Spain.*

His laugh made Pilar warm all over. Pilar was afraid it showed, so she didn't move or look up.

"Bueno, Don Juan, le tengo que hablal d'eso a Pablo," *Well, Don Juan, I have to talk to Pablo about it,* Marta said.

"Las muchachas se van a divertir." *The girls will have fun,* he added.

Pilar knew Marta was looking at her. She didn't move.

"Ehte Juan, le anda detráh a Pilar." *This Juan, he's after Pilar,* Pilar overheard Marta say to Pablo a few days after Juan's invitation.

"¡Qué va ser! Esa es una criatura. No tiene ni dieciséis," Pablo said. *Not true. She's just a child. Not even sixteen.*

"¡Ehtáh ciego! Pero la velda' eh que no sé lo que vé en ella." *You're blind! But I guess I don't know what he see in her.* "Esa no tie' calne en loh huesoh ni colol en la cara y siempre ehtá en lah nubeh. Pero ¿qué carajo tu créh qu'él quiere d'ella? Lo mihmo que quieren to'h loh hombreh, metélsele entre lah pielnah. Y dehpuéh ¿qué? ¿Vamoh a mantenel otra criatura?" Marta went on. *She got no flesh on her bones, no color on her face, and she's always up in the clouds. Lord! And what the hell you think he want from her! Same thing all men want, to get between her legs. And then what! We feed another mouth!*

"Tú siempre pensando mal de la gente, mujer," Pablo grumbled. *You're always thinking the worst of people, woman.*

"¡Carájo! ¡Como ereh blanco y ereh hombre, no te quiereh dal cuenta de na'!" *Damn it! Because you is white and you is a man, you don't see what's happening.*

Marta was getting mad.

"¿Dehde cuándo noh dá ese una tela?" *Since when he give us a piece of cloth for a dress!* she asked.

Pilar could tell her father was angry now.

"¿Qué tela?" *What cloth!* he wanted to know.

"Me dió una tela." *He gave me some cloth.* Marta's voice was lower. Pilar could tell Marta knew she had gone too far.

"¡Me la vas a dar y se la voy a tirar en la cara!" *You're going to give it to me and I'm going to throw it in his face!* Pablo screamed.

"¡Ehtá bien! ¡Ehtá bien, Pablo! Mira, no te preocupeh, eso se va arreglal mañana." *Don't worry! Don't worry, Pablo! We fix it tomorrow,* Marta said.

"¡No va a haber ningún pendejo que va a mantener a mi familia!" *No asshole is going to support my family!* Pablo went on.

Seña Alba squatted at the edge of the sugar cane in the early light and watched her pee trickle on the dust. Was the best time of the day. Seeing the sky get light after a night of screams. That babe don't get born easy. Mother hollering and pushing and that one taking his time like he's too cozy in there to come out to a noisy, bloody world. Can't blame him either.

Seña Alba stood up and took a deep breath in the morning breeze as if to wash away the night of pain still clinging to her thoughts. She listened to the leaves of the breadfruit tree, the baby crying and a voice cooing to him. Then she started walking towards the place where she knew the sun would come up. After a while the ground became sandier and she could hear the surf. The closer she got to the water the deeper she breathed. And when she saw the sea, pale now, quiet, waking up from sleep, she took off her clothes and walked into it.

She wished it were as easy to scrub the inside of her head. Wished she could put the sound of the ocean in there instead of screaming, arguing voices. Instead of pictures that made her eyes sting with tears.

Seña Alba remembered Pilar come telling her Don Juan ask her to the Fiehta de Cruh. Seña Alba wanted to laugh that time but didn't let herself because she catch something in Niña Pilar's eye.

You tell Niña Pilar something and she go somewhere thinking about it. Seña Alba could usually tell what Niña Pilar thought about. But she wasn't sure this time.

"¿Qué piensah, Pilar?" *What you thinking, Pilar?* she finally asked.

Pilar blushed.

"Te puso colol en la cara, lo que piensah." *It put color on your face, what you thinking,* Seña Alba teased her. But Seña Alba was already worried.

"Na', na'," Pilar said and looked away. *Nothing, nothing.*

Seña Alba felt this child pulling away. She tried to reach for her Niña.

"¿Eh Don Juan?" *It's Don Juan?* Seña Alba asked.

"¿Ah ido a una Fiehta de Cruh?" Pilar answered with a question. *You gone to a Feast of the Cross?*

"Fiehtah de pobreh," Seña Alba answered. "Pero una veh me invitó la hija del patrón, la Ramíreh. Mira, no me senté en sala con loh blancoh . . . ." *Poor folks' parties. But one time the mill owner's girl, the Ramírez, she invite me. Look, I don't sit in the living room with the white people . . . .*

Seña Alba's eyes smiled mischievously.

"Me ñangoté en la cocina y me sacaron pa' fuera como el diablo polque se creían que iba hacel mielda. Pelo dehde afuera podía oil lah coplah y hahta me trepé a un palo de pana pa' vel la cruh de ramah pol la ventana." *I squat in the kitchen and they kick me out like I was the devil because they think I'm going to shit. But I hear the songs from out there. I even climb a breadfruit tree to see the cross of branches in the window.*

Seña Alba went on.

"Pero la cosa fué que to' el mundo s'emborrachó y un negro le metió cuchillo a Basilio Péreh. Ni el dotol lo salvó." *Thing is, everybody get drunk and this man stick a knife into Basilio Pérez. Not even the doctor can fix him.*

Seña Alba could tell by the look on Pilar's face that she didn't want to hear that story. She was sure that all Pilar could see right then was the green cross of the feast with Juan's face in front of it.

Seña Alba didn't know what to make of it. Pilar getting sparkly eyes about this Spaniard. Rich too. Family own the store and the cows and most of the land in the village. Not the mill, but pretty much everything else. Everyone in the village owe them money. Every time you need something to put on your body or inside it, you go to that store.

This Juan is a good fifteen years older than Niña Pilar and hasn't wasted them as far as women's concerned. Has more black and brown kids running around than just about anyone else in the village. Except the white doctor who don't run around much anymore because his liver's rotting from the rum.

Seña Alba leaned against the trunk of a palm tree after she put on her clothes over her wet body. She pulled out a pinch of tobacco from her pocket and began spreading it carefully on the cigarette paper. Traded tobacco for herbs with a neighbor. Didn't buy anything at the store, except rum. Didn't feel good about that either. Each time she say she's not going to drink she start thinking about sad things, like a mean voice inside say look how bad things are. Food locked up in the store and folks working so hard for the mill they don't have time to grow their own. Or don't know how anymore.

After they moved to Bocarío, Juan gave the children money for holidays and birthdays. Each of them had a purse with some money in it. It made Pilar very nervous having that money around. She was afraid it would be stolen. There were stories about convicts escaping prison and hiding in the coconut groves. There had been nights when Juan was gone that she had sat up all night with the children, Fernanda and Rosa, the housemaid. All in a big circle in the living room. Telling stories. Seña Alba was there too sometimes. Seña Alba had told them that if there was word of an escaped convict, it was best to leave all the lights on, as if there were many people in the house.

And Pilar was afraid the children would lose their money too. They didn't have any idea what it was worth. She had them count it every once in a while. She told them it helped them learn their numbers. Also told them what the money would buy and how many days of hard work a sugar cane cutter would have to spend in the fields in order to make that kind of money.

She wasn't interested in money for herself. She couldn't put away money when her mother, brothers and sisters had so little. Pilar tried to buy them things with whatever money Juan gave her. It wasn't easy though, they didn't want his money. But she didn't have any money except what he gave her. And Juan didn't like Pilar's family to come to the house. Although he had never said so, Pilar knew.

She went to see them instead when Juan was gone, but it was getting harder and harder for her. She tried to bring them food, which she knew they needed, or sometimes material for her little sisters and a special gift for her mother. Pilar didn't bring anything for Pablo since the time she brought him some tobacco and he had thrown it on the ground and spit on it.

Marta hadn't been well recently. She could hardly see. Pilar had wanted to take her mother to Corona, to the new doctor. That was before Elena's death. But Marta refused. She was very stubborn.

"¿Qué hay que vel en ehte mundo, m'ija? Dehgraciah. Mejol no vel na'," she had said. *What is there to see in this world, child? Misfortune, that's all. Better see nothing.*

Pilar knew Marta was afraid of going to the doctor because she was afraid he might tell her she was going to die.

Pablo too was getting old. He couldn't work as many hours in the sugar cane fields as he used to because of arthritis.

"Eh el reuma," Marta would say. *Rheumatism.*

"Tú no sabes nada, mujer," Pablo said impatiently. *You don't know anything, woman.*

Pilar knew he was angry because he couldn't support his family like he used to when he was younger. But even then he brought home almost nothing. Pilar had known for a long time that he was cheated out of his wages. But he wouldn't even notice.

"Son unoh pilloh." *Thieves,* Marta would say about the people who ran the sugar mill.

Pablo said he didn't want to argue.

Pilar sighed as her mother's dark face emerged in her mind. Poverty had made her mother old. She wore herself out worrying. Poverty was the worst kind of sickness. And not having schooling was a big part of it. Look at her father. It was not that he didn't like to argue with the foreman at the sugar mill; he couldn't argue because he couldn't keep track of how much he worked. He couldn't read the ledgers at the mill's office.

Even his being white didn't do him any good.

Pilar brought food to her mother when Pablo wasn't around. But it was hard. Pablo was home more often. The younger men were hired first to cut the cane and now sometimes there was no work for him.

Pablo didn't look at Pilar when she came. He hadn't talked to her since she left home.

When Pablo wasn't at the house Marta took the food and said, "Graciah, m'ija." *Thanks, child.* Apologetically, as if she wanted to hide.

Marta was quietly bitter. Even when Pilar was able to bring the children to visit. Pilar had thought her parents would be happy to see the children and would be less angry at her, but it was very uncomfortable for everybody. So she didn't bring them very often now.

The last time she had come to visit with the children was about a year before. It was around the time Don Ramiro, the tutor, started coming to Bocarío. Pilar told her parents ahead of time that she was coming because she knew they would feel too embarrassed if she just appeared at the house. When she arrived they were in their best clothes and Marta had fixed food for all of them. Simple things, but Pilar knew it had meant a lot of work for Marta, and her parents wouldn't have much to eat for a while after that. It was difficult for Pilar to eat their food. She felt bad that her children would take bites of things and not finish them.

Elena was not feeling well that day and was in bed. She had never left home because she had tuberculosis. Pilar had each one of the children stand by the door of the room and say hello to her. Pilar was afraid of their coming close to Elena but didn't say anything.

Marta was looking after some of Patria's children. It didn't surprise Pilar that Patria turned up at the end of the afternoon. Pilar's children were a little scared of her. Patria had a sharp tongue.

Clara was only five then. She hadn't seen Patria for a long time.

"¿Quién eh esa mujer fea?" *Who is that ugly woman?* Clara asked her mother.

Pilar said quickly, "¡Shhhh! No hableh así, Clara." *Shhhh! Don't talk like that, Clara!*

Almost slapped her hand. But, of course, there was no way of fixing it.

Pilar apologized to Patria. "Lo siento, Patria. Tú sabeh que loh muchachoh no saben lo que dicen." *I'm sorry, Patria. You know that children don't know what they're saying sometimes.*

Then she turned to Clara and said, "Ehta eh tu tía Patria." *This is your aunt Patria.*

Patria looked at Clara and Pilar angrily. "Bueno ¿se creen que me pue'n insultal polque tie'n chavoh?" *Well, you think you can insult me because you got money?*

Marta tried to fix it by offering them more coffee.

The children sat stiffly by Pilar, except Luisa, who had gone outside with some of Patria's oldest children and was showing them how to make a drawing of a tree.

Pablo didn't say much to the children, but Pilar noticed him looking at them every once in a while.

Patria laughed mockingly, "Bueno, Pilar ¿y el marido cómo ehtá? ¿Siempre de viaje?" *Well, Pilar, how's the husband? Always travelling?*

Pilar just said simply, "Sí." *Yes.*

When Pilar was alone with Patria she could deal with her, but it was hard with the children there. Patria took advantage of it.

"¡Pobrecitoh muchachoh! Son como loh míoh, crecen sin pai." *Poor kids! They're like mine, growing up without a pa!* She went on, "¡Y qué lindah son lah nenah! Vah a tenel que tenel cuidado con ehtah o van a salil como nosotrah, encinta de miralah na' máh." *And the girls are so pretty! You better be careful with them or they turn out like us, pregnant from just being looked at.*

Pilar couldn't think of what to say to stop Patria. She just said, "No te tieneh que preocupar por eso, Patria." *You don't have to worry about that, Patria.*

"Pero me preocupo, polque uhtedeh son familia. En eso somoh diferenteh, Pilar. Tú no te preocupah pol naide, pol eso eh que tieneh chavoh polque ereh egoíhta. Pero cuando uno tie' buenoh sentimientoh como yo to' el mundo abusa de uno. Mira a mamá." *But I worry because you're family. We're different about that, Pilar. You don't worry about anybody. That's why you got money, because you're selfish. But when you got soft feelings like me, everybody take advantage. Look at mamá.*

Patria went over and put her arms around Marta. Marta was obviously uncomfortable. She said, "¡Deja . . . deja, muchacha!" *Go . . . go, girl!*

It was too much for Pilar.

"Noh vamoh a tener que ir temprano hoy. Loh neneh tienen que terminar suh leccioneh. El tutor viene mañana," Pilar said. *We're going to have to leave early today. The children have to finish their lessons. The tutor comes tomorrow.*

"Tutol y to' ¿ah? ¿La ehcuela del pueblo eh muy pobre pa' loh niñoh ricoh? ¿Tie'n miedo que se leh va a pegal la rajita?" *Tutor and everything, eh? Village school's too poor for the rich children? You afraid they're going to catch a little color?*

Pilar remembered how worried she had been the year before because Luisa hadn't wanted to go to the village school. Juan had arranged for all the children to start going to school. He said he wasn't home enough to teach them everything they needed to learn. It was all planned out before he left for one of his trips. The three older children, Mercedes, Luisa and Manuelito, were going to be taken in a buggy to the school. Clara was too young to go. She was only five.

The first day, when it was time to leave, they couldn't find Luisa. She had had breakfast and gone into her room to get dressed, but then they couldn't find her. For most of the morning the servants looked everywhere: by the river, at the beach, in the coconut grove. Then she showed up with her sketchbook under her arm and a sick bird in her hand.

Luisa said she had climbed up in a tree because she had noticed a nest. Forgot about time. She climbed down when she noticed the hurt bird on the ground. No, she didn't hear anyone calling her. And she was very sorry to cause her mother trouble.

The next day she was sick with a sore throat and a high temperature. She was sick for a week. That's when Seña Alba came and put a mustard and linseed pack on Luisa's chest. She was afraid the flu was going into Luisa's lungs.

Mercedes had wanted to stay home to look after Luisa. Manuelito wanted to go to school, but Pilar was afraid he was going to get in trouble if he went by himself. So they all stayed home.

At the beginning of the next week when she was feeling better, Luisa said she didn't want to go to school at all. She said the other children would make fun of her because she was so much older, thirteen already, and tall. And she wouldn't like it if they said things about her mother and father. Besides, she didn't want to be away from Pilar.

Pilar was surprised that Luisa would say that. Luisa cried and pleaded with Pilar not to send her to school. Pilar said that Mercedes was a year older and she didn't mind. And what could the children say about Pilar and Juan anyway? But then Mercedes also began to say she was too old and didn't want the children at school making fun of her either. At that point Manuelito began to make fun of Luisa and Mercedes, imitating what he thought would be the mocking words of the children in the village.

"¡Mírale el moño a Luisa! ¡Mírale el moño a Luisa!" *Look at Luisa's bun! Look at Luisa's funny hair!*

"¡Mercedes camina como una vaca!" *Mercedes walks like a cow!*

Pilar was so upset she sent them all to their rooms.

She decided to wait until Juan came home.

Pilar wondered whether the older girls knew. About Juan. People talked. Maybe they had heard something when they went to the store. Or from the servants. Pilar knew that Fernanda gossiped. Good as she was, she still gossiped.

The girls were getting big. They must be curious about things. Like Pilar used to be. Pilar wished she knew what they were thinking about.

On her way to ask Fernanda for a lemonade, Pilar imagined Luisa listening to a conversation she herself had once overheard in the kitchen.

"¿Cuándo vuelve el Seño' Juan?" *When Mr. Juan come back?* Rosa, the maid, was asking.

"¡Qué voy yo a sabel! Tú sabeh como son loh hombreh cuando andan detráh de mujereh, como loh perroh . . . . Y Doña Pilar ahí senta' ehperándolo . . . . Esa mujel eh una santa." *How should I know? You know how men are when they chase after women. Like dogs . . . . And Doña Pilar sitting there waiting . . . . That woman's a saint,* Fernanda said.

"¿El Seño' Juan tie' mujereh?" *Mr. Juan has women?* Rosa asked curiously.

"No digah na' pero en el pueblo dicen que tie' una mujel en una de lah otrah ihlah y loh viajeh que hace no son siempre de negocioh . . . y qu'el sinvelgüenza hahta tie' hijoh con ella . . . . ¡Shhh! . . . no digah na'." *Don't say anything but in the village they say he has a woman on another island and that his trips are not always about business . . . and that the bastard even has children by her . . . . Shhh! . . . don't say anything.*

Meli couldn't figure out why mami didn't like the dresses papi brought her from his trips. At least at first she didn't seem to. Later she wore them anyway, although she complained that they didn't quite fit right, or they were not the right color. Meli liked her new plaid skirts even if they were too warm.

Abuelita said Arturo was a good father because he often brought books for the children too. Meli noticed that abuelita never criticized papi. Meli was quite sure, like abuelita, that things would be a lot easier at the house if mami didn't get so upset at papi, and if mami went out and did things.

Pilar felt she had to go out of the house. She had had a very hard couple of days with Luisa since the drowning scare. She needed to be alone.

She walked out of the front door without being heard and went around to the side of the house, towards the river, where Santiago had planted the roses. He had pruned them earlier in the year and they were coming up strong now. Whites, yellows and pinks. Pilar wasn't as fond of red ones, but there was one in bloom that dominated the garden.

Against the house there were hydrangeas and geraniums, and a little further away, a bed of carnations and a few gardenia bushes. The flowers made her feel quieter.

Pilar heard Marta's voice. "Nunca vah a ehtal felih, Pilar, si siempre quiereh cosah que no tieneh. Tie'h que confolmalte con lo que Dioh manda." *You never going to be happy, Pilar, if you always want things you don't have. Have to be enough what God send you.*

Maybe she was not happy with what she had. But she tried so hard to be!

As she walked closer to the back of the garden she noticed someone sitting on the ground. It was Luisa.

Pilar was startled. "Luisa ¿qué haceh aquí?" *Luisa, what are you doing here?*

Luisa stood up, dropping her colors.

"¡Nada! ¡Nada! Ehtaba dibujando. Perdóname. Voy a entrar enseguida y termino mih leccioneh." *Nothing! Nothing! I was making pictures. I'm sorry. I'll go in right away and finish my lessons.*

Even though it was Luisa who wasn't supposed to be out, Pilar felt she had to explain what she was doing there.

"Tenía que salir de la casa," she said. *I had to get out of the house.*

Luisa looked at her. The question in Luisa's eyes began to fade as she picked up her sketchbook and colors.

"No te vayah todavía," Pilar heard herself say. *Don't go yet.*

Luisa stood there.

"Ven acá. Siéntate conmigo," Pilar said. *Come here. Sit with me.*

She couldn't send Luisa back in right then, even though Juan had confined Luisa to the house until he came back. Pilar stretched out her hand and led Luisa towards a bench near the fence.

Luisa was getting as big as herself, Pilar thought, but she was bony still, like she wasn't ready to be a woman. Pilar put her arm around Luisa's shoulder and pulled her close. Luisa's body felt stiff, but this time Pilar didn't let go.

Luisa let Pilar hold her.

Pilar knew that Luisa tried to be close sometimes. She tried to help Pilar with the smaller children, or bring Pilar her sewing basket. She even brought flowers for Pilar's room.

Luisa also had a way of knowing how Pilar felt. It made her uneasy. It was as if Luisa saw through her. And Luisa wanted something from her, but Pilar didn't know what it was.

Most of the time now she didn't know how to be with Luisa.

Pilar could feel Luisa relaxing. She seemed little, like she used to be before they moved to Bocarío. Pilar knew that Luisa had been happier at the other house. Maybe because they spent more time together. Pilar was pregnant two times after they moved to the big house. The pregnancy with Manuelito had been hard, and the labor was very long and painful. Seña Alba said that Luisa and Mercedes had been frightened. Luisa had gone into her room when Pilar was in labor and had stopped talking for a few days.

When it was over Luisa didn't let anyone look after Pilar. She wanted to do it all herself: bring Pilar her meals, fix her pillows and come into the room frequently to ask Pilar how she was.

"¿Ehtáh bien?" *Are you all right?* Luisa asked now.

"¿Te sienteh mal porque me dihte un suhto el otro día?" Pilar answered with a question. *Do you feel bad because you scared me the other day?*

Luisa shrugged her shoulders and looked down.

"Yo no sé . . . ." *I don't know . . . .*

"¿Te pasa algo?" *Is there something wrong?* Pilar asked.

"No, nada, ehtoy bien," Luisa said quickly. *No, nothing, I'm fine.* "¿Cuándo viene papá?" *When is papá coming back?*

Pilar smiled. "¿Lo echah de menoh? Ya vuelve dentro de treh semanah . . . . Y ya pronto podráh salir denuevo . . . . Él te quiere ¿tú sabeh?" *Do you miss him? He'll be back in three weeks . . . . You'll be able to go out soon . . . . He loves you, you know.*

"Y ¿él te quiere a tí?" *And he loves you too?* Luisa asked, looking directly into her mother's eyes.

Pilar was startled, but she laughed. "Y ¿qué pregunta eh esa? Seguro que me quiere . . . . Mira como noh cuida . . . y siempre vuelve de suh viajeh cargado de regaloh." *What kind of question is that? Of course he loves me . . . . He looks after us . . . and he always comes back from his trips with a load of presents.*

"¿Y por qué abuela Marta y abuelo Pablo nunca vienen acá?" Luisa wanted to know. *Why don't abuela Marta and abuelo Pablo ever come here?*

Pilar looked at Luisa. She was surprised at her questions.

"Tú sabeh como son. Medioh jíbaroh. Dicen que no tienen qué ponerse y que eh muy lejoh venir acá. Se ehtán poniendo viejoh también y no leh guhta salir." *You know how they are. Shy like country people. They say they don't have anything to wear and that it's too far to come here. And they're getting old too. They don't like to go out.*

"Papá nunca va a verloh. Siempre vamoh sin él." *Papá never goes to see them. We always go without him.*

"Tú sabeh que él siempre ehtá de viajeh. Loh negocioh lo tienen muy ocupado. Cuando viene a casa ehtá cansado y tú sabeh que rarah veceh va de visitah." *You know he's always on trips.*

Business keeps him very busy. When he comes home he's very tired, and you know he hardly goes out to visit.

"Bueno . . . va a ver a Tía Teresa. Pero ella tampoco viene acá. Nadie viene acá. Ya ni siquiera viene Seña Alba. ¿Por qué no viene ya, mamá? ¿Se enfermó?" Luisa wanted to know. *Well . . . he goes to see Tía Teresa. But she doesn't come here either. Nobody comes here. Not even Seña Alba. Why doesn't she come anymore, mamá? Is she sick?*

Pilar didn't want to explain what had happened with Seña Alba. After a while she said, "Yo no sé . . . . Pero uhtedeh se acompañan loh unoh a loh otroh . . . . Y tú ni siquiera queríah ir a la ehcuela. Hubierah conocido muchachitah ahí . . . . Y Don Ramiro viene a darte las lecciones." *I don't know . . . . But you keep each other company . . . . And you didn't even want to go to school. You would have met other girls . . . . Anyway, Don Ramiro comes to give you your lessons.*

Luisa fell into a sullen silence.

"Luisa," Pilar said after a while, "¿por qué salihte sin permiso? ¿Y por qué te metihte en el río dehpuéh que tu papá te dijo que no salierah?" *Why did you go out without permission? And why did you go into the river after your papá said you couldn't go out?*

Luisa moved away. She shrugged her shoulders.

Pilar sighed. She didn't even know why she asked. She should have known that Luisa wasn't going to answer.

"Ehtoy tratando de ayudarte." *I'm trying to help you,* Pilar said.

Luisa started to get up. "¿Me puedo ir ya?" *Can I go now?* she asked.

"No, no, quédate aquí . . . no hablamoh máh de eso ahora." *No, no, stay . . . we won't talk about that now.*

They were both silent for a while.

It was no use trying to talk to mami, Meli thought. She was looking at mami sitting in her rocking chair in the living room. Mami would say yes or no and keep rocking. Meli didn't know whether mami heard. But she must have because she came up with answers. Meli was sure though that mami didn't care who asked or what the question was about.

Meli might as well not be there. She felt very tired all of a sudden. She thought of going to lie on her bed for a while. But that was boring. There was never anything to do and nobody ever came to visit anymore. Except abuelita.

Meli went back into the study and fiddled with papers. She tried to type, but she lost interest quickly. Then she went to the refrigerator to get some lemonade. There was only a little left.

"Mami ¿puedo llamar al colmado a que me manden dulces?" *Mami, can I call the grocery store and have them send me some candy?* Meli asked.

"Sí." *Yes,* mami answered without turning.

The shops were too far away. Meli wasn't supposed to go anywhere except neighbors' houses without a grownup or some-times with older cousins.

After Meli had called for the candy she asked mami, "¿Quiereh ir al cine?" *Do you want to go to the movies?*

"Eh muy tarde ya." *It's too late now,* mami answered.

"No, mira, si noh vehtimoh enseguida y avanzamoh podemoh llegar allá a tiempo . . . y aunque lleguemoh un poquito tarde no importa." *No, look, if we leave right away and we hurry we could get there on time . . . and it doesn't matter if we get there a little late,* Meli said.

"Ay, yo no tengo ganah hoy." *I just don't feel like it today,* mami responded.

Meli went out on the back porch and played with the dog. Then she went outside with her sketchbook. She tried to make pictures of the house and the bushes but they never looked right. After a while she went back inside. Mami was still in her rocking chair.

"Mami, ¿te puedo hacer un dibujo?" *Mami, can I make a picture of you?* Meli asked.

"No, yo me voy a acohtar un rato." *No, I'm going to lie down for a while,* mami answered.

Meli went upstairs to her room. She sat at the vanity. Papi had bought it for her. It had a big round mirror and dark mahogany. Even if it was too big for the room, Meli thought it was pretty.

Meli started drawing her own face.

Pilar felt as if she needed to say something but she didn't know what.

"Luisa," Pilar said.

"Mmmm . . ." Luisa responded without stirring.

Pilar wanted to say something to Luisa about herself. About her life. About sitting on the back stairs of Marta's house *cogiendo fresco, catching the breeze.* About Pablo and Marta and her sisters.

But what could she say? She scanned through the images in her mind. She didn't want to talk about sleeping on the floor, about growing up without shoes, without a bathroom. She didn't want to say that her family didn't sit down to eat at the table and that when Marta and Pablo were angry they cursed at each other. And Pilar didn't want the children to know that Juan didn't want her to see her family and that Doña Teresa didn't like her because Marta was black.

Pilar wanted Luisa to love Juan and Juan's family.

"Tu papá eh un hombre bueno," she said out loud. *Your father is a good man.*

Luisa pulled away again. After a while she said, "Mamá, te voy a hacer una pintura de esa rosa ¿me dah permiso?" *Mamá, I'm going to make a picture for you of that rose. Will you let me?*

Pilar was angry at Luisa now. How was she going to explain all this to Juan? Maybe she shouldn't be sitting outside with Luisa.

Luisa was looking at her mother intently.

Pilar didn't want to hurt Luisa's feelings. She didn't know what to say.

"No sé . . . ." *I don't know . . .* Pilar stalled.

"Bueno, si no quiereh . . . ." *Well, if you don't want me to . . . .* Luisa seemed disappointed.

"No eh que no quiera . . . ." *It's not that I don't want you to . . .* Pilar said quickly.

Luisa looked at her with a question in her eyes.

"Eh que tieneh que hacer lah leccioneh." *It's that you have to do your lessons.*

"Yo lah hago. Yo lah hago," Luisa said impatiently and got up to leave. *I'll do them. I'll do them.*

Pilar couldn't bring herself to say that Juan didn't want Luisa sitting outside in the sun. Last time he came home he had noticed that Luisa looked darker.

One of these days Luisa would have to stop running outside. Would have to. Would have to get married. She wouldn't be able to go running barefooted at the beach.

The thought hurt. Pilar remembered that Marta had to pull Pilar out of the river once. She was looking for shellfish with her sisters. They dug in the mud for them, then made a fire out of sticks by the river and ate them. Pilar fell in and was hanging on to a branch. Her sisters didn't dare get in. It was too deep. One of them ran to get their mother. Marta got right in, grabbing on to the branch to get to Pilar.

Pilar remembered she had never hugged her mother so tight. Both muddy, like sapos. Like the *big frogs* in the river. Sticking to each other. Her mother's heavy breasts and belly against her.

Pilar didn't tell Juan that Luisa didn't want to be away from her. Juan already thought Pilar spoiled Luisa. So, when Juan came back, Pilar said the children had all been sick when it was time for them to start their classes in the village and they couldn't go. Afterwards she was afraid they might catch more sicknesses, there was a bad flu going around. Besides, the older girls were señoritas already, they had *menstruated,* and she wasn't sure that she wanted them going to the village by themselves.

"Uno nunca sabe cuando va a pasar algo . . . . Uno oye unah historiah de raptoh y abuso. Yo no voy a poder ehtarleh pendienteh cuando ehten en el pueblo y me voy a quedar intranquila. No quiero que aprendan cosah feah tampoco." *One never knows what can happen . . . . You hear stories about kidnappings and abuse. I'm not going to be able to look after them when they are in the village and I'm going to worry. I don't want them learning ugly things either.*

"Y hahta pueden coger piojoh . . ." she added. *They can even get lice.*

Juan finally hired Don Ramiro to come teach the children at the house. Don Ramiro was a Spaniard, a very distant relative of the Méndez, who had just arrived from Burgos. From the poor side of the family, Juan had said. Don Ramiro later showed the children where his native city was on the map. He also showed them the walls of the old city from where the Spaniards had defended their island. This made a great impression on Pilar. The children laughed at how he put his face close to the map because he was very near-sighted even with his glasses on. He was not much older than Pilar, but had been sick often as a child and had lost all his hair. He had never grown to his full height either; he gave the impression of having shrunk. And his cheeks, the most lively part of him, were constantly red from the heat.

Juan said he didn't want the girls exposed to all kinds of people at the village school but he wanted them to learn reading and writing. In his family that was part of being a lady. He didn't want to be ashamed of them.

Although Don Ramiro had the best references, Pilar was supposed to sit in on all the lessons. But she didn't know whether Juan wanted her to study reading and writing, so she didn't tell him, or anyone, that she was learning too. She paid attention to Don Ramiro's lessons. Then, early in the morning when she was alone, she would practice her letters.

One would have thought reading would be easier than cooking or sewing, but it wasn't. At first all the letters looked the same. She had to look at them for a long time before she could see that each one was a little different. There was no way to do it except to look hard. But she had made up her mind.

Pilar had taken one of the notebooks Juan brought for the children. She didn't want him to notice. She hid it at the bottom of her drawer where she kept her nightgowns.

Pilar remembered the time Juan gave her a note, the first time they met at the church, when Marta didn't know yet that they were seeing each other. She kept the note hidden in her clothes, pinned to the inside of her dress, next to the herbs Seña Alba gave her for protection.

She had memorized the shapes of the letters but she didn't know what it said. She didn't know who to ask either. Seña Alba didn't read, and Pilar didn't want to show the note to Tía Micaela even though Tía Micaela could read a little.

Pilar knew what one word said: Juan. She knew that the last word of a letter was the name of the person who sent it. Tía Micaela had told her. Pilar wrote that word on the ground with a stick over and over again. And she imagined that the first word of the letter was her own name.

For a long time Pilar thought her name was written: Querida, *Dear*. It wasn't until the children started learning how to write, after Don Ramiro came, that she realized that wasn't how her name was written.

Don Ramiro had the children write their names on the first page of their books. He explained that they would need to sign papers some day and write letters. They might want to write a letter to their father who was travelling again.

Pilar had gone into her room and before going to sleep had written "Querida" on the front page of the notebook she had kept for herself. She was proud that she knew the lesson already.

Until the next day.

Luisa asked Don Ramiro how to write her mother's name. She wanted to put it on the second page of her book and draw some flowers around it. Don Ramiro thought that was a good idea, for all of them to learn both of their parents' names.

"Pilar Clausé de Méndez," he wrote on the small chalkboard which sat on an easel. He went word by word, pronouncing each one slowly with his Castilian accent. Pilar felt herself blushing. She didn't know whether to hide, or be angry, or laugh. She kept thinking: he's wrong, he's wrong. She wanted to say: I learned my name from Juan already. You're wrong. She felt deceived at the same time. But didn't know by what or by whom.

"Juan Méndez y Pilar Clausé de Méndez," all the children kept reciting. All the words together on all their books repeated over and over again. She felt dizzy and had to go into her room. She took her pencil and crossed off the word "Querida" angrily. Many times.

Pilar watched the curtains of her room move with the ocean breeze.

Juan would be back in three weeks or so. She must remember to send Santiago to the village early to see if there was a letter from Juan. One of the girls could read it to her. She was pleased because Mercedes and Luisa could read so well already. They had learned very fast since Don Ramiro had started coming.

A few days after Luisa was pulled out of the river, Pilar woke up very anxious. She kept seeing Luisa muddy and choking. She couldn't get rid of the image, so she got up quickly and went to the kitchen. The children weren't up. Pilar was relieved to see Fernanda already making the thick coffee and steaming the milk.

"Tráeme el café al cuarto, Fernanda, por favor." *Bring the coffee to my room, Fernanda, please,* Pilar said.

She crossed the living room again towards the side of the house where the children's rooms were. She needed to see if they were all right.

When Pilar looked into Mercedes and Luisa's room she was startled because Luisa was not in her bed. Pilar was about to walk into the room when she saw Luisa perched on the window seat looking out. Luisa quickly hid something when she saw Pilar at the door.

Pilar smiled at Luisa but didn't say anything. She didn't want to wake up Mercedes. Luisa waved awkwardly at her mother.

Pilar knew that Luisa was hiding a bird. Luisa didn't dare do that except when Juan was gone. Pilar wasn't sure what to do. She usually gave in or pretended she didn't notice because it was too hard to keep after Luisa. Besides, Luisa was happier when she could have her creatures.

Back in her own room, Pilar realized that Luisa didn't miss Juan. She laughed more when he was gone.

After a while, Pilar heard Luisa and Mercedes giggling in the kitchen and Fernanda trying to scold them. Fernanda had first come to work at the other house. Luisa was her baby. Pilar remembered Fernanda leading Luisa on a horse around and around in the yard when Luisa was only two. Luisa had the pinkest cheeks and was always getting into some mischief.

"¡Miren se van a quemal! ¡Sáquen lah manoh de ahí!" *You going to get burnt! Get your hands out of there!* Pilar heard Fernanda screaming at them. Pilar knew they were teasing Fernanda and trying to pinch the bread before it was done cooling. Fernanda would try to sit them down until it was ready but they would get up behind her back and touch it.

Pilar felt a pang of jealousy.

Luisa preferred to eat in the kitchen. She hated to eat with a fork and to have to put her napkin on her lap. Pilar insisted. She said she didn't want Luisa or any of the children to have to be ashamed when they went to their grand aunt Teresa's house.

Pilar called Luisa to sit at the dining room table. Next to Mercedes and across from Pilar. Luisa was eating very fast without looking up, as if she didn't see anything except the food in front of her. It reminded Pilar of how Pablo used to eat: fast and without saying a word.

"Luisa ¿por qué tieneh tanta prisa?" *Luisa, why are you in such a hurry?* Pilar said.

Luisa stopped and answered without looking up.

"Lo siento, mamá." *I'm sorry, mamá.*

Mercedes looked at Luisa and touched her arm. "Dehpuéh de un rato ¿vámoh a coser?" *Let's go sew after a while, okay?*

Pilar felt tired and discouraged all of a sudden, but she said, "Mercedes, me tieneh qu'enseñar lo qu'ehtáh cosiendo." *Mercedes, you have to show me what you're sewing.*

Pilar used to sew with Luisa and Mercedes on the veranda but she didn't have time recently. She had been spending a lot of time with Manuelito, who was getting in more and more trouble. He was the only boy in a household of women. Pilar felt he needed more attention. She was also having to make sure that Luisa stayed in since Juan had punished her by forbidding her to leave the house. If Pilar didn't keep an eye on her, Luisa would disappear. It was hard to have to keep guard on her that way. It made them strangers to each other.

Pilar was angry at Luisa because she didn't try hard enough to obey her father. But it was hard to admit that to herself. Pilar remembered Marta losing her temper and screaming at the children. It didn't seem to do any good that Marta got angry. Patria still sneaked out. The boys still fought with each other and knocked things down.

Juan didn't shout. Pilar could remember only once or twice when he had raised his voice. Doña Teresa, Juan's aunt, and Doña Saturnina, Juan's cousin, didn't scream and everybody obeyed them. Pilar wanted to be like them.

She wasn't going to shout at Luisa. Luisa should know better. She was almost a woman. Instead, Pilar said quietly, "Luisa, ehtoy muy preocupada por tí. Nadie te va a rehpetar si no tieneh educación y modaleh. Mira la familia mía. Papá todavía ahí trabajando en la caña y loh muchachoh igual." *Luisa, I'm very worried about you. Nobody is going to respect you if you don't have an education and good manners. Look at my family. Papá still cutting cane and the boys will be doing the same.*

Luisa sat in front of her plate, looking down and saying nothing.

Pilar stopped to look at her. "¿Qué diceh, Luisa?" *Luisa, what do you say?*

Luisa shook her head.

"¿Nada?" *Nothing?* Pilar asked.

"A Luisa le guhta hacer otrah cosah." *Luisa likes to do other things,* Mercedes intervened.

"Y ehtá bien que haga otrah cosah." *And it's fine for her to do other things,* Pilar said impatiently. "Pero no tirarse al río y darme un mal rato cuando debería de ehtar haciendo suh lecciones. No ereh una nenita ya, Luisa, y no quiero tener que ehtarte pendiente. Entre tú y Manuelito me acaban." *But not to throw herself in the river and give me a scare when she should have been doing her lessons. You're not a child anymore, Luisa. I don't want to be looking after you all the time. You and Manuelito are wearing me out.*

She stopped herself. It was as if Marta were talking out of her mouth. She quickly added, "Perdóname por levantar la voz, Luisa, pero eh que tengo miedo que vayah a parar como tanta gente pobre por ahí. Yo sé que te vah a casar y Dioh quiera que te salga bueno el hombre. Como Juan. Pero, si no . . . ." *I'm sorry I raised my voice, Luisa. It's just that I'm afraid you're going to end up like so many poor people around. I know you're going to get married and I hope he turns out to be a good man. Like Juan. But if not . . . .*

"Yo no me voy a casar." *I'm not going to get married,* Luisa muttered stubbornly, still looking down at her plate.

"Eso lo diceh ahora, pero dehpuéh . . . ya tú vah a ver, cuando empiecen a andar loh muchachoh detráh de tí." *That's what you say now, but later . . . you'll see when boys start to chase after you.*

Luisa shook her head while still looking down.

"Yo no quiero que mi marido me deje sola mientrah él va de viajeh. Yo quiero una finca." *I don't want my husband to leave me by myself while he goes on trips. I want a farm.*

Pilar was startled.

Mercedes touched Luisa's arm. "No te preocupeh por eso ahora . . . ." *Don't worry about that now . . .* she said.

"¿Me puedo ir de la mesa ya?" *Can I leave the table now?* Luisa asked her mother without looking at her.

Pilar sat at the table and watched Luisa and Mercedes leave the room. Luisa walked away quickly with her back very straight.

"Luisa no sabe lo que eh ser pobre." *Luisa doesn't know what it's like to be poor,* Pilar said aloud to herself. "Debería ehtar agradecida por todo lo que tiene. Juan eh bueno. Quiere qu'ella aprenda cosah. ¿Cuántoh hombreh uno va encontrar que quieren que suh hijah aprendan a leer y ehcribir y coser y tener modaleh?" *She should be thankful for everything she has. Juan is a good man. He wants her to learn things. How many men are there who are going to want their daughters to learn to read and write and to sew and have manners?*

Pilar remembered the last time Juan was home.

They were all sitting at the table having breakfast. Juan always insisted they eat each meal at the table and that they should all be dressed, washed and have their hair combed. Even when they were little. He expected them to eat properly, ask for things to be passed, not play with their food and not fight at the table.

They had to pay more attention to everything when he was there. The children were scared of him, but even though it was hard for them, Pilar liked it that Juan took an interest in what they did. Pablo never had been interested in what his children did. Marta was supposed to do that.

Juan had asked them at the table what they had been doing in his absence. Each one had to answer, even Clara, who was only five.

Mercedes was the first one.

"Ehtoy cosiendo unah fundah para mamá con bordadoh en blanco. También copié la composición que me dejahte y leí loh pasajeh del libro pero habían unah palabrah que yo no entendía." *I'm embroidering some pillowcases for mamá, all in white. I also copied the composition and read the parts of the book you left for me but there were some words I couldn't understand.*

"Bueno. Un poco más tarde me vas a traer el cuaderno y yo te voy a buscar las palabras en el diccionario." *Fine. A little later you can bring your notebook and I will find the words for you in the dictionary*, he said.

Then he turned to Luisa. "Bueno ¿y tú, Luisa?" *And what about you, Luisa?*

Luisa was nervous. "Ehte . . . ." *Ahh . . . .*

"Luisa, no empieces con 'este.' Ya te lo he dicho muchas veces. Piensa lo que vas a decir primero y luego dilo. Cuando empiezas con 'este' pareces tonta," Juan said sternly. *Luisa, don't begin with 'ah.' I have told you many times. Think about what you are going to say first, then say it. When you begin with 'ah' you sound stupid.*

Luisa's face turned very red. Clara and Manuelito giggled.

"Y ustedes cállense. Esto no es para reírse," Juan said to them. *And you be quiet. This is no laughing matter.*

"Luisa, empieza de nuevo," Juan added. *Luisa, start again.*

She was silent for a while. Juan was getting impatient.

"Bueno, Luisa, ya has tenido suficiente tiempo para pensar lo que vas a decir." *Well, Luisa, you have had enough time to think about what you are going to say.*

"L'ehtoy ayudando a Mercedes a coser," she said very softly, looking down. *I've been helping Mercedes with her sewing.*

"Casi no te puedo oir. Levanta la cabeza y mírame." *I can hardly hear you. Lift your head and look at me*, Juan said.

She lifted her head, but was silent and didn't look at him. Everyone at the table sat very still.

Juan's face was somber. "¿Bueno?" he said. *Well?*

Luisa tried to speak but only sounds came out of her. She gasped as if she were drowning.

                        Meli was trying to figure out how one drew a real face. She had only learned to make copies of pictures at school in her drawing class with the Spanish nun. Meli was looking at mami's face carefully now. Mami was sitting in her rocking chair with her eyes closed. There were lots of shadows around the eyes. Meli didn't know whether that was the color of the skin or whether it was the light. Then Meli noticed the scar right above the left eye. She looked quickly at the other small scar above the lip. On the same side.

Meli couldn't remember whether mami had said she had fallen down the stairs when Meli was little or before Meli was born. Mami used to do a lot of things around the house.

It was scary to think of mami falling down those stairs. Banged her nose too. The nose was a little crooked. Didn't notice it too much though.

Meli was glad she didn't remember or wasn't around to watch it. She wondered whether they put a bandage on mami's face. It must have been swollen and she probably looked terrible. Black and blue all over her face.

Meli would be very embarrassed if she had to show up at school with a bandage and her face black and blue. She wouldn't go, probably. She would talk mami into letting her stay home.

Then mami opened her eyes.

"Un día te voy a hacer un retrato." *Someday I'm going to make a picture of you,* Meli said.

"¡Ay no, nena! ¡Tieneh que hacer dibujoh de cosah bonitah!" mami exclaimed. *No, honey! You have to make pictures of pretty things!*

Meli wanted art books. She had seen them advertised in a magazine at Tía Clara's. Books about drawing faces, about oil painting and about anatomy. She wanted to learn to make pictures of real things.

She figured that instead of a present, she wanted money for her birthday. She would order the books by mail.

Mami gave her the money. Those were the first books Meli bought for herself.

Abuelita had said that the only place she had seen books when she was growing up was at the church. Those books had things in them you said to God. She knew you couldn't just tell the God that lived in the church what was on your mind. She thought there was a book that told you what to say to the King of Spain too. She had seen the King of Spain right up there next to God.

Meli liked the story abuelita told about the King of Spain.

As a child abuelita used to think that it was nice of the King of Spain to let them use his road. She knew that even the road belonged to him. She wondered whether she might ever run into him walking.

Seña Alba had said kings didn't walk. Abuelita asked whether there was something wrong with his legs. Seña Alba slapped her thigh and shook with laughter.

Might as well have something wrong with his legs, abuelita told her Seña Alba had said. Don't suppose he ever use them, sitting around in his fancy clothes.

Abuelita had been worried about the King of Spain and about how he felt when the Americans came. There were boats firing cannons at the buildings. Killing people. Lots of them. There were big fires too. Abuelita thought the king must have been angry that someone was burning his island even if he lived far away.

Seña Alba said nothing had happened to the king that she knew of.

"Lo único de que se mueren los reyeh eh de comel," Seña Alba said. *Only thing kings die of is eating.*

Abuelita had hoped, when she was a child, that the kings who brought presents on the Día de Reyes, *Three Kings' Day,* didn't die of eating too much. She wondered whether they knew the King of Spain. Even after she didn't believe anymore that they brought presents, she had thought for a long time that they were real and lived someplace.

When abuelita first knew Juan she had wanted to ask him whether he knew the King of Spain. She was too shy though.

Pilar left the breakfast table and went to her room. She couldn't understand Luisa's lack of interest in improving herself. If Pilar herself had time, she would spend it all learning to read.

She remembered Doña Saturnina. She had books too like the church did. She was a cousin of Juan's. Married to Don Anselmo. They didn't have children and some people were sorry for them. But they had a roomful of books. Pilar had thought it would eat up your eyes to read every page that was there. She couldn't figure out when Doña Saturnina had time to read all of them.

The first time she saw that room Pilar just stood there. That was the first year she and Juan were together. Doña Saturnina was the only one in Juan's family who liked Pilar. The rest of them acted as if she didn't exist.

"¿Qué te pasa, muchacha?" Doña Saturnina said. *What's the matter, girl?*

"¡Ni la iglesia tiene tantoh libroh!" Pilar exclaimed. *Not even the church has so many books!*

Doña Saturnina laughed.

After that she wanted to loan Pilar books each time she came to visit. Pilar refused, saying she didn't have time. She couldn't say she didn't know how to read.

Pilar didn't say anything to Juan about Doña Saturnina wanting to loan her books. She thought Juan wouldn't like it somehow.

Doña Saturnina never asked Pilar whether she could read. She usually read to Pilar when she came to visit every few months. After a while she didn't offer to loan books. Just said Pilar should ask when she had time. They would just sit, Doña Saturnina reading and Pilar listening, on the shaded porch facing the front yard with the flowers behind the iron fence. But her books weren't about what you said to God. They were stories. About people like you and me, Doña Saturnina said.

Juan had books too, like Doña Saturnina and Don Anselmo, but kept them in his room at Doña Teresa's house. Pilar didn't know what those books were about. He still had a room at his aunt's after all these years. He said he didn't want to hurt Doña Teresa's feelings. He had stayed with her when he first came to the island.

Pilar had never seen the room. To this day.

Juan had brought a few books to Bocarío when Don Ramiro had started coming to the house. Juan didn't let anyone use the books though. He had them behind glass shelves in the office room in the house. Juan met with the bookkeeper, the administrator of the finca, the *farm*, and the hired men in the office. Maybe he read the books. Pilar had never asked.

Sometimes Juan would bring out a book and read to the children. Then he asked questions of them to see if they had been listening carefully. He became impatient when they asked questions.

Pilar sat with them, sewing and listening.

Doña Saturnina and Don Anselmo, and Juan too, talked different from her. It seemed to Pilar that it was a nicer way to talk. The books sounded that way too.

It was hard to talk like they did. It was like walking in shoes, when she first started to. Couldn't go as fast. She felt like her feet wanted to run away. It was like that with her mouth. Words just wanted to come out. Not get bent and squeezed like women in those tight things they wore under their clothes. Made them look stiff. Pilar smiled remembering that she used to wonder how they could breathe.

Pilar didn't say much in those days because she couldn't talk like Doña Saturnina and Don Anselmo. Pilar didn't want them to laugh at her.

It was a little different with Juan. In the early days he thought it was charming how she talked.

Seña Alba had told Pilar she should talk the way she talked. The way it comes out. No use trying to make a mango come out like a coconut. No use trying to make a black woman come out white, except by burning out her skin. Seña Alba told her about a black woman who had burnt herself when her mulatto husband had walked out on her with a white woman. The only other way would be to paint herself like the vejigantes, the *masked men* who had yellow faces for the Feast of the Apostle Santiago, Seña Alba said, laughing.

Mostly, Pilar didn't talk very much. She had never talked very much growing up and as she became older, people thought she was reserved. It made them respect her. But she knew she didn't talk much because she felt foolish talking like the Spaniards and ashamed of talking like the *country people,* the jíbaros.

Juan was very angry when the children spoke like that. He didn't say much. It just felt like a cloud had gone over the sun and the air was cooler. She could tell.

So Pilar tried to correct herself and correct them. She tried every day to pay attention.

Pilar sat on her rocking chair facing the veranda, with her sewing on her lap. She remembered that Doña Saturnina read her stories about lovers who had trouble getting together. Their families didn't want them to marry. Like Doña Teresa, Pilar thought. Doña Teresa didn't like her. She had had someone else in mind for Juan. Pilar had figured it out. A Spanish woman by the name of Catalina. Pilar had seen her one of the few times she had been invited to Doña Teresa's at Juan's insistence.

Catalina was a little older than Pilar. Blonde. Pilar hadn't seen a blonde Spaniard before. She hadn't even known there was hair like that. She was trying to think of what looked that soft, but couldn't. Catalina was very pretty to look at. It made you want to do things for her too.

Pilar was afraid Juan would notice Catalina too much. Well, Doña Teresa certainly made sure Juan did. She kept bringing Catalina around to talk to him. Catalina with her pretty way of saying things.

When they were introduced Catalina said how beautiful Pilar was. Pilar could hardly get words out but managed to say that Catalina was very beautiful herself.

That day Pilar wished Catalina could be her friend. But she also knew that it was not possible.

Doña Teresa didn't think Pilar was good enough for Juan. Pilar remembered that from the beginning she didn't want to make trouble for Juan with his family, like it happened in the stories Doña Saturnina read. People ended up shooting each other. Men did, that is; women went to be nuns. Like the Spanish ladies who wore all those hot clothes.

"Ehtan casa'h con Dioh." *They're married to God.* That's what Tía Micaela had told Pilar about nuns when Pilar was little.

"Dioh tie' muchah mujereh," Seña Alba had said. "Debe sel ehpañol." *God sure's got a lot of women. Must be a Spaniard.*

Pilar had thought God must keep nuns from dying in the heat wearing all those clothes.

In the books the women died from loving, Pilar said to herself. Maybe that's what was happening to her. She didn't feel sick or anything, just sad, even when she was busy, like now, sewing. Suddenly, a picture of Seña Alba came to Pilar. Seña Alba's black skin looked like one of the polished stones by the river. And she had a shine in her eyes like she knew something nobody else knew and it was funny.

"Loh pobreh no se ríen así to' el tiempo," Marta had said. "Seña Alba debe ehtal emborrachá'." *Poor people don't laugh like that all the time. Seña Alba's got to be drunk.*

Pilar had never smelled rum on Seña Alba. Not once. Never talked to Seña Alba about it either. Except Seña Alba had said something about rum being the only thing that helped her not hurt. Pilar asked what hurt but got no answer. She had never thought about Seña Alba hurting. Seña Alba didn't talk about herself.

She hadn't seen Seña Alba since the night of Elena's wake earlier in the year. What if Seña Alba never came back? she thought suddenly, looking up from her sewing at the clear sky. It was like thinking there would not be morning. She felt desperate. Nights were just for waiting.

Mami made a scary silence around her. Meli knew what was coming. When papi came home after being gone Saturday night she would scream at him and pull at his clothes. She didn't even wait for him to come in the house sometimes. Meli saw mami once in the glare of the headlights reflected on the garage wall. She was leaning into the car window hitting him. He would never hit back. He would just keep her away and curse angrily at her.

Meli had overheard abuelita say to mami, "Luisa, eso le va a hacer daño a Meli, esah peleah que tieneh con Arturo." *Luisa, those fights you have with Arturo are going to hurt Meli.*

Mami didn't stop. Sometimes she even called him mean names in front of abuelita and Meli's aunts. Meli didn't want to hear so she went up to her room.

The only time Meli had seen mami angry at abuelita was one Sunday morning. Mami and papi had had a fight the night before. Meli was glad abuelita was there.

That morning Meli was in the kitchen getting her café con leche when she heard abuelita on the back terrace saying to mami again, "Luisa, tú no sabeh el daño que le hacen esah peleah a Meli." *Luisa, you don't know how much those fights hurt Meli.*

That time mami snapped back, "¡Fué por tí que yo me casé con Arturo! ¿No te acuerdah? Yo tenía otro pretendiente. El poeta. Pero tú decíah que no me podía mantener; que noh ibamoh a morir de hambre. ¿No te acuerdah? Decíah que Arturo tenía buen trabajo, que era ambicioso. ¡Bien ambicioso y bien mujeriego!" *It was because of you that I married Arturo! Don't you remember? I had another beau. The poet. But you said he couldn't support me, that we were going to starve. Don't you remember? You said Arturo had a good job, that he was ambitious. Very ambitious and very much a woman chaser!*

"¡Cállate que Meli te va a oir!" *Be quiet! Meli's going to hear you,* abuelita said.

For many weeks after that Meli was curious about mami's beau, but she never heard anything about him again. And she didn't ask because she didn't want mami or abuelita to be angry at her.

Mami didn't go out with papi anymore. It used to be that abuelita would stay with Meli, her brother and a cousin or two at night while mami and papi went to the movies. Abuelita let them turn off all the lights and they had rubber band wars. When it got late they would play a game of 'counting cars.' Abuelita would have them guess how many cars would go by on the street before mami and papi came back. The person who came closest to the right number got a little prize.

Lying on her bed, Meli tried to remember what the prizes had been but kept getting distracted by the sound of the wind in the leaves. When she turned to look out of her bedroom window she saw Seña Alba standing at the foot of the flamboyán looking at a spray of orchids which grew from the place where a big branch came out of the trunk.

Meli noticed again how the trunk looked like a body with muscles and tight, smooth skin. Seña Alba seemed to be standing next to a giant. Meli wished she were Aladdin and could rub a lamp and make the tree turn into a giant who would grant her three wishes. She had seen the movie.

Suddenly, Seña Alba was squatting in front of Meli.

"¿Cuáleh son loh treh deseoh que tieneh?" *What are your three wishes?*

Meli was surprised every time Seña Alba read her thoughts. But Meli didn't know the answer. There were so many things! It was hard to know what was most important to ask for. In fairy tales you got punished if you asked for the wrong things.

She looked out to the yard. The rabbit cages. The orange tree. Palms, hibiscus, papaya.

"Una cámara de películah." *A movie camera,* she said suddenly.

"¿Y qué máh?" *And what else?* Seña Alba asked.

"Que no tenga miedo de noche." *That I'm not afraid at night,* she answered, wondering whether she should have asked that she not be afraid of anything. Then she thought that might be too much to ask. Meli also knew from stories that it was not okay to be too greedy.

"¿Y el último deseo?" *And the last wish?*

The last one was always the hardest. What if it wasn't right and then you felt sorry you had asked for the wrong thing? Then you didn't have any more wishes left.

"¿Lo puedo guardar para máh tarde?" *Can I save it for later?* Meli asked. She didn't want to take any chances. She had to think about it some more.

She didn't want mami to have any more fights with papi. But what if the tidal wave came? She had to keep an emergency wish to be rescued. She hoped to go away to the United States too. It was a good thing she had asked not to be afraid at night because she didn't know how she could go to the United States by herself if she were afraid at night. And Meli wished her mother was like the American mothers who bought store dresses, read magazines in English, drove cars and didn't hide when people came to the house.

Pilar remembered how good it felt to sit on the porch all afternoon and listen to Doña Saturnina read. Pilar liked to look at her too. She was a pretty lady in a shiny black dress that must have cost many months of wages. Pilar wondered who sewed so nice for her. She wore lace too, not where it showed the breasts, she blushed to think of Doña Saturnina being so exposed, but just neatly around the face. It made her face sweeter somehow. And she had the whitest, softest skin you ever saw. Like the inside of a new coconut. She didn't know how these Spaniard women kept looking so pretty and white in the heat. And Doña Saturnina smelled like she had flowers hidden in her clothes. Pilar could never figure out where. Made it nice to sit next to her.

Doña Saturnina once asked Pilar to come stay for a few days. That was when Mercedes was almost a year old and Doña Teresa hadn't seen her yet. Juan was going to take Mercedes to Doña Teresa's. Pilar was not invited. She wondered years later whether Doña Saturnina found out and invited Pilar so that her feelings wouldn't be hurt.

"Para que descanses de esa niña," she said. "Ser madre debe agotar." *So you can get a rest from looking after that child. Being a mother must be exhausting.*

So Pilar came to visit.

There she felt like a child herself. Doña Saturnina fussed over her. She made sure Pilar got enough sleep. She had the maid bring a tray with steaming milk to her room each night.

During the day someone came to fit her for a dress. Doña Saturnina gave her several. Shoes and underwear too. And perfume. It made her smell like flowers too. Pilar felt like she was sitting in the middle of a field.

Doña Saturnina didn't tell Pilar what to do but Pilar learned just from watching. Watching how Doña Saturnina ate. At first, Pilar said she didn't want anything to eat. She was worried she might break the pretty plates out of nervousness. Her hands were shaking. She didn't know where to put them.

So she just sat there the first time. She watched Doña Saturnina never touch food with her hands. Pilar figured that's why her hands were so clean and pretty. And she listened to Doña Saturnina tell stories about crossing the ocean. Pilar couldn't imagine being in the middle of all that water without any land around. She thought Doña Saturnina was very brave. Doña Saturnina showed her pictures of big buildings too. She had been inside them. Pilar thought she would never do that. She would be afraid the building would fall down.

Pilar wondered why Doña Saturnina came to the island when there were so many other places she liked so well.

It was hard for Pilar to go back to her mother's house at first after visiting Doña Saturnina. She didn't want to say it to herself but it was true. After being in town, she noticed how Marta smelled and how dirty her hands were. And how loud her voice was too.

The children running around. Peeing outside. Nobody said very much to anybody else either. Pablo came from the fields and he sat on the front steps without his shirt on until it was time to eat. He ate, then got up to sit on the steps again, chewing tobacco and spitting until it got dark, then went to sleep.

One morning Meli noticed mami more than usual. How mami looked.

Meli had invited a schoolmate to come to the house after school. She didn't have people over very much. Her school friends lived far away. But Meli knew it had more to do with mami.

She noticed mami's bare feet with the long toenails. They had dirt in them. The old sandals were in a corner. And mami's dress had buttons missing. It was held with a safety pin at the breasts. She didn't want to think of it, but mami didn't have on any underwear. Meli guessed that's how they did it in the country, but she also knew abuelita didn't do that.

Mami was scary, sitting in the rocking chair with her legs spread open. Her rough feet. Hair not combed. Meli stood at the door to the back porch for a moment. Mami sat there rocking and humming.

"¡Mami!" Meli called.

Mami turned. "¡Qué linda!" she said. *How pretty you look!*

Mami got up and hugged Meli. Meli wished she wouldn't. She pulled away a little. Mami smelled of sweat. It was good that mami went into the kitchen right away to heat the milk for Meli's coffee.

Meli went and sat down at the dining room table, wondering how it was going to be when her friend came after school. She could go directly to the yard. Show her the ducks and rabbits. Play ball. Maybe mami would go upstairs and lie on her bed in the afternoon, like she did sometimes, until it was time to fix supper.

Meli's mind wandered from mami to the fried egg in front of her that she didn't feel like eating to what was going to happen when she brought her friend over. And the school bus was late. It was always breaking down. She hoped papi didn't have to take her to school. She felt embarrassed when she had to walk into class late. She didn't like it when people looked at her. But she was proud of papi's big, new car. She secretly hoped her school friends would notice it.

Mami stood behind her and started combing her hair. She had to undo Meli's braids and then do them again. Pulled her hair.

"¡Aauuu!" Meli screamed.

Mami let go for a minute then started again. Meli thought that as soon as she was old enough she would cut all her hair off. Then mami wouldn't have to make her braids anymore.

"Ya ehtá." *All done,* mami said, and bent down to kiss Meli on the cheek.

Meli just didn't like her smell. And mami's cheeks were always sticky from sweat. Abuelita sweated too when she was out sweeping the front terrace, but it was a kind of clean sweat. She had a man's handkerchief hanging from her belt that she wiped her face with. Abuelita smelled of powder, like her nightgowns.

Meli liked sleeping with abuelita when abuelita stayed over a couple of nights in the week. The rest of the time she stayed with her other daughters. Abuelita told her stories after they turned off the lights. But Meli never liked being in bed with mami even when she was real scared in the night. Mami made blood spots on her sheets sometimes and even on her dress. And she didn't cover herself.

It made Meli angry at mami.

Meli was staring at the frayed place on the rug. Right next to the front door. Right where everybody could see it. Maybe she could put something over it.

But it wasn't just that. There was dog hair everywhere and the arms of the chairs were stained with grease.

It would be better to stay in the yard with her friend. And when her friend's mother came to pick her up, they could wait out in front of the house so the mother wouldn't have to come in and say hello to mami.

Meli was good at imagining things. Most times it was okay, but when she was scared she wished she didn't. She put pillows on her head at night to try to keep out the pictures. But it was no use. The pictures were inside. The only way they would go away was if someone was right there next to her. Especially abuelita. No bad pictures ever came up when she was around.

With mami it was different; it was like mami wasn't there. Even when she called mami in the night and mami answered. She didn't really wake up. She answered in her sleep, Meli thought.

It was at night mostly that Meli was scared. The pictures hid in dark corners. Especially in the closet. She was afraid scary ghosts would come out of there.

She loved stories about being invisible. She thought that would be a good way not to be scared. She wouldn't be afraid of anybody doing anything to her because they wouldn't know where she was. And she could watch them without their knowing.

It would be like peeking through the nail holes in the fence at the back of the yard. She could see little black kids squatting on the ground; fat women in dirty dresses carrying water, sitting on front steps smoking, or arguing with old men without shirts.

She didn't think she was supposed to look, so she didn't very often.

It was scary too how those people lived.

"Esoh negroh," mami would say. *Niggers!*

BOOK
THREE
□

☐ Seña Alba lay on the ground. It was cool.

She could see the whole night sky. So big you could get lost looking. But close too.

She wondered what it would be like to touch the sky.

She closed her eyes and reached up. Felt something very soft touching her fingers. As soft as a mother's breasts. Or a baby's lips.

She opened her eyes suddenly to erase the feelings. Felt like something sharp growing out of the ground had cut into her back. Was stuck in her chest.

There it was again. The scream trapped inside her. Like bloody wings beating her ribs.

She wanted to go to the store, get a bottle of rum and drink it all at once. Until the rum burnt the sound of tearing in her. But she knew that the next day her body would be like a tree after a hurricane, bent on its side with its roots in the air. And she would get so busy mending herself that she would forget the fury of what had come loose in her. For a while.

Tonight there was a break in the rain. She was happy to sleep outside. Didn't mind the wet ground. Felt warm after a while. Like somebody was holding her. She didn't want to put things between herself and the ground. Between herself and the sky and trees. Got nothing to hide.

"Pero, Seña Alba ¿polqué t'ehcondeh?" she heard Pilar ask at the beach, first time they met. *But, Seña Alba, why you hide!* With eyes that wanted to take everything in. Bigger than this night sky.

Don't see that look much, Seña Alba thought. Like every-thing's new and nothing hurt yet. Seen that look in the newborn goat she deliver yesterday. Holler like she got her leg stuck some-place. Seña Alba had held the kid against her chest to quiet it.

She felt that way now remembering Niña Pilar, which is what she called Pilar even now when she had her own children. To herself mostly. She thought maybe Pilar wouldn't want to be called niña anymore. *Girl.* Didn't want to be made little.

Yes, she felt warm in her chest like she was holding a new baby.

Seña Alba, why you hide? Pilar had asked.

The question sank into her like a smooth stone into a pool. Rolled in easy and sank deep. Hardly left any ripples you could see. But went directly to the bottom and sat there.

Seña Alba could feel the question in her. Could feel Niña Pilar finding her. Didn't even know she was hiding until this child find her. At the beach.

Rain pouring down her face and body like the sky's kissing her. This feeling coming into her. Like loving. Feeling so full of it like you can't breathe. But it keep coming in. Through her feet. Her hands. The skin on her arms. Her cheeks.

Like there's rivers piling on her head, below her matted hair. Pouring into her ears. Turning into a roar. Don't know anymore whether it's inside or outside.

She follow where it take her. The sounds. The feeling.

Suddenly it all stop. Pour out of her. Not like she's empty. Don't make sense. Full of quiet. Like in the morning when the ocean's sleeping. Except she look around, at the beach, and the ocean's still loud. The quiet is inside her.

Don't have to do with ears and sound, Seña Alba thought. Have to do with something inside.

Different kind of quiet now, hiding in the sugar cane. Like after her baby die. Feel there's no air and not even the trees is breathing. Nothing's breathing.

She feel she is dying. Everybody have it wrong about the light going out and everything being black. Everything's the same. Like a shell you find at the beach. Except nothing's living in it.

Shell's quiet because something's gone that talk to it.

She didn't know how long that went on. Don't matter about time, she thought. She never care about time much anyway. Not people's time. Like the men cutting sugar cane between the morning whistle and the afternoon whistle. You whistle for dogs, not people. And even dogs you treat more careful than mill people treat the cutters. Even praying, people do at the sound of a bell.

She know better. She know the kind of time makes sense. Time it takes to shape a baby inside you. Time it takes the sugar cane to grow and the ocean to get quiet and pull into itself, then come back up and clean the beach. Ocean has a job too. People don't understand that. Think it's just mean like they are. Ocean grows things inside itself. Some of it she leaves on the beach for people to find. Some of it you have to ask her for.

Ocean don't go by no whistle.

After her baby stop breathing she get hard. Like a shell. A hollow sound in her. Nothing sit in there and feel it belong.

She remembered that the only thing that kept moving was the ocean. So she sat by it day after day.

Don't even know when one day begin and the last one stop. Only thing she see is the ocean moving. It teach her to breathe.

She breathe with it. Sometimes quiet. Sometimes loud. Teach her to cry again too, after sitting there forever, it seem like, looking back on it. Rain coming down. Coming down and coming down. Then she feel it's coming down warm on her face. Like fingers touching her. Eyes feel warm too. And the ocean's a little brighter. Lights dancing on it.

She look around. No sun out. Not even any shine in the sky. Piles and piles of clouds on the sun. Like you bury something so good you can't find it. She reach up to touch her eye. Think something's got into it.

It's tears what's got into it.

She figure it's a gift from the ocean, the tears. Salty like it.

Different kind of quiet after you cry too. Washed clean on the inside. Like a baby that wake up in her mother's arms after sleeping.

The ache began to grow inside Seña Alba again like a vine choking her heart.

Never hurt anything in her life. But she hurt her Niña Pilar bad.

It's a curse. You hurt most what you love most. She wanted to be cut down like the sugar cane and crushed between the teeth of the mill into pulp and bagasse.

If she could feed the ground, she might feel good again. Then her blood would be washed clean.

Images of blood on a white sheet swam through her head. A priest was praying. Her ma screamed. Then there were roads and roads until she saw the ocean. And Pilar.

It had started to get very cloudy at Bocarío. By lunch time it was already raining. Manuelito cut his finger trying to help Fernanda peel potatoes, and Clara broke Pilar's favorite vase.

She was thinking of things for the children to do when she heard a horse galloping on the road. Pilar went to the front of the house to look in the direction of the sound. She didn't recognize the man, but opened the door and stood on the porch to greet him.

He brought a letter from Juan marked urgent. It had postage from Spain. Pilar opened it immediately after telling the messenger to go around to the kitchen to get some coffee.

"Querida Pilar . . . ." *Dear Pilar . . . .* It was dated one month earlier.

Pilar was frightened. She read the words slowly.

"Ehtán todos bien en esta. Los . . . ." *Everyone is well here. The . . . .*

She couldn't understand the next word. She stood staring at the page and her whole body began to sweat.

"¡Luisa!" she called.

Luisa answered, "Dime, mamá." *Yes, mamá.*

"Ven acá." *Come here.*

Pilar walked into the living room and stood by the window staring at the letter without seeing it. Luisa followed her.

"¿Qué te pasa, mamá?" *What's the matter, mamá?* Luisa was frightened.

"Eh una carta de Juan. Mira a ver si la puedeh leer. Eh urgente." *It's a letter from Juan. See if you can read it. It's urgent.*

Luisa began to read. "Están todos bien en esta. Los negocios pro-gre-san. He tenido tiempo de visitar a mis padres en la vieja casa y hablar de mi niñez." *Everyone is well here. Business is good. I have taken time to visit my parents at the old family home and hear their stories about my childhood.*

"La mala no-ti-cia es qué he estado en-fer-mo con una tos que no se me-jo-ra-ba. Cuando fuí al doctor me dijo que en-con-tró un tu-mor . . . ." *The bad news is that I have been ill with a cough which has not im-proved. When I went to the doctor he said he had found a tu-mor . . . .*

Luisa stopped reading and looked at her mother.

"Sigue, sigue," Pilar said. *Go on, go on.*

"Encontró un tumor en la gar-gan-ta. Espera que no sea nada serio. Pero, quiere o-pe-rar en un par de se-ma-nas, así que no voy a poder volver a la isla tan pron-to como es-pe-ra-ba hacer-lo . . . ." *He found a tumor in my thro . . . throat. He hopes it is no-thing se-ri-ous. But he wants to o-per-ate in a couple of weeks, so I will not be able to re-turn to the island as soon as I had hoped . . . .*

That's almost two weeks ago, Pilar kept thinking. Almost two weeks ago. How is he? How is he? The question repeated itself with each deafening heartbeat.

"Te echo de menos a tí y a todos los niños . . . ." *I miss you and the children . . . .*

He had never said that before. He must be upset. Pilar's whole body ached to hold him.

"Dale a todos un a-bra-zo y díles que re-cen por mí. A-fec-tuo-sa-mente, Juan." *Give everyone a hug and tell them to pray for me. Af-fec-tion-ate-ly, Juan.*

He added at the end, "Te es-cri-bi-ré en cuanto sepa los re-sul-ta-dos de la opera-ción." *I will write as soon as I know the re-sults of the oper-ation.*

"¡Ay, Dioh mío!" *Oh, my God!* Pilar exclaimed, turning her back to Luisa.

She looked out of the window towards the river, not seeing anything.

"¡Juan! ¡Juan!" she whispered. She felt Luisa's arms around her waist. Luisa's face leaning against her back.

"Mamá, te quiero mucho." *Mamá, I love you very much.*

Pilar thought it was a comfort to feel this body against hers.

It seemed dark all of a sudden. The rain was coming down hard. She felt as if the house were pressing down against her. She had to move away from Luisa.

Luisa stood there in the dimming light, not knowing what to do.

Meli waited for papi to come with the magazines still smelling of newsprint.

Meli loved to read at night before dinner when it was raining outside. That was her favorite time, when the magazines came and everybody was around, even papi. The house didn't seem as dark.

And when abuelita was there it was even nicer. Meli didn't have to be scared because abuelita always checked to see if the doors were locked before they went to bed, and the windows latched and the gas stove turned off. And abuelita didn't fall asleep before Meli did. She told Meli stories.

"Abuelita, cuéntame de cuando te enamorahte de Juan." *Abuelita, tell me about falling in love with Juan,* Meli asked.

Meli didn't know what to call her grandfather. Meli never knew him, so she didn't feel comfortable calling him abuelo, *grandfather.* He had never been her grandfather really. She only knew him as Juan, which is what abuelita called him, or papá, as mami called him.

There was a picture of him with the other photographs in the closet. He looked like something out of a history book. Kind of stern. Somebody who would make you feel bad if you wore dungarees and a big shirt and loafers. Meli was suddenly glad he wasn't her father. Papi liked American things too.

"Cuéntame, cuéntame," Meli insisted. *Tell me, tell me.*

Abuelita laughed. "Lo conocí en una Fiehta de Cruh," she started. "Bueno, no exactamente, él trabajaba en la tienda de suh tíoh, loh Méndez. Esa gente tenía muchah propiedadeh. Ademáh de la tienda tenían ganado, fincah de cocoh, y hahta ehportaban cocoh para Europa." *I met him at a Feast of the Cross. Well, not exactly. He worked at the store owned by his aunt and uncle. The*

Méndez. *Those people had a lot of land. Besides the store, they had cattle, coconut farms, and even exported coconuts to Europe.*

Meli could see the coconuts stacked in piles on ships, ending up on cakes and cookies all over the world. She didn't like coconut except when the skin was soft and you could spoon it out of the inside.

"Traían loh productoh a la tienda en carretah de bueyeh. Teníamoh un cuarto en Bocarío con jamoneh ehpañoleh colgadoh del plafón, aceite de oliva en latah grandeh, aceitunah, sacoh de papah . . . ." *They brought the products to the store in carts drawn by oxen. At the house in Bocarío we had a room with Spanish hams hanging from the ceiling, big cans of olive oil, olives, big sacks of potatoes . . .* abuelita went on.

Meli thought of mice. There was probably a lot of mice in that room too. Like in their own pantry. Papi brought lots of fancy foods. Meli could hear the traps that mami set up snapping at night.

"No noh faltaba nada." *We lacked nothing,* abuelita said, turning towards the open window.

Pilar kept looking at pieces of ocean framed by the windows, as if the ocean could yield the answer.

"Juan, Juan ¿cómo ehtáh?" *Juan, Juan, how are you!*

In the afternoon her anguish and the ocean had the same rhythm. Their sounds beat her down in the silence of the house.

The children had grown very quiet after hearing the news. They sat in their rooms. Waiting.

Listening to abuelita's story, Meli could see the ocean at a great distance from the window of her bedroom. The moon was out. She felt like she was way up on top of the mango tree.

She imagined that the tree had grown silver leaves after a blonde fairy godmother had touched it with her wand. Meli would climb the tree to the top, fearful that the smaller branches would break, but she would succeed in getting the silver leaves. Then she would sell some of them and get a movie camera. She would give some money to mami too, to pay for a chauffeur so they wouldn't have to take buses anymore. Papi didn't take them anywhere in the car and mami didn't drive.

Pilar remembered Tía Micaela saying to Marta as they hung up the wash under the mango tree, "No le va a faltal ná' si se casa con ése. Eh buen paltido." *She won't need nothing if she marry that one. Good catch.*

"Pero mujel ¿tú te créh qu'ese hombre se va a casal con una muchachita que no tié' ná' y con su rajita? ¿Tú ehtáh loca?" Marta said. *You think that man going to marry a girl's got nothing 'cept nigger blood? You crazy, woman!*

She went on, "¿Y lah ehpañolah pol ahí saliéndoseleh lah babah pol ese hombre? ¿Y con to' esoh chavoh?" *And Spaniard women around drooling for that man! With all that money!*

"Pilar eh bien linda, Marta. Tú no lo veh. To' el mundo lo dice. Y pálida. Pasa pol blanca. Tú lo sabeh," Tía Micaela responded. *Pilar's very pretty, Marta. You don't see it. Everybody say it. And pale. She pass for white. You know that.*

"Tie' el pelo malo. Esa gente no se olvida d'eso. ¿Y qué van a hacel conmigo? ¿Pintálme de blanco y ehtiralme el pelo? ¿Tú te créh que loh hijoh del ehpañol van a tenel una abuela prieta? ¡Ay, Micaela, tú ereh idiota!" *She got kinky hair. Those people not going to forget that. And what they going to do with me? Paint me white and straighten my hair? You think the Spaniard's children going to have a nigger grandma? You stupid, Micaela!* Marta laughed, but Pilar could tell she was getting angry.

"No sé . . . Pilar eh diferente. Eh lihta. ¿Y qué malo tié' si va a la fiehta? Va gozal. Mira, yo lah pue'o lleval a lah treh nenah. Noh sentamoh afuera a oil la música." *Don't know . . . Pilar's different. She smart. It don't hurt anything to go to the party. She going to*

*have fun. Look, I can take the three girls. We sit outside to hear
the music.*

Pilar didn't know how many days
went by. Every day before the sky was light she was awakened by
the rain on the roof and the window panes. Every day the heat
clung to her skin like wet rags. There was only a brief respite
when the rain came. Suddenly. Big drops making the flowers bend
down towards the red ground.

She felt very alone. As if time had gone on without her. She
felt betrayed by the distance between herself and Juan. And she
had no one to ask the questions that tore at her inside. Where was
this voice, these words, coming from? Could they be trusted? And
what right did they have to make a pronouncement about Juan's
life?

Over and over she had to look at the letter which lay on top
of her night clothes in her dresser, to make sure that it was true.

But was it? Was it true?

Or she sat and rocked on the veranda, with Luisa on a low
stool next to her. Watching her.

"¿Quiereh algo, mamá?" *Do you want something, mamá?* Luisa
asked.

"No necesito nada, graciah, m'ija," Pilar answered. *Thanks,
honey, I don't need anything.*

"¿Ehtáh bien hoy?" *Are you all right today?* Luisa asked.

Pilar stopped rocking and reached for Luisa's hand. She knew
Luisa was trying to take care of her.

"Te veh cansada . . . . Tú ehtáh segura que ehtáh bien?" Luisa
asked again. *You look tired . . . . Are you sure you're all right?*

"Sí, ehtoy bien. No te preocupeh tanto por mí." *Yes, I'm fine.
Don't worry so much about me,* Pilar answered, and touched Luisa's forehead. "Tú ereh la qu'ehtáh un poco caliente. Vete a acohtar
un rato y cuando te levanteh pídele a Fernanda que te haga una
limonada," Pilar said. *You're the one who's a little warm. Go lie
down for a while, and when you get up ask Fernanda to fix you a
lemonade.*

"Yo no quiero limonada." *I don't want lemonade,* Luisa said stubbornly.

"Ehtá bien, pero acuéhtate un rato." *All right, but lie down for a while,* Pilar said.

Luisa left the room dragging her feet.

Seña Alba watched from a distance. She chuckled to herself. Good thing about being black is nobody see you in the dark.

Lots of people coming to the Fiehta de Cruh at Doña Teresa's. You forget there's so many rich white folks around, or poor ones making like they have money. House lit up and all this hollering and running around. Boys going from the big house to the cook house carrying food all piled up. You don't know how they do it. And the pigs turning and turning slow on the spit and dripping and the fire spitting like it's slurping all that fat.

Big barrels of rum they's got out there for poor folks, Seña Alba thought, and the Spaniards licking their wine inside and sweating like everybody else.

Seña Alba's mouth began to water. But she said to herself she wasn't going to. Was there to look out for Niña Pilar. They wasn't there yet. Pilar coming with Micaela, Asunción and Elena. Pablo make a stink about the cloth Don Juan give Marta. Micaela is so damn smart she make up a story about she don't know where she put the stupid cloth and she felt so bad about it and all that. She made like she got some other cloth put away her ma give her for some curtains long time before and how she not going to make them because the sun fade them and on and on about getting so damn old and forgetting where she put things. Goddammit! Marta and her make Pablo so sick and tired from talking about it he don't care about no fucking cloth old dead ma of that Micaela given her anyhow, and how Marta can stand all that talk he can't understand. That's how Micaela got to make skirts for the girls.

Seña Alba was getting thirsty from standing by the hot fire. Maybe she could have a little rum. Didn't have any for a couple of weeks. But better wait 'til after the girls come because she want to see what they look like in the new skirts.

Men come on horses and women in buggies and she worry the girls' going to get mud all over their feet before they get to the village. She don't want anybody saying mean things to her Niña Pilar. Wipe their faces in the mud, that's what she's going to do. She wish the girls got there already, because the pig's smelling awful good and the rum barrels' getting empty in a hurry, seeing how those boys carrying food are taking swipes at them every time they go past. And the neighbors gathering around to look get their nips in too. Besides, Seña Alba thought, just one swig's not going to do harm and they're going to be there anytime now.

Seña Alba put her mouth to the spout and felt the warm sweetness going down her throat all the way into her belly. People were egging her on and laughing. She called back at them, "¡Miren, déjen eso, compais!" *Look, stop that, folks!*

She don't want to miss her Niña Pilar coming, but she sure feel easier. Whole body warm and waked up.

Then she saw Micaela standing at the gate with the three girls. Pilar stood out.

Seña Alba didn't know what Micaela had done with that cloth. She thought: that woman make miracles with her hands. But maybe it's not the cloth because the other two don't look like her Niña Pilar look. Niña Pilar stand behind the others and she's shy but tall and there's something about that child like she's taking everything in and putting the whole world inside. You can't help looking at her because she's got the night and the candles and the songs all in her eyes.

People turn to look at Niña Pilar too.

Pilar stood at the gate.

The house looked so pretty she almost forgot to be scared. She wanted to notice everything to tell Seña Alba. And Marta. About the ladies' dresses and the men with hair so shiny you didn't know what they polished it with. Even the horses looked shiny, and the windows of the big house too. There were tables all over the grass with white cloths, and candles everywhere on the ground in big cans full of sand. It was so bright! Like they had washed the night away.

Pilar kept looking at Tía Micaela and her sisters to make sure it was true they were really there. The mud on her shoes reminded her. She'd borrowed them from Tía Micaela. Tía Micaela had gone around from neighbor to neighbor looking for shoes to borrow. Got enough of them for all the girls. Mostly from black women who worked as maids for rich people.

Pilar was wondering how they were going to get that mud off before going in. And where were they going to go anyway? She didn't know whether they were supposed to sit outside. Pilar got scared again. She hadn't thought about what she was going to do once she got there. Only thought of getting there.

She looked at Tía Micaela. It seemed like she didn't know what to do either.

Then Pilar heard Don Juan's voice. "¡Doña Micaela! ¡Qué mucho me alegro de que haya podido venir y traer a las muchachas!" *Doña Micaela, how glad I am that you could come and bring the girls!* But all the time he was talking, his eyes were on Pilar.

Pilar knew her face was burning.

"Oiga, yo no las he conocido formalmente. Yo soy Juan Méndez." *I have not met them formally. I am Juan Méndez*, he said, stretching his hand towards Pilar.

Pilar only saw her muddy shoes and his shiny boots.

"Pilar, mira, ehte eh Don Juan Méndez." *Pilar, look, this is Don Juan Méndez*, Tía Micaela said, and she took Pilar's hand and moved it towards Juan's.

Pilar was sure he must have felt her shake when he took her hand. Made her feel quiet too right away, like when you stroke a cat that's frightened.

It seemed to take a long time for him to move his hand. Pilar didn't know whether he had said anything to her or not. She heard Tía Micaela's voice instead.

"Ehta eh Elena, y ehta eh Asunción . . . . Pilar ¿qué le diceh a Don Juan?" *This is Elena and this is Asunción . . . . Pilar, what you say to Don Juan?*

Pilar looked at Tía Micaela. "No sé . . . ." *I don't know*, she said.

Juan laughed. "Una muchacha tan bonita no tiene que decir nada. Encantado de conocerte, Pilar." *A beautiful girl doesn't need to say anything. Pleased to meet you, Pilar,* Juan said.

When he let her hand go she felt alone.

"Pero entren, entren a la casa. Vámos a darle unos refrescos a las muchachas y usted, Doña Micaela ¿quiere un vinito?" *But come in, come into the house. Let's get some refreshments for the girls, and you, Doña Micaela, would you like some wine!* Juan said.

"Pero, abuelita ¡cuéntame, cuéntame de cuando Juan se enamoró de tí!" Meli asked. *But, abuelita, tell me, tell me about Juan falling in love with you!*

She didn't want to hear about the farm and the coconuts. She wanted to hear about the romance.

Abuelita turned towards her in the dark. "Tú sabeh como eran lah cosah en esoh díah. No eh como ahora." *You know how things were in those days. Not like now.*

"¿Como en lah novelah? ¿Él pasaba por la calle y miraba la casa y tuh papáh no querían que lo vierah?" *Like in the soaps? He would go by on the street looking at your house, and your parents wouldn't let you see him!*

"No exactamente . . . . Esa era una gente de dinero, tú sabeh . . . y papá . . . bueno, papá trabajaba en fincah . . . ." *Not exactly . . . . Those people had money, you know . . . and papá . . . well, papá worked on the farms . . ."* abuelita said.

Meli imagined abuelita's family in one of those country houses she had seen when she went for drives with papi. They saw houses with wide verandas. That's how Spaniards had lived in the country. They had a lot of banana and orange trees around and gravel walks bordered with flowers. Inside the houses there were big wood fans hanging from the ceiling and mahogany rocking chairs.

"¿Y qué pasó?" *And what happened?* Meli asked. She wanted to get to the part about the romance.

"Bueno, fuí a ehta Fiehta de Cruh y él me cantó unah coplah . . . ." *Well, I went to this Feast of the Cross and he sang some couplets for me . . .* abuelita continued.

Like a musical comedy, Meli thought. They are about to kiss and they start singing right away.

.

Pilar walk to the house between Juan and Tía Micaela.

People look too. Because Pilar's pretty, that's why, Seña Alba thought.

Never seen her far away like this with people around her. Can tell there's something special about her. Not silly like other girls. Like there's something inside her that make her walk straight.

She was proud of her Niña Pilar.

"¡Miren, miren ahí 'htá Pilar!" *Look! Look, there's Pilar!* She wanted all the folks out there to know. "¡Vamoh a celebral!" *Going to celebrate!*

Seña Alba put her mouth to the spout of the barrel like it's July and she's been running through the sugar cane and sweat's coming down her face.

She sat on the ground. Through the windows she could see the people in the big house laughing and singing. Outside, the jíbaros and the black folks played bongos, palitos, *sticks* and guitars. They sat around the fire pit with their hats on.

Seña Alba kept saying to herself: if he hurt her, I kill him.

Walking down the path to the house with Juan next to her, Pilar noticed people looking. Their eyes went to her shoes, her skirt, Tía Micaela, and to her and Juan.

She would have hidden if Juan hadn't been there. She would have gone outside with the servants. But Juan kept having her meet people that looked at her like they were looking for something. She tried to smile because he looked so pleased. She watched Tía Micaela too. She always seemed to know what to say. And she noticed that Tía Micaela and her sisters were darker than these people. Darker than herself. Everyone else around looked like they had been living in a room without windows. They were so pale you thought maybe they were sick.

"Tía Teresa, mire, quiero presentarle a Pilar . . ." she heard Juan say. *Tía Teresa, may I introduce Pilar . . . .*

Pilar got scared suddenly. Doña Teresa was his aunt. The Spaniard lady that worked at the store. She was always there and was always afraid black folks were going to steal from her. She was short and fat and had a smooth round face, very white, and green eyes. Pilar almost laughed out of nervousness. She felt like a mango being peeled.

"Y ¿cuál es su apellido?" Doña Teresa asked her without a smile. *And what is your family name?*

"Clausé," Pilar responded, looking straight into Doña Teresa's green eyes. It was like falling into something.

"¿Qué clase de nombre es ese? No es español." *What kind of name is that? It is not Spanish,* Doña Teresa said.

"Don Pablo, el papá de Pilar, es de descendencia francesa," Juan answered. *Don Pablo, Pilar's father, is of French descent.* Pilar was surprised Juan knew that.

"Y ¿cómo se deletrea ese nombre?" Doña Teresa insisted. *And how do you spell that name?*

Pilar didn't know what to say. She didn't know how to spell.

"Con una 'c.' Ce, ele, a, u, ese, e." *With a 'c.' C, l, a, u, s, e,* Juan answered.

"Y la abuela de palte de la mamá era ehpañola. Helnándeh," Tía Micaela added. *And her grandma, on her mother's side, was a Spaniard woman, Hernández.*

Doña Teresa looked at Tía Micaela like she was ready to send Tía Micaela on an errand. Then she looked down at their shoes.

"Siento que se le ensuciaran los zapatos tanto. Pueden pasar por la cocina y los sirvientes se los pueden limpiar." *I am so sorry you soiled your shoes. You can go to the kitchen and have the servants clean them for you.*

"Tía, no es el momento de limpiar zapatos, sino de empezar la fiesta," Juan said, smiling. *Aunt, it is not time to clean shoes, it is time to start the celebration.*

Then he led Pilar, Tía Micaela and the girls to the room where the cross was.

"Cortaban unoh ganchoh de un árbol que se llamaba granadillo . . . yo no sé como le llaman a eso ahora . . . y loh ponían en forma de cruh, entonceh loh ataban con un lazo en el medio . . ." Meli heard abuelita say. *They cut branches from the granadillo tree . . . I don't know what they call it now . . . and held them together in the shape of a cross, then tied them and made a bow in the middle.*

Meli didn't quite know where to put this cross of branches in the picture she had in her mind. But she could see the two of them tying the bow together and Juan putting his hand on hers.

"¿Y te cogió la mano?" Meli asked. *And did he take your hand?*

Abuelita seemed a little embarrassed. "Solamente cuando me lo presentaron. Yo creo que ya él ehtaba interesado en mí. Yo era una muchachita. Tenía solo quince añoh, y él ya era de treinta." *Only when we were introduced. I think he was already interested in me. I was just a girl. I was only fifteen and he was already thirty.*

"¿Era viejo?" Meli was a little disappointed. *He was old?* In Meli's mind Juan suddenly turned into an old man.

Abuelita laughed. "No, tenía máh añoh que yo, pero era muy guapo, ehpecialmente cuando pasaba a caballo en su uniforme." *No, he was older than I, but he was very handsome, especially when he rode by on his horse in his uniform.*

Meli was relieved.

"Ehtaba en la milicia cuando llegaron loh americanoh. Ehtaban bombardeando la capital con cañoneh que tenían en loh barcoh. Habían invadido la bahía y salía la gente de la ciudad en unah filah largah. Decían que hubieron muchoh fuegoh," abuelita went on. *He was in the militia when the Americans arrived. They were bombing the capital with cannons from ships. They had invaded the bay and there were long lines of people leaving the city. I heard there were many fires.*

Meli saw Juan going off to war. Abuelita was at a window looking longingly towards the spirals of smoke at the horizon. Meli had seen a lot of war movies, but they were not her favorites. She liked romances best.

"Pero ¿y qué pasó con Juan?" *But what happened with Juan?* Meli was getting very impatient.

Pilar felt light-headed.

The room was very crowded already, but she didn't see anything except the cross. The branches were held together with a
white bow and decorated with thin strips of colored paper which
had been curled, and different kinds of pink and violet flowers.
The only light in the room came from the candles which surrounded the cross and were reflected in the windows and the
mirrors.

Pilar could not take her eyes off the reflections. It was a little
scary. Like the whole room was in flames and people were laughing and talking in the middle of it. Everything was shining, the
tables and floors and the glasses of wine. She didn't know how
those skinny stems held up the cup where they poured the wine.
They were like the palm trees. The trunks growing tall and skinny
with the big pencas, *fronds,* up above making a swooshy sound in
the wind.

All of a sudden it was very quiet. Then an older man spoke.
"Para la Virgen." *For the Virgin.* He put some coins on a plate, then
sang.

> "Enero, febrero y marzo,
> abril y mayo
> son los primeros meses
> del año."
> *January, February, March,*
> *April and May*
> *are the first months*
> *of the year.*

He looked pleased, but it seemed like nobody else was very
excited about the song. Asunción and Elena giggled behind Pilar.
Tía Micaela turned towards them with a scowl.

Then another man stood up and put money on the plate. This
one was very fat and had a very red face.

> "Junio y julio
> son calientes,

agosto y septiembre
las lluvias sientes."
June and July
are hot,
August and September
you feel the rains.

A tall white-haired man sang, after bowing to the lady next to him.

"La Virgen es bella
y mi señora
es una estrella."
The Virgin is beautiful
and my lady
is a star.

The plate kept going around and the older men kept putting money in it. Ladies took out their fans as the room grew hot. Men's faces began to look damp with sweat.

"En la bahía
las bombas vienen
y mi corazón
tus palabras hieren."
In the bay
bombs fall
and you wound my heart
with your words.

A young man sang this song not looking anywhere in particular. A couple of men standing by him, probably his friends, Pilar thought, turned to look towards a young woman who was standing in a corner of the room next to an older man. She was busy with her handkerchief. Pilar couldn't see her face.

It looked like the more money you had to put in the plate, the more chances you got to sing. Pilar wanted to ask Tía Micaela, but Tía Micaela had fallen asleep after a couple of glasses of wine. Asunción and Elena were busy whispering to each other and giggling. Pilar noticed there were a couple of men who kept looking at them.

Then Juan stood up. He bowed slightly towards the cross, then looking straight at Pilar he sang,

"Si tú me quieres, te quiero.
Si tú me amas, te amo.
Si tú me olvidas, te olvido.
Y yo bonito lo hago."
If you want me, I want you.
If you love me, I love you.
If you forget me, I forget you.
And I will make it beautiful.

People clapped and laughed. Pilar was looking at her hands the whole time. She wished she had a fan like the ladies did, to play with. Elena and Asunción giggled loudly, and Tía Micaela woke up with a start and knocked down her wine glass, which broke on the floor.

The room was silent.

Tía Micaela bent down to start picking up the pieces, mumbling apologies under her breath. But Juan walked quickly across the room and said, "No es necesario, Doña Micaela. Yo llamo a uno de los sirvientes a recogerlo." *That's not necessary, Doña Micaela. I'll call one of the servants to pick it up.*

Seña Alba told herself she don't like it. She say so to Pilar too. It's one thing to go to a party, it's something else to sneak around after a man. End up no good. She think that girl have more sense. Don't think much of a grown man chasing after her Niña Pilar. Not going to say that to Pilar because she look like someone put a spell on her. But she's afraid her Niña going to get hurt.

And she was angry about Pablo not letting Juan come to the house. He should let Juan come where they can keep an eye on him. But this pendejo, *asshole,* Pablo is ashamed of being poor. That's what happening. Don't have anything to do with looking after Pilar.

And what's that Niña Pilar going to do? Going to get pregnant, that's what always happen.

"Yo no soy como Patria," *I'm not like Patria,* Pilar had said, looking at Seña Alba straight in the eye. "¿Y pol qué ehtáh en contra de Don Juan?" *And why are you so set against Don Juan?*

White part coming out, Seña Alba said to herself. Proud like her papá. But stubborn like her ma too. Had plenty of pride herself, Seña Alba thought, but what matter most now is that Niña Pilar don't get hurt. Can't say nothing bad about Juan. Not now. Don't want Pilar to run away from her. She going to lie if she have to.

"No tengo na' en contra de Juan, m'ija, eh que cuando tú ereh jóven el cuelpo manda. No tie' tiempo pa' pensal na'." *Don't have anything against Juan, child, but when you're young your body boss you around and you don't got time to think or nothing.*

"No soy Patria." *I'm not Patria,* Pilar repeated.

"¿Y pol qué te tie' qu'ehcondel pa' velo?" *And why you got to hide to see him?* Seña Alba asked.

"Papá no lo quiere en la casa. Y dice que si lo veo en casa de Tía Micaela no le va a hablal a ella máh nunca. Así que ¿adónde lo voy a vel?" *Papá don't want him at the house. And he say he never talk to Tía Micaela again if I see him at her house. So where am I going to see him?*

"¿Te venía a visitar?" *Did he come to visit you?* Meli asked.

Abuelita didn't answer right away. "No . . . papá no quería . . . . Pero la noche de la fiehta, cuando llegó la hora de irnoh, Juan me dijo, tú sabeh, en el oído para que nadie lo oyera, que noh podíamoh encontrar al día siguiente al medio día en la iglesia cuando tocara la campana." *No . . . papá didn't want it . . . . But the night of the feast, when it was time to leave, Juan said, you know, in my ear so that nobody could hear him, that we could meet the next day at noon at the church when the bell rang.*

Meli could see the church at a distance across the town square. Heard the bell ringing.

"Pero yo no pude ir. No había forma de salir sin que mamá lo supiera. Me ehtaba velando. Le fuí a hablar a Tía Micaela. No le conté todo, pero le dije que Juan me quería ver." *But I couldn't go. There was no way of going out without mamá knowing. She was watching me. I just went to talk to Tía Micaela. I didn't tell her everything, but I did say Juan wanted to see me.*

"¿Te encerraron en tu cuarto?" *Did they lock you up in your room?* Meli asked.

"No, no, loh cuartoh no tenían puertah," abuelita said. *No, no, the rooms didn't have doors.*

"¿No tenían puertah?" Meli was surprised. "¿Dónde se dehvehtían? ¿En el baño?" *They didn't have doors? Where did you undress? In the bathroom?*

"Era diferente en esoh díah . . . . Pero, de todoh modoh, lo que pasó fué . . . ." *It was different in those days . . . . But, anyway, what happened was . . . .*

Abuelita was very eager to go on with the story.

Seña Alba thought she like it best if Juan just go away somewhere with some woman and don't ever come back, or fall off his horse and die. She know Pilar is going to hurt about this man. But it's no use. If her Niña love him, Seña Alba best keep an eye on her.

Seña Alba was shaking as she walked into the church. Last time she was in a church . . . but, she didn't want to think about it now. It made her angry. She kept telling herself she had to be there for her Niña Pilar. Had to be there. Had to be there. She repeated the words like the incantations the old curandera, *healer,* had taught her to keep evil spirits away.

Seña Alba broke into a sweat and grabbed the greasy armrest of the pew near where she squatted. She was afraid she was going to faint. She reached for herbs in her pocket and began to chew a leaf. The bitter taste calmed her.

She cursed under her breath at the priests in the sacristy. "¡Puelcoh! ¡Criminaleh! ¡Pilloh! ¡Hipócritah!" *Pigs! Cons! Thieves! Hypocrites!*

Then Pilar came with Elena. They didn't see Seña Alba. They sat close to each other on the far side of the aisle, with their heads bowed. Seña Alba could tell they were scared.

Juan came soon after. Took off his hat and kneeled before entering the aisle. He sat next to Pilar. Whispered to her.

Seña Alba was relieved he didn't stay long because the smell of the church made her feel like vomiting. The girls left quickly through a side door.

Seña Alba leaned on the outside wall of the church to steady herself. She saw Pilar and Elena walk away. Then she couldn't hold it back any longer, the vomit surged out of her and splattered the white wall. A stray dog began to sniff at it.

Seña Alba walked quickly around the side of the church and then disappeared into the bushes. She ran through the thick underbrush as if she were being chased.

"Seña Alba ¿qué va hacel con el ron? ¿Va cocinal un cabrito?" *Seña Alba, what you doing with the rum? Gonna cook a goat?* a man called out at her outside the store, laughing loudly.

"Negra ¡échame loh caracoleh!" *Negra, read them shells for me!* said a tired-looking mulatto girl.

Seña Alba didn't answer. They thought she was a santera![2] She smiled at everyone as she walked into the store.

To the man she said, "¿Cómo ehtá tu mujel? ¿Se le quitó la toh?" *How's your woman? Her cough gone?*

And to the girl, "Siento que peldihte el muchacho." *Sorry you lost your baby.*

When she went inside the store Seña Alba was glad Juan wasn't around. She knew she was going to have a hard time not opening her mouth and saying something mean.

Doña Teresa was there in her apron. Never said hello. Just "¿Qué quieres hoy?" *What do you want today?*

Seña Alba pulled out an empty bottle from under her skirt. Handed it to Doña Teresa.

"Ron," she said. *Rum.*

Doña Teresa went and filled the bottle from the barrel. She put out her hand for the money before she handed it to Seña Alba. Seña Alba put the change on the counter. Doña Teresa counted it carefully.

"Te faltan tres centavos," she said, looking sharply at Seña Alba. "Ha subido el precio." *You are three cents short. The price has gone up.*

"No tengo máh chavoh," Seña Alba said. *Don't got more money.*

Doña Teresa took the bottle away without a word and emptied a cupful out of it. Then she put it back in front of Seña Alba and walked away.

Seña Alba felt her body get hot. Every part of it. Like she had been drinking rum for a while already. She cursed herself for having to buy rum from the white store.

Seña Alba hid the bottle in her skirt and walked through the high sugar cane. She went deep into it, away from the road and away from the cutters. Then she sat down on the ground in the cool shade.

After she finished the bottle she began to remember things.

She saw herself squatting with her eyes half closed in the corner of a room. Against a wall with bare studs. Not exactly looking at anything. Sometimes she smoked. Only a drag or two at a time. There was smoke too from other herbs burning.

A woman lay on the bed. There was only silence around her. Like prayer. Seña Alba was very still.

Outside, the rain had softened into a drizzle. There were puddles on the clay ground. But she only noticed the shape on the bed. Her eyes were fixed on the heartbeat at the throat. She felt that if she stopped looking, the heartbeat would also stop.

Alba spoke to the trees and the rain. She spoke to the fields, and most of all to the ocean. Sometimes the ocean was a god and sometimes it was a goddess. She called them ehpírituh. *Spirits.* Everything has an ehpíritu, the curandera had told her. Some of them are very powerful. She knew you can tell by the sound. It isn't just loudness either. Some sounds get inside you and you can't get them out. Those are the powerful ehpírituh. Like the ocean. Even when Alba went into town and couldn't hear it, she felt it inside her.

Different sounds at different times too, she thought. The ehpíritu of the ocean have different feelings, like people. Sometimes it just make a plain mean sound. She can almost feel it coming. The ocean get dull and sullen all day.

She had known people like that too, she thought while looking through the stems of the sugar cane. Like José. He was after her. But she could see it coming. He was going to smash her against the rocks and spit her up in the air and she was going to end up like dry seaweed at the beach.

Her mother had been worried about her. What was going to happen to Alba when she died? Her mother hadn't wanted her to end up alone. But they both had known that men didn't stay.

At the sick bed she had been suddenly startled by a sound of birds. The mango tree had been loaded with song all morning. Happy sounds that made her feel almost hopeful. They quieted down in the afternoon. She had forgotten they were there. Until now.

They all flew off the tree at once. Like a scream.

She looked for the heartbeat at the woman's throat. It had stopped.

Her mother was dead.

Alba felt as if the birds had left her body. She could feel the air blowing through her. She thought the trees must be sad too.

"¡Bruja! ¡Bruja! La gente le gritaba . . . ." *Witch! Witch! Folks shout at her . . . .*

Pilar remembered the story Seña Alba told the children a couple of years ago. The story of Leona.

"¡Bruja! ¡Bruja! Le gritaba la gente a Leona cuando ella iba pol la calle. Elloh no sabían que ella podía vel loh pensamientoh de la gente de solo oileh lah voceh . . . ." *Witch! Witch! Folks shout at Leona when she go on the street. They don't know she can see people's thoughts from just hearing their voices . . . .*

The children were sitting in a circle on the floor of the dining room. It had been raining hard for a few days. They were afraid there would be a hurricane, but so far no one had come from the village to warn them. Seña Alba had shown up on the second day and it was a good thing because the children had been nervous and restless. She always calmed them down with her stories.

They sat together, closed in. With two kerosene lamps. Pilar had ordered farm hands to board the windows on the ocean side just in case the wind got worse.

"Y Leona también podía vel el pasa'o y el futuro en loh ojoh de la gente . . . ." *And Leona can see the past and the future in folks' eyes too . . .* Seña Alba said, making her eyes bigger and bigger.

The children were absorbed in the story. But then Manuelito shouted, "¡Yo quiero saber lo que me va a pasar en el futuro!" *I want to know what's going to happen to me in the future!*

"¡Ay, yo no!" *Not me!* Luisa said, shaking her head.

"Yo no quiero que hagah cuentoh de brujah." *I don't want you to tell stories about witches,* Clara said, covering her ears.

"Leona no era bruja, m'ijita. Pero la gente le tenía miedo polque sabía mucho." *Leona is no witch, child. But people is scared of her because she know too much,* Seña Alba said kindly.

Pilar felt like crying when she remembered Seña Alba's gentleness. She needed her now. Why didn't she come? Pilar kept asking herself the question like a complaint, even though she knew the answer.

"Esa mujel veía tanto que cuando pasaba pol la calle la gente se cubrían loh ojoh. No querían que Leona viera to'h suh secretoh, to' lo que ehcondían y to'ah lah cosah que leh daban velgüenza." *That woman see so much that when she go on the street people cover their eyes. They don't want her to see all their secrets, the things they hide and the things they's ashamed of.*

"La gente pol ahí decía que Leona, que era el nombre que le dieron en el pueblo polque tenía el pelo como un león, decían qu'ella daba el mal de ojo. Así que to' el mundo s'ehcondía cuando la veían venil." *Folks around say that Leona, that's the name folks call her in the town because she has hair like a lion, they say she give the evil eye. So they hide when they see her coming.*

"Decían en el pueblo que Leona se había chupa'o el alma de una nenita de treh añoh. Leona le había da'o un remedio cuando la nena tenía una fiebre tremenda y dehpuéh la nena salió boba. No entendía bien lah cosah y había que repetílselah. Así que naide dejaba que loh neneh se acelcaran a Leona." *In the village they say Leona suck out the spirit of a three year old girl. Leona give her a remedy when the girl have a bad fever and after that the girl turn dumb. She don't understand things and you have to say things over and over to her. So nobody let their children get close to Leona.*

"La única que se atrevió a venil celca d'ella fué una niñita de doce o trece añoh. Máh o menoh como tú, Luisa. Ella no le tenía miedo a Leona polque no tenía na' qu'ehcondel." *Only one gets close is a girl, twelve or thirteen. A little like you, Luisa. She's not scared because she don't have nothing to hide.*

"Leona le miró loh ojoh y vió el sol, loh álboleh y el mar. A Leona le guhtaba ehtal celca de loh niñoh polque loh niñoh to'avía sentían alegría. La gente grande solo se acoldaban de sentil el dolol polque habían sufrido mucho. Y naide sabía el peso que Leona llevaba de su vida y de sabel tantah cosah de la gente. Ehtaba trihte polque había tanta gente pobre y tanta gente desehperá'." *Leona look in her eyes and she see the sun, the trees and the sea. Leona like to be near children because they still feel happy. Big people only remember to feel pain because they suffer so much. And no one see what big weight Leona carry from her life and from knowing so many things about people. She's sad because there is so many poor folks that is desperate.*

"A Leona le guhtaba andal sola ehpecialmente pol la playa. Podía oil loh sueñoh de to'ah lah criaturah, de loh álboleh, loh animaleh y hahta lah piedrah. Pa' ella to' tenía vi'a, y lah cosah que no hablaban como la gente, tenían sueñoh. Hahta lah piedrah hablaban con imágeneh." *Leona like to walk alone. Most of all at the beach. She can hear the dreams of all creatures, of trees, of animals and of stones. For her everything have life. And things that don't talk like people, they have dreams. Even stones talk with pictures.*

"Pueh ehta niña que Leona s'encontró en la playa no le dió miedo polque ehtaba en esa eda' mágica entre sel una niñita y una mujel. A esa eda' a uno le parece que to' eh posible y uno siente to' y cré' en cuentoh." *Well, the girl Leona find don't get scared because she's at the magic age between being a child and being a woman. When you're that age you think you can do everything. You feel everything and still believe in stories.*

"Leona vió en loh ojoh d'esa niña que to' el mundo la iba querel polque tenía el corazón lleno de amol pa' to' el mundo. Y Leona vió que a ehta niña le guhtaba aprendel cosah y que le iba a enseñal a suh hijoh y nietoh qu'era bien impoltante aprendel cosah." *Leona see in the girl's eyes that everybody's going to love*

*her because her heart is full to the brim from loving people. And
Leona see this girl want to learn things and she's going to teach
her children and grandchildren about how you got to learn things.*

Seña Alba continued. Her eyes were brighter than Pilar ever
remembered. Pilar didn't know whether it was because she was
seeing Seña Alba through her own tears.

"Y cuando la niñita miró a Leona, Leona se dió cuenta que era
la primera vez que alguien la había vihto. Y la única vez que sintió
que alguien la quería dehde que su mai murió." *And when the
little girl look at Leona, Leona know that it's the first time somebody see her. And the only time she feel someone love her since
her ma die.*

The heavy grass was shining in the midday sun. It had no right to,
Pilar thought. Had no right to be so healthy and happy when Juan
was sick and so far away. She didn't even have a picture in her
mind of where he was.

It was a relief that it had stopped raining, but it was also cruel.
The ocean and the sky looked fierce in their colors. They didn't
care.

Everything was the same as always. It made Pilar feel trapped
and alone.

She looked out of the window or went out on the veranda
over and over again. Without thinking, as if looking for some
change. Something to speak to her.

She remembered how Marta had found out she had been
meeting Juan at the church. Doña Bochinche told her. Laughed
too. She said everybody in the village knew. That Seña Alba was
chaperoning them.

"La negra loh vela," Doña Bochinche said. "Dioh sabe lo qu'esa
vé polque siempre ehtá picá." *The nigger woman watch them.
Lord know what she see because she's drunk most times.*

The hardest part for Marta was that she found out from Doña
Bochinche. Pilar knew it made Marta feel ashamed.

"¡Qué velgüenza! ¡Y yo creía que tú erah diferente! ¡Me hah
salí'o puta también! ¡Ay, bendito! ¿A quién salen ehtah criaturah?"
*Shame! And I think you's different! You turn into a whore too!
Lord! Who these children take after!*

"¡Mamá, peldóname! ¡Te juro que no hago na' malo!" *Mamá, forgive me! I swear I done nothing bad!*

Elena tried to convince her mother too.

"¡To'ah me van a salil putah!" Marta kept screaming. *All's going to turn out whores!*

"¡Mamá, mamá! ¡Óyeme! ¡Pregúntale a Seña Alba!" Pilar pleaded. *Mamá, mamá! Listen to me! Ask Seña Alba!*

"¡La puta negra borrachona! ¿Qué t'enseña esa de putería? ¿Y ehtáh bebiendo ron también? ¡La hija de la gran puta! ¡Negra sucia!" *Drunk nigger whore! What she teach you about whoring? You drinking rum too? Son of a bitch! Dirty nigger woman!* Marta kept screaming.

"¡Mamá! ¡Mamá! ¡Óyeme! ¡Don Juan me quiere ponel casa!" *Mamá! Mamá! Listen! Don Juan want to get me a house!*

"Eso eh lo que to'h loh hombreh dicen. ¿Y pol qué te va ponel casa a tí dehpuéh que t'embarra? ¡Ereh idiota, Pilar!" Marta was crying. *All men say that. Why he going to set up house after he get you all messed up? You just dumb, Pilar!*

Pilar didn't like to make her mother cry.

"¡Peldóname, mamá! ¡No hice na'!" *Forgive me, mamá! I done nothing!* Pilar kept repeating.

"Cuéntame de cuando te casahte," Meli said to abuelita. *Tell me about getting married.*

They were sitting on the window seat next to the milk glass panels.

Abuelita looked out of the window for a long time. Meli wondered whether she had heard. She seemed far away. It made Meli scared. Abuelita was never like that.

Meli was about to ask again when mami came. Meli had to go and study her piano lesson.

"Pero ehpérate, ehpérate . . . abuelita m'ehtá contando de cuando se casó . . ." she said to mami. *Wait . . . wait . . . abuelita is telling me about getting married . . . .*

Mami frowned. She looked angry.

Meli didn't want to study the piano. It was mami's idea anyway. Mami thought it would be nice for Meli to be able to play the piano if she were on a transatlantic ship sometime. She had seen it in a movie.

But why was she so mad about it right now?

Outside the theatre there were life-size cutouts of the stars. A big crowd pressed towards the doors. Meli stood close to her mother. She felt she needed to look after mami when they were out.

Meli held mami's hand in the dark theatre. The air conditioning was cold but Meli liked it. It made her feel cool and clean. She felt American when she saw movies in English. She felt special.

Meli's eyes were on Ingrid Bergman, her favorite actress. Meli liked love scenes best. Swordfights and pirates came next.

Cary Grant and Ingrid Bergman were kissing on the screen while he tried to make a telephone call. The kiss went on and on. Meli started shifting in her seat. She felt a familiar warm feeling. Meli didn't want it to stop even though she felt as if she couldn't breathe.

Meli tried to feel the way she thought Ingrid must feel. Then like Cary Grant must feel when Ingrid kisses him. She shifted back and forth between the two. Then Cary Grant became a shadow and all Meli saw was Ingrid's glowing face, her eyes half closed, her mouth ready to be kissed again. And her upper lip slightly touched with hurt.

Meli tried to keep herself in the picture, but the scene shifted.

Going to the movies was the only thing Meli and mami did together, except go to piano lessons. They didn't talk about what they saw either, just sat there eating candy and popcorn. But Meli had seen mami cry at movies. Meli cried too sometimes but she didn't blow her nose because she didn't want anybody to know. She just blotted her tears with her handkerchief.

Meli wished she could ask mami about things.

Going home on the bus mami said, "En lah películah todo eh tan bonito . . . lah casah, loh jardineh, loh romanceh. La vida no eh así." *In the movies everything's so pretty . . . the houses, the gardens, the romances. Life is not like that.*

"Pero, a veces tú lloras," Meli said. *But sometimes you cry.*

Mami seemed a little embarrassed. "Aunque uno llore en el cine todo eh bonito . . . romántico. Ay, pero en la vida . . . lah cosah son feah . . . loh hombreh . . . lah cosah feah que hay en el periódico. A mí no me guhta hablar de eso . . . . Y qué buena vida se dan esah ehtrellah! Que bueno sería tener dinero, ir de viaje, tener todo." *Even if you cry at the movies it is all so pretty . . . romantic. But in real life . . . things are so ugly . . . men . . . ugly things in the paper. I don't like to talk about it . . . . And what a life those stars have! It would be wonderful to have money, go on trips, have everything.*

"Yo quiero ir de viaje," Meli said emphatically. "Voy a ir a todoh los sitioh . . . y no en guagua tampoco." *I want to travel. I'm going to go everywhere . . . and not on the bus either.*

"Y uno eh tan feo . . ." mami went on, "con la narih torcida y el cutih manchado. Aquí el sol le hace daño a uno . . . y uno siempre sudando . . . . Si uno tuviera buen servicio y uno no tuviera que hacer nada más que ocuparse de si mihma . . . . Yo le daría dinero a mamá y a la familia también . . . . Pero ¿dónde uno va encontrar servicio como en lah películah? Aquí en ehte paíh la gente ehtá muy mala, loh jíbaroh y esoh negroh. Son muy atrevidoh. Ya nadie le tiene rehpeto a nada . . . . Que bueno sería tener dinero y servicio rehpetuoso, como anteh . . . ." *One is so ugly . . . with a crooked nose and discolored skin. Here the sun hurts you . . . and you're always sweating . . . . If one had good servants and didn't have anything to do except look after oneself . . . . I would still give money to mamá and the family too . . . . But where are you going to find servants like in the movies? People in this country are getting so bad, the jíbaros and those black ones. They are insolent. There is no respect . . . . It would be so good to have money and servants that are respectful, like in the old days . . . .*

Meli imagined mami in a white dress. Mami was young, like in the picture in the closet. She was standing stiffly to the side in a big room. Other people danced. A young man came and asked her to dance.

"Yo no sé bailar." *I don't know how to dance,* she said awkwardly.

Meli realized that the young man wasn't her father.

"La danza es fácil de aprender." *The danza is easy to learn,* he said.

"No . . . eh mejor que no . . . . " *No, I'd rather not . . . .* She shook her head. Her face was red.

"Pues entonces ¿nos podemos sentar a hablar en la terraza?" *Well then, can we sit outside on the terrace to talk?*

He led her outside. He was smiling. Mami, on the other hand, looked very serious.

"¿Qué te gusta hacer?" the young man asked. *What do you like to do?*

"Coser . . ." mami said. *Sew . . . .*

"¿Por qué te gusta coser?" *Why do you like to sew?* he wanted to know.

Luisa was surprised by the question. "Me guhta . . ." she said, looking at him. *I like it . . . .*

"Sí ¿pero por qué? ¿Qué es lo que hace que te guste?" he insisted. *Yes, but why? What makes you like it?*

"Me guhtan loh coloreh." *I like the colors,* mami answered.

"¡Ahh! ¡Muy bien! ¡Los colores! ¿Cuáles colores te gustan más?" he wanted to know. *Ah! Very good! Colors! What are your favorite colors?* he persisted.

"Mmm . . . loh verdeh . . . rosa . . . diferenteh coloreh rosadoh . . . . Tengo muchoh hiloh de coloreh diferenteh . . . ." *Mmm . . . greens . . . rose . . . different pinks . . . . I have threads of many different colors.* She was getting more animated.

"¿Rosa como las flores, o como las nubes del crepúsculo, o como las mejillas de una niña?" *Rose-colored like flowers, or clouds at sunset, or the cheeks of a young girl?*

He made her smile. "¿Ereh poeta?" *Are you a poet?* she asked.

He became more serious for a moment. "Sí, pero estabamos hablando de tí." *Yes, but we were talking about you,* he said.

"Lo que hago no eh muy interesante." *What I do is not very interesting,* she said, looking away.

"¿Tú crées que no es interesante crear imágenes en colores? Es lo más bello del mundo. Imagínate lo que sería la vida si todo fuera en blanco y negro y gris. Me dá miedo pensarlo." *You think it is not interesting to create images in color? It is the most beautiful thing there is! Can you imagine what life would be like without*

colors? If everything were black, white and grey? It is frightening to
think about it. *He shuddered.*

"¿Tú no crées?" *Don't you think so?* he said, smiling broadly
and looking at her directly in the eyes.

Meli thought she wanted to make a movie sometime. But mami
didn't think much of the idea of Meli making a movie. She only
wanted Meli to practice the piano. Play danzas. It was almost the
only thing her mother cared about that Meli did. She didn't like
practicing the piano. It was boring. But she wanted to go to a
concert sometime. Everybody all dressed up, in a big hall with a
red velvet curtain.

"No quiero ehtudiar el piano," Meli said stubbornly when
they got home from the movie. *I don't want to study the piano.*

Mami ignored her and sat in the rocking chair next to the
piano.

"Practíca la danza," mami said. *Practice the danza.*

Juan had said he was going to
teach Pilar the steps of the danza sometime.

Pilar thought she was too shy for that, but she didn't want to
disappoint him so she didn't say anything. She told him instead
that Marta had found out they were meeting at the church and
that she was very angry. She was threatening to tell Pablo. Pilar
was afraid her father would come looking for Juan and there
would be a fight.

"Voy a hablarle," Juan said. *I am going to talk to him.*

"¡No, no! Yo creo que a él no le va a guhtal que uhté' vaya a la
casa." *No, no! I think he don't want you at the house,* Pilar said.

"No me llames 'usted,' Pilar, es muy formal," he said. *Don't call
me 'usted,' Pilar, it is too formal.*

He had said that many times, but Pilar couldn't bring herself
to call him 'tú.' Out of respect.

"Yo no quiero pelear con Pablo. Yo quiero estar contigo," Juan
went on. *I don't want to fight with Pablo. I want to be with you.*

Two days later Juan showed up at the house on his horse. He got off it and stood in front of the wood steps facing Pablo. Pablo sat at the top of the steps chewing his tobacco. Juan took off his hat.

"Pablo, yo quiero ver a Pilar." *Pablo, I want to see Pilar.*

Pablo didn't move. "Ya la estás viendo." *You're already seeing her.* His expression didn't change.

"Nos queremos." *We love each other,* Juan said.

Pilar's heart jumped.

She had been inside the house when Juan came. She went to hide in her room. She was afraid of what was going to happen if her father got angry at Juan. All the other children were watching from the open doorway and from the windows. Pilar could hear every word from inside the house.

"¿Y las otras mujeres, Don Juan?" *And the other women, Don Juan?* Pilar heard Pablo say.

She didn't want to hear anymore. She went and hid in the bushes behind the house.

Elena told Pilar later that Don Juan got real pale after Pablo said that. He got back on his horse and said to Pablo, "Yo respeto a la Pilar. No he venido aquí a recibir insultos. Si hay mala sangre entre nosotros va a ser tu propia culpa. De ahora en adelante, si me tienes que decir algo me vas a tener que venir a buscar." *I respect Pilar. I didn't come here to be insulted. If there is bad blood between us, it is going to be your fault. If you have something to say to me from now on, you are going to have to come find me.*

That was the last time Juan and Pablo stood face to face with each other.

Pilar didn't get any news for weeks. Then, one day, Juan's brother Aurelio came to Bocarío.

Juan was dead.

That was all she heard. She stood there. Like a rock or a tree. Like all silent things that watch over beginnings and endings.

"¡Mamá! ¡Mamá!" She heard Luisa as if from very far away. Luisa was leaning over her. Mercedes and Fernanda were standing at the foot of the bed. Pilar couldn't remember what had happened.

"¿Ehtáh bien?" *Are you all right?* Luisa wanted to know.

Pilar looked around. "¿Qué pasó?" *What happened?* she asked.

"Te dehmayahteh. Fernanda y Mercedes me ayudaron a traerte a la cama. Mandamoh a Santiago a buhcar a Seña Alba." *You fainted. Fernanda and Mercedes helped me carry you to bed. We sent Santiago to get Seña Alba.*

Pilar began to shake her head. Then she remembered. A look of profound pain came over her face. She began to sob, "¡Ay, Dioh mío! ¡Juan! ¡Juan!" *Oh, my God! Juan! Juan!*

Luisa stood by the bed with tears in her eyes. "Mamá, yo ehtoy aquí," she said softly. *Mamá, I'm here.*

Pilar couldn't hear her.

Pilar didn't leave her room. The hours had no shape, they hung limply around the chasm that divided her past and her present. In the agonizing silence she reached out for words, but the words that came tortured her: tumor, cancer, death. They beat inside her head without mercy.

From one moment to the next something had ended. Forever. And she didn't know how it had happened. Juan was gone. Her life with him had stopped. She would never see him again.

Then a desperation rose like the crest of a wave, higher and higher, as if it would cover the house and the palm trees and swallow everything into darkness.

Juan. Juan. She called in the night, as if she could bring him back. Her voice returned to her without resonance. He would never answer.

After a few days Pilar found herself wandering through the house to escape the anguish that had taken hold of her. She remembered Juan and her life with him, then always came back to what she was going to do next. And to Seña Alba. She wasn't there to help her.

Pilar would stop herself in the middle of doing something and try to remember why she was doing it. Nothing made sense.

She found herself one day staring at her sewing. "Mamá, mamá . . ." she heard Luisa calling.

When Pilar looked up she saw Luisa's worried expression.

"Mamá t'ehtaba llamando. No me oiah. Hace rato que t'ehtaba llamando . . . . ¿Qué te pasa?" *Mamá, I was calling you. You didn't hear me. I've been calling you for a while . . . . What's the matter?*

Pilar shook her head. "No sé . . . no sé." *I don't know . . . I don't know.*

That same afternoon Santiago came to the back door.

"Seña Alba se desapareció'. Naide l'a vihto. La gente dice que se fué del pueblo, o que se la llevó el diablo, o que alguien le hizo mal de ojo," Pilar heard Santiago telling Fernanda. *Seña Alba disappear. Nobody see her. People say she leave town, or the devil take her, or somebody give her the evil eye.*

"¡Fernanda!" Pilar called from her bed. "Dile a Santiago que entre acá." *Fernanda, tell Santiago to come here!*

Santiago stood at her door looking at everything. He had never been in the house, except for the kitchen.

"Santiago, muchah graciah por buhcar a Seña Alba, pero ya no la buhqueh máh. Yo creo que nadie la va a encontrar. Dile a Fernanda que te dé un café. Y toma . . . ." *Santiago, thank you for looking for Seña Alba, but I don't want you to look for her anymore. I don't think anyone is going to find her. Tell Fernanda to give you some coffee. And take this . . . .* She reached out and gave Santiago some coins.

Pilar didn't know what to do.

At night she cried. She didn't want the children to see her crying all the time. She wanted to be strong for them. But the truth was that she was uncertain about what needed to be done next. Juan had taken care of everything. Pilar didn't even know whether she was supposed to talk to Doña Teresa. No one from Juan's family had come to see her or spoken to her. No one from her own family. And Seña Alba was gone.

On the fifth day after Pilar received the news of Juan's death, Fernanda heard through Santiago, who heard it in the village, that they were having rosarios, *rosaries,* for Juan and a memorial service at Doña Teresa's.

Pilar couldn't decide whether she should go.

"Doña Pilar, uhte' tié' que il. No ehtá bien eso de que no le han dicho na'," Fernanda said. *Doña Pilar, you got to go. It's not right they don't tell you.*

Luisa and Mercedes said they would go with her.

Juan's family didn't expect her. When Pilar arrived at Doña Teresa's house, heads turned towards her and people whispered.

Pilar was all in black, pale and tall, with her young daughters one on each side. She stood at the doorway and no one came to greet her. She found herself looking for Doña Saturnina's sweet face. Then remembered she had taken ill the year Pilar and Juan moved to Bocarío. She had gone to Spain for treatment and had never returned. Pilar wished she were there to help her get through this room of strange faces.

Then she saw Doña Teresa and Don Rafael standing across the room with their backs turned towards her. They were talking to guests. Pilar walked directly to them and stood behind Doña Teresa.

Doña Teresa was forced to turn and greet Pilar. The two women stood facing each other for the first time since the day Elena had to be taken to the hospital.

Pilar felt as if she had stepped into a country without rain. She wanted to scurry away and hide under a rock. Lick the ground for moisture; find kinship with creatures underground. But she couldn't move. Her eyes were fixed on Doña Teresa's face.

The Spanish woman looked at Pilar without expression, then turned towards the girls. She touched them both on the head without saying a word, then walked away. Pilar saw the walls of the old city rise up in front of her. Her anguish reached towards Doña Teresa's back with the violence of surf. But silent. Suspended. Stillborn.

"¿Por qué Tía Teresa no noh quiere?" *Why doesn't Tía Teresa like us?* Luisa wanted to know as they rode back to Bocarío.

"No eh verdad, Luisa. Tía Teresa ehtá bien trihte por la muerte de Juan. Ehtá dihtraída," Pilar responded. *It's not true, Luisa. Tía Teresa is very sad because of Juan's death. She's distracted.*

After practicing the piano Meli hoped abuelita would come. But it was getting late. Meli thought of calling Tía Clara's house. She hated to call because if abuelita weren't coming she would be very disappointed. She wouldn't have anything to look forward to in the evening except mami being angry. It was Saturday, and Saturday was when papi went out. Mami would start getting upset if he didn't come back.

It was like getting ready for a hurricane. Pilar knew that everything would change fast. She knew it in her body.

Aurelio, Juan's brother, hadn't been friendly. He had always been cool towards her, but now his real feelings could come out in the open, even though he said something about her taking her time at the house and about her getting a pension. And that he would make all the arrangements. She wouldn't have to worry about any of it.

But she did worry. Juan had protected her. With Juan gone she felt like a stranger in his world.

Now everything had a price.

When she sent servants to the store to get food or household items, a clerk would write down everything that was sent to the big house. It was Aurelio's orders.

Aurelio came every day to talk to the foreman. He rarely came to the house. Pilar began to feel more and more like an unwelcome guest.

She gathered all the money in the house. The children were upset that they had to give up their money purses. It wasn't a lot, but it was good to set aside in case they had to go someplace. Besides, she didn't know when Aurelio would start the pension.

Then a letter came from Juan.

It was frightening. Maybe it wasn't true he had died. What if everybody had been making it up because they wanted to keep her away from him?

She stood there shaking for a while before she dared open it.

"Mi querida Pilar," it started. *My dear Pilar.*

It was dated after the operation, about ten days before he died.

"Espero te encuentres bien al recibir esta. Siento tener que darte malas noticias." *I hope you are well when you receive this letter. I regret having to give you bad news.*

Pilar struggled with the words. She wanted to have him all to herself for the last time. She had to look at the lines over and over again to make sure of the words. She couldn't see through her tears.

She started perspiring and felt faint. Then she remembered the dictionary in Juan's study. Don Ramiro wanted the children to look up words, so Juan had brought the dictionary from Doña Teresa's house. But he rarely left it out where they could use it. When he went on trips he would leave it in his study. Locked. Only the accountant was supposed to go in there.

Aurelio had said something in the past week about needing to get to the books. He was going to bring his own accountant to go over everything and move the business books to his own office.

Pilar knew she was not supposed to go into the study, but she also knew that this time she had to. She knew where the key was.

"Perdóname Juan, pero tengo que hacerlo." *Forgive me, Juan, but I have to do it,* she said as she walked into their bedroom and reached into a drawer of Juan's dresser, under his shirts, for the key. She felt as if she were stealing something.

The children were in their rooms, resting after lunch. She was afraid that they would hear the sound of her heart pounding as she crossed the dining room towards the study, and the sound of the key in the lock.

Pilar closed the door behind her and walked into the dark, musty smell. Here she felt Juan's presence so strongly that tears began to roll out of her eyes uncontrollably.

"¡Juan, Juan, amor mío! ¡No me dejeh!" she whispered. *Juan, Juan, my love! Don't leave me!*

Pilar had to sit down and rest her head on the desk, and sob. But she stopped herself soon. She had to get the dictionary and get out. She didn't want anyone to know she was there. She felt as if she were breaking into a church. She feared she was going to be punished.

When she lifted her head to look for the dictionary her eyes fell on a book with a piece of paper stuck between its pages. It was a beautifully bound book.

She was drawn to it, as if it could tell her something about Juan. Maybe he had marked some passage he particularly liked.

She opened the book. It was a book of poetry. Doña Saturnina had shown Pilar books of poetry.

The piece of paper had something written on it in handwriting which was not Juan's. She read: Amor de mi vida . . . . *Love of my life* . . . .

With a stab of recognition, Pilar knew this was a note and a present from another woman. It was signed: Catalina.

"¡No! ¡No! ¡No quiero saberlo! ¡Déjenme en paz!" *No! No! I don't want to know about it! Let me be!* Pilar cried.

She slammed the book shut, put it back in place and grabbed the dictionary which was standing close to it. She was ready to close the shutter and walk out when she realized that she didn't want anyone else to see that note. She would feel too humiliated if Aurelio or the accountant saw it when they went through Juan's books.

Pilar grabbed the note and crushed it in her fist. Then walked out with the dictionary.

She collapsed on her bed. What else was going to happen? What else was she going to have to go through? She wanted the ocean to swallow her. She wanted to go into a place where there was no air. Even breathing reminded her of a life where there was no home.

Pilar got up, lit a match and held it to the note. She prayed for death silently while she watched it burn.

Luisa was shaking her. Pilar moved. She tried to speak. Luisa held her, crying and calling, "¿Qué pasó?" *What happened?*

Pilar whispered, "Llegó una carta . . . ." *A letter came* . . . .

Luisa took the letter that lay next to Pilar. When she saw that it was from Juan she became pale.

"¿De papá?" *From papá?* She looked at Pilar uncomprehendingly.

Seeing Luisa's anguish, Pilar forced herself to speak. "Yo no entiendo tampoco porqué llegó ahora. Saqué el diccionario . . . ." *I don't understand either why it came now. I took out the dictionary . . . .*

Luisa began to read. "Siento darte malas noticias. El doctor ha encontrado un cancer . . . ." *I regret having to give you bad news. The doctor found cancer . . . .*

Luisa held her breath and stopped for a moment.

"Ha encontrado un cancer en mi garganta. Se ha es-par-cido por otras partes de mi cuerpo, así que hemos decidido no tratar de . . . ." *He has found cancer in my throat. It has s-spread to other parts of my body. We have decided not to try to . . . .* Luisa couldn't understand the next word. She had to stop and look it up.

"Es-tir-par, e-rra-di-car, ex-tra-er . . . sacar." *Ex-tir-pate, e-ra-di-cate, ex-tract . . . take out.*

She looked triumphant.

"Sacar. Sacar, eso eh lo que quiere decir." *Take out. Take out, that's what it means.*

Luisa turned energetically to the letter again. "Hemos deci-dido no tratar de extirpar, de sacar, los tumores. Dice que si des-canso podré vivir hasta seis meses." *We have decided not to try to extirpate, to take out, the tumors. He says that if I rest I will be able to live as long as six months.*

Pilar stared at the ocean.

The words seemed distant. As if this had happened to some-one else some other time. Like one of those Spanish stories Doña Saturnina used to read to her.

"Voy a hacer arreglos para volver a la isla." *I am going to arrange to return to the island.*

It was strange to Pilar to watch herself hurt.

"Deseo que tomemos los . . . ." *I would like for us to take our . . . .* Luisa stopped.

". . . vo-tos . . ." *. . . vo- . . . vows . . .*

Luisa opened the dictionary again. "Vo-to, pro-mesa." *Vow, pro-mise.*

Luisa looked at the letter again as if she couldn't understand.

". . . ma-tri-mo-nia-les . . ." *. . . ma-tri-mon-ial . . .*

She looked up at her mother questioningly. "Tiene que ver algo con el matrimonio . . . ." *It has something to do with marriage . . . .*

Suddenly Pilar's body was burning. Curses, ugly words came up inside her. Words she had heard her mother use. Her father. The hired men.

She covered her mouth. She was afraid she was going to vomit.

Luisa watched her mother.

"No ehtabamoh casadoh," Pilar blurted out to Luisa. *We were not married.*

Luisa was very frightened. Pilar softened, seeing the look on her face. Pilar knew how Luisa felt.

"Siento darte pena," Pilar said with tears in her eyes. *I'm sorry to hurt you.*

She tried to hold Luisa. Luisa pulled away.

Meli couldn't understand why they hadn't fought for what was theirs. Her aunts, and mami too, said Aurelio got all the money and all the land.

Meli thought she was going to grow up and find a lawyer and a detective to find all those papers that told about where the land was. The land that was by the ocean and had all the coconut groves on it. Bocarío. It made her mad to think that Aurelio had stolen it.

Tía Clara had said too that there had been a letter from abuelo Juan about all the property that he was leaving abuelita and his children. But the letter had been lost. They didn't know how.

"Hay gente mala. Pero no voy a dejar que nadie me haga eso a mí," Meli said to abuelita. *There are bad people. But I'm not going to let anybody do that to me.* She was angry.

"Y un día, abuelita, yo voy a encontrar esah tierrah y te lah voy a dar. Y vah a tener tu casa de nuevo." *Abuelita, some day I'm going to find that land and I'm going to give it back to you. And you're going to have your house again.*

But Meli couldn't imagine abuelita in her own house. During the whole time Meli was growing up abuelita had stayed with her daughters.

Meli secretly wished that abuelita had a house. She could stay with her. Then she wouldn't have to watch mami get angry and hear her fights with papi in the middle of the night.

But abuelita didn't seem to want things.

BOOK
FOUR
□

◻ "¿Cuándo viene Meli?" Pilar asked Luisa from her hospital bed. *When is Meli coming?*

"¿Le avisaron a Meli de que ehtoy en el hohpital?" *Did you let Meli know I'm in the hospital?* she insisted.

"Sí." *Yes,* Luisa answered.

"¿Cuándo?" *When?* Pilar asked.

"Hace unoh díah." *A few days ago,* Luisa responded.

"¿En qué avión llega?" *What flight is she taking?* Pilar wanted to know.

"No hemoh sabido de ella todavía," Luisa said. *We haven't heard from her yet.*

Days later Pilar asked again.

Luisa was angry.

"Ya se le avisó, mamá." *We let her know already, mamá,* she said impatiently.

"¿Le habrá pasado algo?" *Do you think something happened to her?* Pilar asked.

"No sé." *I don't know,* Luisa answered.

Pilar hoped Meli would come. She had been gone for a long time. "Se olvida uno de lah cosah," she murmured to herself. *One forgets things.*

She tried to remember when Meli had left for el Norte. For the U.S. Was she only sixteen? By the time she left, Pilar had been glad. It wasn't good for Meli to be there. Luisa wasn't well.

"La vida eh diferente por allá." *Life's different over there,* she had said to Clara.

But she had been afraid she would not see Meli again. Even though she told herself it was silly.

Meli sent things throughout the years: letters, photos. Were the felt-lined slippers for her birthday? Or the knitted wrap? There was a painting too. It was sunny and had a lot of color.

Pilar tried to remember where the picture was. Her head wasn't working as well as it used to. It did what it wanted to, like an unruly child. Went where it wanted, whenever it wanted to, or hid from her altogether. There were times when it felt as if there were nothing there. The clock was one time, then when she looked again it was a very different time.

When I arrived at the airport I realized how long I had been gone. I felt like a tourist in my own past: arriving by plane, in the morning dampness which clings to the skin. The cement defeated by rain. Becoming mold. Becoming ruins to be looked at.

In my body I knew already she had died. I didn't need to be told that they were driving directly to the funeral home. A building with many rooms, hushed voices and men in dark suits standing in small groups. I felt uncomfortable with the sudden intimacy which death brings to relatives and friends. Most of them I had not seen for many years. As I stood next to mami, I remembered how I hadn't liked to think about abuelita dying.

Meli had learned a poem she was supposed to recite at school. It made her sad. In it a grandchild kept asking her grandmother, "¿Abuelita, qué horas son?" *Abuelita, what time is it?* Then the grandmother died and there was no one there to ask.

The night before she was going to recite the poem in the school chapel, Meli woke up. The ceiling light was on. Abuelita was in her cotton nightgown that mami had made for her. She was holding her belly in pain.

Meli thought of going into her parents' bedroom to get mami. She didn't do that anymore since the time she had walked in when she was scared and her mother called out from a corner of the room, "No mires, nena." *Don't look, honey.*

Meli didn't know what it was she wasn't supposed to see. But she got the idea she wasn't supposed to come into their bedroom even though the door was always open. When she was scared now she just called mami from down the hallway. Sometimes mami didn't even hear.

Meli couldn't sleep well unless there was someone else around who made her feel safe. More than anybody else, abuelita made Meli feel safe.

Except that night abuelita was bending over with pain. She didn't even cry or anything. She was just bent over.

Meli called mami from down the hallway. Mami phoned the doctor. He didn't live far away. He came right away, in his shirt sleeves.

The doctor said it looked like a gallstone, whatever that was. It hurt when it was trying to come out. It would be better to put her in the hospital.

Abuelita went from one daughter's house to the next with only her purse. She stayed only two or three days at each place. She didn't carry anything else. That was all she brought to the hospital too. Meli didn't know what was in the purse. But she was curious. She knew abuelita kept one cigarette in it. Meli could smell it. And there was another one under abuelita's cotton nightgowns on the shelf in Meli's closet where abuelita kept her things: her underwear, and men's handkerchiefs which she wore hanging from her belt when she was sweeping, to wipe the perspiration from her face. But on her shelf she also had a couple of small handkerchiefs with violet prints and lace around the edges. And there were some dresses hanging in the back of the closet. Mami had made most of them, but there were one or two that Tía Clara had bought for abuelita at the department store.

Meli came every day after school to see abuelita at the hospital. She liked that she could walk to the hospital by herself. Mami said it was okay.

Meli didn't remember ever seeing abuelita sick. She looked old and thin in the hospital bed. She had always seen abuelita doing things: sweeping, ironing, walking places. Except when she sat on the window seat in the dining room and told Meli stories about growing up.

What if abuelita died? Meli looked at abuelita, who had fallen asleep with her mouth open. Abuelita never liked to wear her lower teeth because they were too uncomfortable. She looked very pale. It was scary. What if abuelita couldn't come and be with her at night? And take her places? Meli didn't want to think about it.

She was glad she brought her sketchbook. She got bored when abuelita went to sleep. The thought kept popping into her head even as she tried to draw the view from the window: what if she dies? It would be even more scary at night in her room if abuelita died.

Meli remembered when the neighbor, Don Julio, had died. The coffin was right there in the living room. She could see it through the windows from her house. There were people coming in, all dressed up to look at the body. She didn't go over there. It was a good thing that papi didn't ask her to go. But she didn't like to be alone at home either. She was afraid something was going to appear suddenly when she wasn't looking and startle her.

Seña Alba came and squatted on the linoleum floor of the hospital next to Meli. Abuelita was sleeping.

"¿Qué hay?" *What's happening?* Seña Alba said, grinning.

Meli was pleased to see her but didn't want to say she had been bored. It didn't seem right to be bored when abuelita was sick. Besides, abuelita always said that there was no reason for children to be bored.

"¿Por qué abuelita dice que los niños no tienen porqué aburrirse?" *Why does abuelita say that there's no reason for children to be bored?*

Seña Alba didn't answer, instead she began to tell a story.

"Había una veh . . . ." *Once upon a time . . . .*

In her fitful sleep Pilar dreamed of herself sitting on the top step in back of her parents' house. A breeze came up from the ocean. She felt light. Like she could take off into the air and perch on the mango tree. Move with the branches. The leaves made a soft sound.

She didn't know how come birds didn't get dizzy. They would pick away at the ripe mangos way up on the high branches. The ones that fell to the ground with holes pecked in them. They were too soft to eat.

Sometimes she felt the tree was part of the house. She woke up and saw the leaves in the window. First thing. She had been watching every morning one mango getting ripe. She didn't want the boys to notice. They would climb up and grab it when it was still too green. Marta screamed at them when they did that.

"¡Dehpeldiciando la comí'a, dehgracia'oh!" *Wasting food, shameless runts!*

But they would do it anyway.

Pilar saw her herself as a child hiding up there in the leaves. Watching Marta through the windows. For hours. Laughing. Seeing Patria try to sneak out. The boys chasing a lagartijo, a *small lizard*, out of the house.

"Había una veh," Seña Alba started, "una negrita que vivía en una casita debajo de unah palmah de coco. La casita era chiquita y así monta' en paloh. La negrita no tenía na' que hacel to' el día polque no tenía helmanoh ni helmanah y su mai se pasaba el día sentá' en una silla ehperando a su negro que hacía un pal de añoh no había vení'o. Un vecino leh daba unah limohnah pa' que no se murieran de hambre." *Once upon a time, there's a little black girl that live in a house under coconut trees. The house is little and up on sticks. The little black girl do nothing all day because she have no brothers or sisters and her ma sit all day waiting for her man. He gone two years now. A neighbor give them money so they don't starve.*

"La negrita se aburría de pasalse el día en la ventana mirando al mar. Un día se quedó mirando un lagaltijo que había debajo 'el techo y de pronto el lagaltijo empezó a bajal pol la paré' y empezó a ponelse máh grande. Tenía un colol velde amarillo y loh ojoh eran como el cielo, niña, y como si l'ehtuviera saliendo luh pol loh ojoh." *The little black girl is bored just sitting there by the window looking at the ocean. One day she look at this lizard that is sitting under the roof, then suddenly the lizard start coming down the wall, getting bigger. It's green and yellow and it has eyes blue like the sky, child, like light come out of them.*

"La negrita se asuhtó . . . ." *The little black girl get scared . . . .* Seña Alba's eyes twinkled and she laughed loudly. Meli looked towards abuelita to see if she had been awakened by the laughter. Abuelita stirred but she didn't wake up. Meli got scared again. What if abuelita didn't wake up?

Seña Alba went on. "S'ehcondió detráh de la paré' pero deh-puéh de un ratito se asomó un chihpito. El lagaltijo ehtaba to'avía allí. La negrita s'ehcondió de nuevo, pero dehpuéh de otro rato se asomó y ehta veh no ehtaba tan asuhtá' como la primera veh, así que se quedó mirando al lagaltijo un ratito máh lalgo." *She hide behind the wall, but after a little while she peek. The lizard is still there. The little black girl hide again, but after a little while she peek again and this time she's not as scared as the first time so she look at the lizard for a while longer.*

"Ehto pasa unah cuantah veceh y ca' veh ella se pone un poco máh brava. Y el lagaltijo eh tan bonito que era difícil quitále loh ojoh de'encima. Bueno, en una d'esah la negrita oye una voh que dice, '¿Cómo ehtáh, negrita?'" *This happen a few times and each time she get a little braver. And the lizard is so pretty it's hard to take her eyes off it. Then she look one time and she hear a voice that say, 'How are you, negrita?'*

"Miró pa'lante y pa'tráh y salió pa'l otro cualto a vel si su pai había llega'o. Y le dice a su mai, 'Mai ¿dónde ehtá mi pai? Le oí la voh.'" *She look this way and that and she go to the other room to see if her pa just come. And she tell her ma, 'Ma, where's my pa? I hear his voice.'*

"Bueno, la mai se cae pa'tráh gritando y llorando, '¿Dónde ehtá mi negro? ¿Dónde ehtá mi negro?' Y le dá un patatú y allí mihmo se murió." *Well, her ma fall down screaming and yelling, 'Where's my man? Where's my man?' And she have a stroke and she die right there.*

"¡No digah eso!" *Don't say that!* Meli said to Seña Alba. "Me asuhta." *It scares me.*

Meli got up and looked anxiously at abuelita. She seemed to be sleeping okay.

Seña Alba said apologetically, "Bueno, ehtá bien muchacha, no se murió la negra. La negrita se creyó que su mai se había muelto polque se cayó al piso gritando, pero la mai no se murió, se dehmayó na máh." *Okay, child, the black woman don't die. The little black girl think her mother die because she fall down screaming, but her ma don't die, she just faint.*

Meli was relieved.

Seña Alba started again. "La negrita no sabía qué hacel hahta que oyó la voh de nuevo." *The little black girl don't know what to do until she hear the voice again.*

"'Ven acá, negrita,' la voh le decía." *'Come here, negrita,' the voice say.*

"La muchachita se dió cuenta que era el lagaltijo que hablaba. Bueno, quería correr pa' fuera, del suhto que le dió, pero el lagaltijo le decía, 'Ven acá, negrita' en una voh tan dulce que a ella se le empezó a quital el miedo." *The girl notice that it's the lizard that's talking. Well, she want to run outside, she's so scared, but the lizard keep saying, 'Come here, negrita,' so sweet she start not being scared.*

"Entonceh el lagaltijo le dijo, 'Mila, si le dah un beso a tu mai se va a dehpeltal bien contenta, pero primero tieneh que dálme un beso a mí.'" *Then the lizard tell her, 'If you kiss your ma, she wake up real happy, but first you have to give me a kiss.'*

"Bueno, eh una cosa miral un lagaltijo y eh otra cosa dále un beso. Ella hizo una cara fea y se fué a sental al la'o de su mai y empezó a dále besoh, pero la mai no se dehpeltaba." *Well, it's one thing to look at a lizard and it's another to kiss it. She make a face and go sit by her ma and start giving her kisses. But her ma don't wake up.*

"La negrita empezó a lloral y lloró y lloró y dehpuéh de un rato paró de lloral y oyó unoh gemi'oh del otro cualto. Cuando fué a vel lo que era vió al lagaltijo llorando y ella le dijo, 'Yo nunca he vihto un lagaltijo llorando. ¿Pol qué llorah?'" *The black girl begin to cry and cry and cry and after a while she stop crying and she hear moaning in the other room. When she go look, she find the lizard crying and she say, 'I never seen a lizard crying. Why you cry?'*

"'Polque tú créh que yo soy feo,' él le dice." *'Because you think I'm ugly,' he say.*

"'Yo no creo que tú ereh feo,' ella contehtó." *'I don't think you're ugly,' she answered.*

"'Bueno, ¿y pol qué no me quiereh besal?' él le pregunta." *'Then why don't you want to kiss me?' he ask.*

"'Polque ereh un lagaltijo,' ella le dijo." *'Because you're a lizard,' she answer.*

"El lagaltijo empezó a lloral y lloró tanto que se le fué el colol y se dehmayó. La negrita no sabía qué hacel con su mai y el lagaltijo dehmaya'oh y ella solita allí." *The lizard begin to cry and he cry so much he faint. The little black girl don't know what to do with her ma and the lizard fainted and she all by herself there.*

"La negrita se sentó en el sillón de su mai y s'empezó a mecel. Dehpuéh de un ratito empezó a cantal un son que su mai le cantaba cuando ella era chiquita. Eso fué anteh de que su pai se fuera, cuando la mai to'avía ehtaba contenta." *The little black girl sit in her ma's rocking chair and she begin to rock. After a little while she begin to sing a song her ma used to sing when she was little. That's before her pa leave, when her ma is still happy.*

"Entonceh la mai se dehpeltó y dijo, '¡Adioh! ¿Pol qué ehtoy yo pol el piso y tú sentá en mi sillón?'" *Then her ma wake up and say, 'Lord! Why I'm on the floor and you sitting on my rocking chair?'*

"La negrita dijo, 'Te dió un suhto cuando el lagaltijo me empezó a hablal. Él quería que yo le diera un beso pero yo no quería.'" *The little black girl say, 'You get scared when the lizard start talking to me. He want me to kiss him but I don't want to.'*

"La mai le dijo, 'Tú ehtáh loca o mentirosa. Ahora mihmo te vah a sacal eso de la cabeza.'" *Her ma say, 'You crazy or you a liar. Going to get that stuff out of your head right now.'*

"Y allí mihmo le dió una paliza." *And right there she give her a beating.*

"Entonceh la mai se sentó de nuevo a ehperal a su negro y a mecelse en el sillón. La negrita se fué al cualto a miral pol la ventana. Dehpuéh de un ratito la negrita oyó una voz que la decía,

'¿Cómo ehtáh, negrita?'" *Then her ma sit again to wait for her man and to rock in her rocking chair. The little black girl go to the other room to look out the window. After a little while the little black girl hear a voice saying, 'How are you, negrita.'*

"No me guhta ese cuento," Meli said to Seña Alba. *I don't like that story.*

"¿Y pol qué, niña?" *Why, child?* Seña Alba asked.

"Porque la mamá le dió una paliza." *Because the mother gave her a beating,* Meli said.

"Bueno, niña, puéh cuéntame tú un cuento." *Well, child, you tell me a story,* Seña Alba said.

"Yo no sé hacer cuentoh," Meli protested. *I don't know how to tell stories.*

Seña Alba just sat there smiling at her.

Meli was curious. "Seña Alba, ¿por qué empiezan loh cuentoh con 'había una vez?'" *Seña Alba, why do they always start stories with 'once upon a time'?*

"Esah son palabrah mágicah," Seña Alba said. "Eh como si le echarah un fufú a la gente, entonceh elloh entran pol una ventana al paíh de loh cuentoh. Enseguí'a que diceh 'había una veh' ya ehtán ahí. Y tú también." *They's magic words. Like you cast a spell on people then, they go through a window into the country of stories. As soon as you say 'once upon a time,' they're there and you too.*

Meli took a deep breath and turned towards abuelita, who was still asleep. She began very softly, "Abuelita, había una veh un lagartijo maravilloso que vivía en una palma de coco en una playa de arena bien blanca." *Abuelita, once upon a time there was a magic lizard that lived in a coconut palm at a beach that had very white sand.*

Seña Alba looked pleased.

Meli found herself walking down the beach. She stopped in front of the palm tree, which she recognized instantly among all the many other palm trees because when Meli approached it she felt like singing. She also noticed that the palm moved very gracefully.

"¡Rey Lagartijo! ¡Rey Lagartijo!" *King Lizard! King Lizard!* Meli called at the foot of the palm tree.

Soon a creature of many colors came walking down the palm trunk, slowly and solemnly. He was yellow and bright green and had eyes that shone like gems. Meli's mouth dropped open and she bowed.

The lizard said, "Eso no se hace aquí. Levánta la cabeza y mírame. Yo no puedo hablar con gente que no me enseña la cara." *We don't do that here. Lift your head and look at me. I can't talk to people who don't show me their face.*

Meli blushed. She didn't like to do the wrong thing.

When she looked up the lizard asked, "¿Qué piensah?" *What do you think?*

"¿De qué?" *About what?* Meli said.

"De cualquier cosa. Yo me aburro aquí. No hay con quién hablar. Dime lo que te venga a la cabeza. Eso eh lo máh importante." *Whatever. I get bored here. There's no one to talk to. Just tell me what comes into your head. That's the most important.*

Meli blushed again.

"Debe ser interesante lo que piensah." *It must be interesting what you're thinking,* the lizard said.

"No sé si debo decirlo." Meli was shy. *I don't know whether I should say it.*

"Lo que no debemoh decir eh siempre lo que debemoh decir." *What we shouldn't say is always what we should say,* the lizard said with great authority.

Meli giggled nervously. The lizard waited.

"Bueno, lo que pensé eh que ... te veh ridículo en todoh ehtoh coloreh ... eh bien jíbaro." *Well, I thought that ... you look ridiculous in all those colors ... like a country hick.*

Now it was the King Lizard who blushed. He got all bright red and kind of puffy and started breathing hard like he was going to suffocate.

Meli thought, Oh, my God! This story is turning out like Seña Alba's. He's going to die, then I'm going to feel like it's my fault.

Then she heard Seña Alba's voice coming from behind the palm tree. "Esah cosah pasan ...." *Those things happen ...* Seña Alba was saying.

"¡Yo no quiero que pasen!" *I don't want them to happen!* Meli screamed.

The lizard was so startled by the scream that all the color went out of his body and he stood there looking kind of plain and regular.

"¡Ay, pobrecito lagartijo! ¡Perdóname! Yo creía que te ibah a morir. Me asuhté. ¿Dónde ehtán tuh coloreh? Seña Alba te debe haber hecho un fufú." *Poor little lizard! Forgive me! I thought you were going to die. Where did your colors go? Seña Alba must have cast a spell on you,* Meli said.

Seña Alba peered from behind the coconut palm. "Mira, niña, no m'echeh la culpa a mí. Si te vah a metel a hacel cuentoh vah a tenel que tenel cuida'o." *Look, child, don't blame me. If you going to mess with telling stories you got to be careful.*

"¿Cuidado con qué . . . ?" *Careful with what . . . ?* Meli asked.

Seña Alba's face faded. In its place was abuelita's face in the hospital bed. Meli stared. Abuelita looked very pale and kind of shaky, but she was smiling at Meli.

"Graciah por cuidarme tan bien." *Thanks for looking after me so well,* she said.

Meli was surprised.

"Me siento mejor cuando tú vieneh a verme." *I feel better when you come visit me,* abuelita said.

Meli blushed. She was pleased.

"Y uno de ehtoh díah te voy a hacer un cuento." *And one of these days I'm going to tell you a story,* Meli said.

That was the only time Meli remembered abuelita being sick, when she got her gallstone. Soon after that they were able to go on their walks again.

Meli had never been allowed to go places by herself. She had to go with mami, abuelita, or an older cousin. To her, anything that happened outside of the metal gate of her house was an adventure. Even things that happened at the gate were exciting. Like the masons pouring the concrete for the sidewalk and smoothing it out with a long board. They poured small amounts of water on the surface and smoothed it and smoothed it until it was perfect. She remembered when she hid behind the stone fence to watch the lame beggar they called el Cuco come up the street. Meli was afraid of him. When she got her mail order telescope for $1.98, she put it together herself and would sit on the fence and look through it as far as she could down the street, to the point where the street curved out of sight.

She had pictures in her head of everywhere she had gone and everything she had seen. She liked to go places, but she didn't always like to walk there. She didn't like people to look at her, or talk to her. She didn't like it either when the buses were full and you had to stand right next to somebody you didn't even know, rubbing against some part of them. And she didn't like to wait for buses, especially when she was hot and tired.

"¿Cuándo viene Meli?" Tía Clara asked on the phone. *When is Meli coming?*

"Esta tarde," abuelita answered. *This afternoon.*

Meli was very happy that she was going to stay overnight at Tía Clara's new apartment. It was on the top floor of a four-story building that had an elevator. Abuelita was going to take her there that day. Meli was already thinking about how much fun she was going to have exploring the building.

She put her pajamas in her purse like abuelita did with her nightgown when she went someplace. Meli also took the money mami had given her for a comic book.

Abuelita and Meli had to go down the hill to take the bus to Tía Clara's house. The bus stop was about a mile and a half away from Meli's house. Meli didn't like it that papi had the car and she had to take buses most of the time.

"Abuelita ¿te guhta caminar?" *Abuelita, do you like to walk?* Meli asked.

"Sí." *Yes,* abuelita said, smiling at Meli.

"¿Por qué?" *Why?* Meli wanted to know.

"Yo no sé . . . . Creo que eh porque no tengo que ehperar por nadie." *I don't know . . . . I think that it's because I don't have to wait for anyone,* abuelita answered.

"Pero, tú me ehperah en la ehcuela." *But you wait for me at school*, Meli said.

Abuelita always came to get her after Meli's drawing class. Waited for her in front of the building. Meli didn't know what abuelita thought about when she sat there waiting.

"Eso eh diferente," abuelita was saying, "a mí me guhta venir a buhcarte y pasar tiempo contigo." *That's different, I like to come get you and spend time with you.*

Meli was pleased. She walked closer to abuelita and took abuelita's hand. But she was still mad that they had to walk.

"Me da coraje de que tenemoh que caminar y papi siempre anda en carro," Meli said. *It makes me mad that we have to walk and papi's always using the car.*

"Bueno, si Luisa fuera diferente ya ella aprendería a guiar." *Well, if Luisa were different she would learn to drive*, abuelita said.

That time Meli didn't want to think about how mami was. It just wasn't right that papi had the car all the time.

The part of town where they had to go to catch the bus was ugly. Meli didn't like to walk through it. There were men standing at the cafetínes, *coffee shops*, and they looked at her. She didn't like it. They said things.

She learned from abuelita. Just from watching her. On the streets when men said things or walked close trying to get your attention you didn't look right or left. You looked straight ahead, far away, not at anything in particular. You acted like they weren't there. But you noticed everything so you could tell which men would say things, which would just look, which would laugh. You could tell by the clothes and how they stood. She learned when was the best time to cross the street before getting to the corner where men stood. When to hurry her steps without seeming as if she were running away, when to slow down, or when to go into a store so as not to run into a drunk coming down the street. Meli was glad abuelita was always with her.

On the way to the bus they went to Doña Mirta's store. Doña Mirta had a small counter with candies she made herself. The bright-colored pirulí shone inside the glass jars. The *cone-shaped suckers* were not Meli's favorites. They were too sticky. Meli looked past the coconut candy to the guava paste, orange paste and gofio, a *sweet powder,* until she found the pasta de batata, the *sweet potato paste.* Her favorite. Doña Mirta wrapped it in pale-colored tissue paper. The kind Meli used to make kites. The ends of the paper were cut into fine ribbons. Meli opened the paper carefully like it was a surprise.

Abuelita took her purse in one hand and Meli's hand in the other and off they went. Abuelita's hand was cool and bony. And she had big veins. Abuelita showed Meli once how one of the big veins on the back of her hand made the shape of a 'c,' the first letter of abuelita's last name.

Abuelita hummed as they went. Meli watched the telephone lines against the blue sky, the clouds that made shapes of giant cows lying in a field, and wondered about the stories behind the windows and balconies they passed.

When she was little and people still came to the house, Meli was always allowed to listen to the stories that visitors told about their lives. Stories of the relatives that sat on the front terrace and of the poor people who came around the back asking for food and money.

Meli heard abuelita say sometimes, "Ave María ¡lah cosah que pasan!" *God, the things that happen!*

Meli knew from early on that things happened and that part of what she was supposed to do was to keep things from happening to her. Imagining them was like a preparation.

Mami said she didn't want to know. She hated to read the paper. She said there were a lot of sad things happening in her life already, why add to it. Meli knew that abuelita thought mami didn't know how to protect herself from things. Abuelita often said to mami, "Luisa, tú no te dah cuenta . . . ." *Luisa, you don't notice . . . .*

Meli tried to notice and she tried to imagine. She could never imagine altogether what it would be like to go places alone. Crossing the ocean seemed at times impossible. She thought maybe there was nothing else out there past the ocean, that all other places were imaginary. And that she was trapped forever on the island.

Now, as I write this, I am on the other side of that ocean. Meli is asking a question which I have feared to ask myself. Why didn't I go see abuelita before she died?

I sit at my writing desk and close my eyes. I see abuelita in bed at Tía Clara's house. Clara brought abuelita to her house because she knew abuelita didn't want to die at the hospital. There wasn't much the hospital could do anyway.

Abuelita is very thin. It is still hard for me to think about her dying even though my own hair is grey now.

Meli's question hovers over my desk like a ghost: why didn't I go back to the island to see abuelita before she died?

It was cancer.

She hadn't felt so much pain since her gallstone. They found out that the cancer had spread through her intestines.

Pilar didn't like the hospital. She didn't like people fussing with her. And having no privacy. That was the worst part of being sick. When you're sick nobody leaves you alone.

Pilar thought about dying. What's dying anyway? You just stop. But it made her afraid. She didn't know of what exactly.

She kept remembering things. Didn't know where one memory started and another ended. All mixed together like trees on the hills. All thick green and soft-looking like something you could lie on.

Pilar closed her eyes, attempting to get away from the pain in her belly. She saw the children all lined up on the front veranda at Bocarío to watch Juan come up the road. He had sent someone from the village ahead of him to alert Pilar that he was coming. This time he had been on another island for months buying land and setting up a business.

The children and the servants were all dressed up. Pilar was very nervous and kept asking Fernanda whether everything was ready. She even sent Santiago down the road to see if Juan was coming.

They heard a horse galloping. It was Santiago wrapped in dust and sweat.

"¡Ya viene!" he called out as he approached the front of the house. *He come now!*

Then they saw Juan at the turn of the road. He was very small and far away. Pilar wanted to reach out and pull him to her breast. The road had never seemed so long. But little by little she could see his face. The broad forehead under the wide-rimmed hat, and the dark moustache. He looked very handsome sitting so straight on his horse.

Pilar was always surprised to see him come home. She didn't totally expect him to come back to her.

The children surrounded him. He picked up Clara. She squirmed and laughed. The other children stood a little stiffly near him. He kissed each one on the cheek and patted Manuelito on the head. Then walked up the stairs, saying hello to the servants.

Pilar watched every movement and every gesture he made to see if he was the same as when he had left. She wanted to touch his face and hold his head in her arms. Bring him home.

He stood in front of her, smiling, and said, "Te ves bien." *You look well.*

Then he hugged her and kissed her on the forehead.

Pilar didn't want him to move away even for an instant, but he turned and started to go into the house. She followed him.

"¿Quiereh algo?" *Do you want anything?* she asked.

He looked tired, especially around the eyes, and he had lost some weight. But she was going to look after him.

They all sat at the dining room table. Fernanda brought coffee for Juan and Pilar and sweets for the children.

"Todos se ven bien." *Everybody looks well,* Juan said, looking at the children.

Then suddenly he called to Luisa, "¡Luisa!"

Pilar jumped. Luisa's face turned red.

"Estás siempre distraída." *You are always distracted,* Juan said. She dropped her head.

"Trae la valija que dejé cerca de la puerta." *Bring the bag I left near the door.*

"Yo te la traigo." *I'll bring it to you,* Pilar said.

Juan frowned at Pilar. "Tienes que dejar que las niñas te ayuden. No quiero que las malcríes." *You must let the girls help you. I don't want you to spoil them.*

Pilar didn't say anything. Luisa went for the bag. The other children sat quietly, except for Manuelito who squirmed in his chair.

"Manuelito, después de un rato vamos a salir a caballo. Tengo que hablar con el capataz a ver cómo andan las cosas. Pero tienes que quedarte quieto, porque si nó, no vas a poder ir conmigo." *Manuelito, after a while we are going for a horse ride. I have to talk to the foreman to see how things are going. But you have to be still, otherwise you won't be able to come with me.*

Pilar wished Juan would take Luisa too. Luisa wasn't allowed to take her horse out anymore except when someone could go with her. Juan had forbidden Luisa from going out on the farm by herself because she had gone off to the beach alone and without asking permission. He had found out when Clara happened to mention it at the table.

Seña Alba never came around to Bocarío when Juan was home. But this time she had to. That was about five months before Juan died.

Elena was very sick and Pablo didn't want Marta to let Pilar know. Pablo didn't want to ask anything of Pilar or Juan. Everybody knew that Pablo was very angry because Juan didn't want Pilar's family visiting at the big house.

Juan didn't want Seña Alba at the house either.

"Ese sabe que yo veo suh mañah." *He know I see his tricks,* Seña Alba said to herself.

She tried to come to the house when Juan wasn't there. She didn't want to make trouble for Pilar. But if there was something important to tell Pilar, nothing would stop her.

Seña Alba came to the kitchen door. Fernanda frowned at her. "Don Juan ehtá en casa." *Don Juan's home,* Fernanda said.

"Yo no vengo a vel a Don Juan. Vengo a vel a Pilar." *I don't come to see Don Juan, I come to see Pilar,* Seña Alba snapped.

"Ehtá ocupá'. Ehpera afuera." *She busy. Wait outside,* Fernanda snapped back.

Seña Alba waited near the back door until she saw Juan riding away with Manuelito, then she knocked again.

"Don Juan se fué." *Juan's gone,* she said to Fernanda.

Fernanda was angry. "Si no fuera pol Doña Pilar . . . y límpiate loh pieh." *If it weren't for Doña Pilar . . . and clean your feet.*

"¿Me qui'e dal un trapo?" *Want to give me a rag?* Seña Alba asked.

Fernanda dropped a dirty rag next to Seña Alba's feet.

"Ehtá muy seco." *It's too dry,* Seña Alba said.

"Pueh ehcupe en él y no me molehteh máh. Tengo demasia'o que hacel." *So spit on it and don't bother me. I got too much to do.*

Seña Alba went outside looking for water. After a while she came back, smiling mischievously. She stood at the door and showed Fernanda her feet.

Fernanda went to tell Pilar, reluctantly, that Seña Alba was there.

Pilar came out to greet her. She was very alarmed about Elena after Seña Alba told her.

"Son loh pulmoneh." *It's the lungs,* Seña Alba said.

Elena had suffered from tuberculosis all her life. Nothing seemed to clear it altogether.

"Ehta veh eh pulmonía." *This time it's pneumonia,* Seña Alba went on.

"¿Bien mala?" *Very sick?* Pilar was very worried now.

"Sí." *Yes,* Seña Alba answered.

From her bed at Clara's Pilar could see the deep blue sky trapped between the blinds, the strong shadows on the red tiles of the terrace. She could feel the breeze and the endless afternoon stretching into her past. She saw herself riding sidesaddle with Seña Alba straddling the horse in back of her. She didn't want Juan to know about her going to see Elena, but she also knew that someone was probably going to tell him. She had left instructions with Fernanda not to tell anyone, just to say that she was talking to Seña Alba in her room. She would be back before Juan returned at sundown.

Pilar didn't talk much on the way to Marta's house. She felt soothed by the sound of the wind in the palm fronds. Then she realized it was Seña Alba humming.

Pilar began crying. It had been a very long time since she had gone somewhere with Seña Alba. The tears rolled down her cheeks and fell on the dusty ground.

Pablo wasn't home and Marta didn't want to let Seña Alba in, but Pilar insisted.

"Mamá, Elena necesita tratamiento." *Mamá, Elena needs treatment.*

"¿Qué t'impolta tí?" *What do you care?* Marta snapped.

Pilar held back her hurt feelings. "Ehtoy aquí porque me importa." *I'm here because it matters to me,* she answered. Then she turned towards Seña Alba and said, "Entra a ver a Elena." *Go in and see Elena.*

Marta wouldn't even look at Seña Alba. She went on, "El dotol no se consiguió. Emborracha'o pol ahí." *Can't find the doctor. He's drunk someplace.*

Then she lowered her voice and pointed towards Seña Alba. "Como la negra esa." *Like that nigger woman.*

Pilar knew that Marta was jealous of Seña Alba and jealous of Pilar's life. Pilar felt ashamed of her mother.

It was hard to be there now. Pilar tried not to think about it. But the place smelled of pee and there were flies everywhere. Marta's old dress was dirty on the belly where she rubbed her hands to dry them.

She remembered her mother saying, "Vamoh a sel negroh limpioh." *We going to be clean black folks.*

Seña Alba came out of the room, the same room where Pilar used to sleep. She was looking worried.

"Hay que llevala al hopital." *Have to take her to the hospital.*

"¡Ay bendito! ¡Qué lucha en ehta vida!" *Lord! Life's such a struggle!* Marta sobbed loudly.

Pilar was trying to think about the fastest way to get Elena to the hospital without Juan or Pablo knowing. At least until after it was done. It would take too long to go back to the house and send Santiago to make arrangements. She would have to go to the village herself and rent a buggy to take Elena to the hospital.

Maybe Tía Micaela would go with her and Marta could stay home. If Marta wasn't home when Pablo came, he would take it out on her later. It would be better if he were angry only at Pilar and Seña Alba.

Pilar didn't want to leave Seña Alba there either, in case Pablo showed up. She knew Seña Alba could take care of herself, but she needed Seña Alba. Felt safer with her.

It was useless. Everybody was going to know. She would have to talk to Doña Teresa at the store about renting a buggy. There was no way out.

But it didn't matter what anybody said, Elena was very sick. That's what was important.

It was beginning to get dark. Meli heard the metal gate to the driveway open and the door of a car slam. Her heart was pounding.

Meli had been thinking about it all day, what she was going to say to papi. It was hard to talk to him. Every time.

She heard him come in.

"¡Ya ehtá en la mesa!" *It's on the table!* she heard mami call out.

Meli waited until she heard papi go to the dining room.

She sat at the table across from her father. He was already eating. Meli's brother came downstairs carrying a book. He sat down next to Meli. Mami brought a plate for each of them with white rice, ground beef and slices of tomato. Her brother's plate also had red beans. Meli didn't like beans.

Mami set the plates down and went back to the kitchen. She didn't sit down to eat with them.

"¿Cómo está la escuela?" *How's school?* papi asked her brother.

"Bien." *Okay,* he said. They all continued eating in silence.

Suddenly papi pounded his fist on the table. "¡Mierda!" *Shit!*

Meli sat very still. She looked at her rice.

"¡Luisa!" He pounded again on the table.

Mami answered from the door to the dining room. "¡Coño! ¿Y qu'eh lo que quiereh ahora?" *Damn! And what do you want now?* she said.

"¿Cuantas veces te voy a decir que no me des mangós pudridos? ¡Carájo!" *How many times do I have to tell you not to give me rotten mangos? Damn it!*

"¡Pudrido ehtáh tú, sinvergüenza!" *You're the rotten one, you bastard!* she screamed.

Papi pushed the plate away, stood up and walked towards the front porch. Her brother got up and went back upstairs with his book. Meli pushed the white rice around with her fork. She picked up her plate and took it to the kitchen.

Mami was sitting on the back porch in the dark. Meli could hear her rocking chair.

Pilar rode into the village with Seña Alba and went directly to the store. Doña Teresa was not happy to see her, especially with Seña Alba.

"Pilar ¿qué haces aquí?" *Pilar, what are you doing here!* Doña Teresa asked.

"Mi hermana Elena tiene que ir al hohpital. Necesito una caleza." *My sister Elena has to go to the hospital. I need a buggy.*

"Están todas alquiladas, pero tenemos una carreta." *They are all rented, but we have a cart,* Doña Teresa answered.

Pilar knew it was a lie. She had seen a buggy in the back of the building.

"Doña Teresa, yo creo que le devolvielon uno polque hay uno ahí afuera." *Doña Teresa, I think they return one because there's one in the back,* Seña Alba said.

Doña Teresa's face turned deep red. "Pués, no lo sabía. Deja ver si hay alguien para engancharla." *Well, I didn't know. Let me see if there's someone to hitch it.*

She returned quickly from the back of the store and said, "Se han ido todos a comer. No hay quién lo haga. ¿Por qué no vienen más tarde?" *Everyone has gone to eat. There's no one to do it. Why don't you come later!*

Seña Alba said, "Yo lo pue'o hacel." *I do it.*

Doña Teresa's face became hard. "Yo no puedo permitir eso porque el caballo puede destrozar la caleza si no se engancha bien. Y puede ser un peligro para los pasajeros." *I cannot allow it because the horse could destroy the buggy if it is not hitched properly. And it can be very dangerous for the passengers.*

"Yo seré rehponsable, Doña Teresa. Seña Alba, vete a buhcar el caballo y empieza a ponerle el arnéh." *I will be responsible, Doña*

Teresa. Seña Alba, go get the horse and start harnessing it, Pilar said.

Doña Teresa was angry. "Voy a tener que hablarle a Juan de esto." *I will have to talk to Juan about this*, Doña Teresa said.

"Y yo también." *And me too*, Pilar said under her breath as she walked out.

Seña Alba not only found the horse and the buggy but also a couple of men in the stable. They joked with Seña Alba while hitching the horse. When they were done one of them pulled a bottle from his pocket and offered Seña Alba a swig. She gestured with her hand that she didn't want any.

The image of the man offering Seña Alba a bottle of rum stayed with Pilar even after she had gone back to Marta's with the buggy and had arranged with Tía Micaela to go to Corona with Elena.

The sun was low over the ocean and the sky was getting rose-colored as she rode back alone towards Bocarío. Seña Alba had wanted to ride back with her, but Pilar said Juan was going to be back soon anyway.

She felt a familiar feeling. There was something between them. Something between herself and Seña Alba that she couldn't talk about. She felt bad that Juan didn't want Seña Alba or Pilar's family at the house. She felt bad that she couldn't do anything about it, and today she also felt scared about what was going to happen when she told Juan about going to Marta's. She knew she had to tell him before someone else did.

Papi turned on the radio and went to sit on the front porch as he usually did every evening after work.

"¡Un vaso de agua!" *A glass of water!* he called out. To no one in particular.

Meli usually tried to hide when he asked for things. It made her feel like a servant to take things to him. But this time she went to the kitchen and filled a glass with filtered water from the refrigerator. She put it on a saucer.

Meli stood at the door looking towards her father who was behind the newspaper. He didn't notice that she was standing there.

She always had to get his attention. "¿Papi?" she said.

"Ponlo ahí," he said from behind the paper. *Put it down.*

She put the glass of water down.

"Papi," she said. Her heart was pounding again.

He put the paper down. Looked at her with slight impatience. He was still in his white office shirt with the stiff collar which abuelita ironed.

Everybody thought papi was very handsome. His picture was in the papers sometimes.

Meli thought of how it felt to kiss him. She only did it on his birthday or holidays. His short moustache was bristly against her cheek and he smelled of cologne and cigarettes.

His face was brown from sitting outside in the yard on the weekend, but where the shirt opened he was very white. It was always surprising to Meli to notice how white he was. Kind of soft and white. Meli didn't like it. And his arms were hairy.

Now he looked at her with an amused look.

"Ehte . . ." Meli hesitated, ". . . quería saber si podíah . . . llevarnoh al concierto . . . ." *Ah . . . I wanted to know if you could . . . take us to the concert . . . .*

"¿Qué concierto?" He seemed amused at her awkwardness. *What concert?*

"El domingo . . . en la Universidad." *Sunday . . . at the University,* Meli said haltingly. "Un recital de piano." *A piano recital.* "A las ocho de la noche." *At eight p.m.*

"Bueno." *Fine,* papi said and returned to his paper.

Meli stood there, not knowing what else to say.

When Pilar returned to Bocarío, Juan was already there. He was sitting at the dining room table looking at some papers and drinking a glass of sherry.

Pilar came in through the kitchen and caught Fernanda's worried look. She said that Luisa had asked for Pilar. Fernanda had told her that Pilar was in her room talking to Seña Alba.

"¿Y dónde ehtabah tú?" *And where were you?* Juan said with irritation. He sounded like he did with the hired men.

"Elena ehtaba bien enferma . . . . Tuve que ir al pueblo a buhcar una caleza." *Elena is very sick . . . . I had to go to the village to get a buggy.* She was breathless and scared.

"¿Y por qué no mandaste a Santiago?" *And why didn't you send Santiago?* Juan asked.

Pilar was silent for a while. The truth was hard to say.

"Tenía que verla." *I had to see her.* She barely got the words out.

"¿Aunque sábes que no quiero que vayas allá?" *Even though you know I don't want you to go there?* Juan's eyes were angry.

Pilar didn't know how to say what was pounding in her head. He wouldn't understand.

"¿No me vas a contestar?" *You are not going to answer me?* His voice was harsh.

"Tenía que verla, Juan. Ehtá bien enferma . . ." she pleaded. *I had to see her, Juan. She's very sick . . . .*

"¿Y tenías que irte por mi espalda acabando yo de llegar?" *And you had to go behind my back? Just when I came home?*

Her body felt the weight of his words. She felt beaten. Her head was full of screams, but in her throat there was just a dull feeling.

"Lo siento." *I'm sorry,* she said without seeing him. She only noticed it was getting dark.

"No permitas que vuelva a pasar." *Don't allow it to ever happen again,* he said and returned to his papers.

Pilar just stood there for a while.

Then Juan said, "Te ves estúpida parada ahí. Vete al cuarto." *You look stupid standing there. Go to the bedroom.*

She went into the bedroom and lay on the bed in her clothes. After a while Juan came in and without a word he took off his pants and lay on top of her.

Sunday came.

Meli took a bath early in the afternoon. Washed her hair over the sink. Mami ironed her dress.

Mami always wore the same thing. A dark dress which had powder stains around the collar and smelled kind of stale. She didn't send it to the cleaners with papi's suits because she wanted to save money.

Meli went and sat in the yard to let her hair dry. She imagined a roomful of people in fancy dresses at the auditorium. She had never been to the University. There were all these places that she had heard about and never been to.

She had had to talk mami into going to the concert. It hadn't been easy. Meli said it would just be like taking her to her piano lesson. And besides, her piano teacher had said Meli should go.

Meli liked to go places. Like papi did. Papi was gone for the afternoon in the car.

After dinner Mercedes wanted to talk to Pilar. Pilar went into Mercedes' room.

"Luisa dijo que te vió salir a caballo con Seña Alba. Ehtaba bien preocupada. Dijo que Fernanda le había dicho que tú ehtabah en el cuarto hablando con Seña Alba pero que ella te vió salir. Ella tenía miedo que había pasado algo." *Luisa said that she saw you go out on a horse with Seña Alba. She was very worried. She also said Fernanda told her you were in your room talking to Seña Alba but that she saw you go out. She was afraid something had happened.*

Mercedes continued, "Oímoh cuando llegahte." *We heard you come back.* There was a question in her eyes.

At that point Clara ran into the room followed by Manuelito who was teasing her.

"¡Clara eh una idiota! ¡Clara eh una idiota!" *Clara's dumb! Clara's dumb!* he was saying in a sing-song voice.

Clara jumped into Mercedes' bed and put a pillow over her head.

Pilar was paralyzed. Mercedes yelled at Manuelito, "¡Déjala en pah, Manuelito!" *Leave her alone, Manuelito!*

Pilar tried to intervene. "Manuelito ¿a dónde fueron tú y Juan?" *Manuelito, where did you and Juan go?*

"Bien aburrido. ¡Fuimoh a ver caña y máh caña! ¡Me importa un carájo esa caña!" *Very boring. Went to see sugar cane and more sugar cane! I give a damn about that sugar cane!* Manuelito had begun to swear, and he enjoyed getting his mother and sisters upset about it.

"¡Cállate, que si te oye Juan te va a cahtigar!" Pilar said. *Be quiet! If Juan hears you, you're going to be punished.*

Luisa appeared at the door of the room.

"Por lo menoh tú saleh a caballo con papá. Nosotrah siempre metidah aquí," she said angrily to Manuelito. *At least you go out to ride with papá. We are always stuck here.*

Pilar was startled by Luisa's outburst.

"Lah mujereh tienen que ehtar en la casa." *Women have to be in the house,* Manuelito said. He already knew how to get Luisa.

Before Pilar could intervene, Luisa said, "¡Mira, te voy a poner mierda en la boca!" *I'm going to put shit in your mouth!* Luisa grabbed him and sat on him.

Pilar tried to separate them. Manuelito started screaming.

"Cállense, que loh va a oir su papá," Pilar said. *Be quiet, both of you, or your father's going to hear you.*

Papi wasn't back by dinner time.

Meli ate quickly and went upstairs to get dressed. Mami finished up in the kitchen and came upstairs too. She went into the bathroom and turned off one light. She began to put on make-up.

"Mami ¿por qué apagah la luh cuando te arreglah la cara?" Meli had asked once. *Mami, why do you turn off the light when you put make-up on?*

"No quiero ver lah arrugah." *I don't want to see the wrinkles,* she had said. She put on a heavy layer of pancake. It made her skin look coarser. After it dried it made little cracks all over mami's face. Beads of sweat sat on top of it.

After they dressed they sat in the living room to wait. Meli counted the cars. She watched the headlights come and go. Mami sat in the rocking chair, rocking with her hand over her mouth. Meli was straining hard to make papi's car come. The concert began at eight. It was seven already.

Meli tried to sit very still so as not to wrinkle her dress. She spread the skirt out and sat up straight. She opened her purse, which matched her black patent-leather shoes, to see if she had the handkerchief abuelita had given her. The compact was from Tía Clara. Meli took it out to look at herself.

She didn't like her eyebrows. Didn't like to have so much hair either. She never wore her hair loose because it stood up. The braids were a lot of trouble but they kept her hair smooth. When she was bigger she was going to pluck her eyebrows and cut her hair real short and shave her legs and underarms. Her Tía Clara shaved. It was embarrassing to Meli that mami didn't shave under her arms.

Meli looked in the mirror. Her face was too rounded too. She couldn't wait to get older and have deep set eyes like mami. And cheekbones. She turned her head to look at her mother.

Mami said without looking at Meli, "Yo creo que él no viene." *I think he's not coming.*

Meli's heart jumped. "Todavía eh temprano." *It's still early,* she said.

She decided that papi was going to come after the next seven cars.

Meli heard the sound of the first car approach and saw the headlights get brighter on the street. She couldn't make up her mind whether it would be seven cars coming from both directions or from just one direction.

The second car came from the opposite direction. Now she would really need to decide. Well, okay, from both sides. Otherwise it would take fourteen cars and that might make it too late to get to the concert.

She started praying too to help papi hurry up. She said the words carefully. "Padre nuehtro qu'ehtáh en loh cieloh . . . ." *Our Father who art in heaven . . . .*

She really wanted to make sure God heard her this time. She was going to think about each word.

Four cars already. She repeated the prayer over and over.

". . . santificado sea el tu nombre." *. . . hallowed be thy name.* "Venga a noh el tu reino . . . ." *Thy kingdom come . . . .*

After the fifth car Meli really concentrated on the words.

"Hágase tu voluntad . . . pero, por favor, por favor, Dioh, hah que papi venga . . . y si él viene, yo voy a . . . ." *Thy will be done . . . but please, please, God, make papi come . . . and if he comes I'm going to . . . .*

She didn't know what to offer. She didn't know what would be the one thing that would make God most pleased. To promise to go to church on Sundays? But that was real hard because nobody could ever take her. Mami and papi didn't go . . . . Well, maybe she wouldn't fight with her cousin . . . that was too easy. She didn't see him much anyway . . . . Okay, okay. She knew what she would offer God.

Meli wasn't going to buy any candy for four Thursdays. That was the day she went to the movies with mami after the piano lesson. Meli and mami always bought candy at the movies. Meli hoped it was all right with God if she didn't give up her ice cream soda too.

They heard a knock at the door.

It was Juan.

Luisa stood up quickly. Everyone was silent.

"¿Qué pasa aquí?" *What's going on?* Juan asked when he walked in.

Manuelito said quickly, "Luisa ehtá diciendo malah palabrah. Dijo 'mierda.'" *Luisa's saying dirty words. She said 'shit.'*

"Y tú no lo tieneh que repetir," Juan said. *And you don't have to repeat it.*

"Eso no fué lo que pasó," Pilar said. *That's not what happened.*

Juan looked at Pilar without any expression on his face. Then he turned away.

Mercedes said, "Mamá tiene razón. Manuelito eh él que dijo una mala palabra y yo no la voy a repetir." *Mamá's right. Manuelito was the one who said a dirty word and I'm not going to repeat it.*

"Loh doh dijeron malah palabrah y yo tampoco lah voy a repetir. Y Luisa le dió una paliza a Manuelito porque él dijo que lah mujereh tienen que ehtar en la casa," Clara said. *They both said dirty words and I'm not going to repeat them. And Luisa gave Manuelito a beating because he said that women should be in the house.*

"¿Eso es verdad, Luisa?" Juan asked. *Is that true, Luisa?*

Luisa didn't answer.

"¡Eh verda'! ¡Eh verda'!" both Manuelito and Clara were saying. *It's true! It's true!*

Mercedes was silent too. Pilar could not bring herself to speak again.

"¿Qué dices tú, Mercedes?" *What do you say, Mercedes?* Juan asked.

"No le dió una paliza, solamente se le sentó encima . . . ." *She didn't beat him, she only sat on him . . .* Mercedes answered.

"¿Porque él dijo que las mujeres tienen que estar en la casa?" *Because he said women should be in the house!* Juan wanted to know.

Mercedes looked down and said, "Sí." *Yes.*

Juan spoke. "Luisa, ven conmigo." *Luisa, you come with me.*

Pilar forced the words out of herself. "¿Qué le vah a hacer, Juan?" *What are you going to do to her, Juan!*

He didn't answer.

Pilar followed them into the dining room. Juan sat down in front of Luisa who was still standing.

"Luisa, no quiero tener que avergonzarme de tí. Ya eres una señorita y no puedes portarte como si fueras un peón. Manuelito es un muchacho. Tú no te puedes permitir esas cosas. Yo no entiendo lo que pasa aquí en mi ausencia. Tu madre no te está enseñando lo que tienes que aprender. Te está permitiendo tener ideas que te van a hacer daño. Y como ella parece que no te puede dar un buen ejemplo, yo voy a tener que darte un castigo para corregir tu forma de actuar. Algún día vas a agradecer que tienes un padre que toma interés en educarte. De castigo no vas a poder salir del cuarto desde ahora hasta que yo vuelva de mi próximo viaje. Y quiero que en ese tiempo pienses mucho en lo que es apropiado para una señorita." *Luisa, I don't want to have to be ashamed of you. You are a young lady already and you cannot behave like a hired hand. Manuelito is a boy. You cannot permit yourself such behavior. I don't know what happens here during my absence. Your mother is not teaching you the things you need to learn. She is allowing you to have ideas that are going to be harmful to you. And since it seems that she cannot give you a good example, I will have to punish you to correct your behavior. Some day you will be thankful that you have a father who takes an interest in educating you. Your punishment is going to be that you cannot leave your room from now until I return from my next trip. During that time I want you to think carefully about what is appropriate for a young lady.*

Mami got up from her chair and said, without looking at Meli, "Me voy a acohtar un rato." *I'm going to lie down for a while.*

Meli didn't like to sit there by herself at night with the door open. Once, a drunk had just walked in off the street. It was a good thing papi had been home that night.

Then she heard the sixth car. Its headlights got bright and it slowed down in front of the house. God heard her!

As the car turned into the driveway Meli went running to the bottom of the stairs and called mami to let her know that papi had arrived. It was close to seven-thirty already.

Meli stood waiting in the dining room. When papi saw her he said, smiling, "¿A dónde fueron hoy?" *Where did you go today?* He was looking at her clothes.

"Vamoh al concierto. Ya mami ehtá lista." *We're going to the concert. Mami's ready.*

"¿Qué concierto?" *What concert?* He seemed curious.

Meli held her breath.

"El concierto al que noh ibah a llevar." *The concert you were going to take us to.*

He was amused. "¿El concierto al que yo te iba a llevar?" *The concert I was going to take you to?* he repeated.

Meli's face was getting hot. Why did he think it was so funny? Papi laughed.

"Yo no te dije que te iba a llevar a ningún concierto . . . y si fuera más temprano . . . pero, es muy tarde y estoy muy cansado." *I didn't say I was going to take you to a concert . . . and, well, if it were earlier . . . but it is very late and I'm tired.*

"¡Pero tú dijihte que noh ibah a llevar!" *But you said you were going to take us!* Her throat was tight and her eyes were filling with tears.

Papi wasn't smiling anymore.

"Yo no me acuerdo de eso." *I don't remember that,* he said and turned to walk away.

Meli couldn't stand to have him walk away. She followed him and stood in front of him. Tears were running down her face.

"¡Yo no voy a ser como mami! ¡Sentada ahí ehperando que tú vengah! ¡Yo nunca voy a ser como ella!" *I'm not going to be like mami! Sitting there waiting for you to come! I'm never going to be like her!*

          Pilar watched Luisa rearrange the sheets on her bed at Clara's. Luisa was good to her. It was hard now to think this was the same woman who swore and fought with her husband for years before Meli left.

Pilar remembered one night. She was awakened abruptly by Meli who was shaking with fear. She sat up in the bed and held her. There was some light coming from the hallway. Loud voices. Meli covered her ears and curled up in Pilar's arms, trembling. She was silent but her eyes were open wide.

Then there was a crashing sound. Through the half-open door she could see pieces of a hand mirror scattered on the floor of the hallway. Pilar was afraid of what Meli would see. Of finding blood. Then she saw Luisa. She had Arturo by the shirt and was tugging at him angrily.

That was the night Meli missed the concert.

The next morning the house felt musty and dark. Meli was sitting on the railing of the back porch looking towards the yard. Arturo was in bed upstairs with a cold. Calling for something. Luisa was sitting on her rocking chair on the other side of the porch. She didn't seem to hear.

Pilar said to Luisa, "Él te llama." *He's calling you.*

Meli got up and went out to the yard.

Meli hid behind the hibiscus hedge. The ground was hard. It hadn't rained for a while. It was March. She saw the yard through the stems and leaves of the bushes, and after a while, mami coming down the back steps of the house to feed the dog.

Meli sat there waiting for something. Not doing anything. Pretending that she was escaping through a tunnel. She didn't know what she was escaping from. It was exciting not to be seen. She just sat there looking at things and making pictures in her head.

She remembered when she had gotten lice. She really wanted to hide then. She felt that she was not like las pobres, the *girls who were poor* and were in a different part of the school. Meli used to see them through the high wire fence which separated the paying students from the charity students. They stood in line with their dusty brown legs, in old sandals.

Abuelita had combed Meli's hair with a very fine comb over a white pillow case, so she would see the lice and the eggs and kill them by putting them between her two thumbnails. That's the gesture the girls at school made when they thought someone had lice. Meli knew that the lice came out when you sat in the sun. She had seen lice crawl on some of the girls' hair. So when Meli went on the school bus she made sure she didn't sit by the window so the sun didn't hit her head. She didn't like anyone sitting behind her either. And if her head itched, she tried very hard not to scratch it.

Pilar remembered now how Meli used to lie on the ground behind the hibiscus. It was one of her hiding places. Pilar sighed. Meli had grown a lot that year. Luisa had noticed too. Sometimes Pilar thought Luisa didn't want Meli to grow older. She would tell Meli a little poem she had made up.

> "Aún cuando no seas niña,
> aún cuando seas grande,
> siempre, mi vida,
> serás mi bebé."
> *Even when you're not a child,*
> *even when you're big,*
> *always, my dearest,*
> *you will be my baby.*

Pilar remembered Luisa when she was a child asking whether Seña Alba could stop her from growing.

Images drifted past Pilar's eyes. She saw a girl running through a palm grove, skipping over small bushes. She came to a place where there were some pencas, *coconut fronds,* which had fallen. They were leaning against bushes so that they made a kind of tent.

It was Luisa. She was about twelve. Pilar didn't remember seeing Luisa that happy again after they left Bocarío. Luisa was busy working. She dragged a frond next to the other ones and made a place big enough to sit under. She put leaves and branches on the sandy ground, then crawled under the tent. She lay down on the cool mat of leaves and looked like she was daydreaming.

Suddenly, there were steps outside. Luisa lay very still. Scared.

Pilar felt anxious, but the images seemed to have a life of their own.

Then Pilar heard a man's voice. "¡Mira, ahí hay una chosa de palmah! ¡Ven acá!" *Look! There's a palm hut there. Come here!*

"No quiero." *I don't want to,* a girl's voice responded.

"No tengah miedo. Te voy a enseñal algo." *Don't be afraid. I show you something.*

"Yo quiero ilme a casa." *I want to go home,* she said.

"Te pue'h il enseguí'a, pero ven acá un momentito." *You can go right away, but come here a minute,* the man said.

Luisa couldn't get out without being seen. Her eyes looked very frightened as she crawled frantically under the bushes that the coconut fronds were leaning against. She couldn't move more than an arm's length away because the branches of the bush were too thick and low. She put her face on the ground and lay very still.

"Ven acá, negrita." *Come here, negrita,* the man was saying.

In the dim light Pilar could see a man pulling a girl under the coconut branches. They were so close to Luisa that Pilar was sure she could smell his sweat and feel the girl's breathing.

"Mira, te voy a enseñal algo." *Look, I'm going to show you something,* the man was saying.

Luisa held her breath and closed her eyes tight. Pilar was afraid he could hear her breathing.

The girl kept struggling and saying, "¡No! ¡No!" while the man grunted and groaned. The girl gasped as if she were going to choke. Pilar was anguished. She wanted to call out but no sounds came out of her throat.

Then it all stopped. He said, "Límpiate con eso y vente." *Clean yourself with this and let's go.*

The girl was crying.

"¡Vente! ¡Vente! ¡Que tengo que volvel al trabajo!" *Come on! Come on! I got to get back to work!*

The girl kept crying.

"¡Vente!" *Come on!* he yelled.

He tried to pull her out of the tent.

"Y si se lo diceh a alguien te voy a coltal la cara." *And if you tell I'm gonna cut your face.*

They left. Luisa just lay there. Pilar wanted desperately to hold her.

Finally, when Luisa moved, she looked pale and sick and as if her whole body were bruised. She got up slowly, but once she was out of the hut she ran. All the way home.

"¿Qué te pasó?" *What happened?* Mercedes was startled when she saw Luisa.

Luisa responded quickly, "Me caí de un árbol." *I fell off a tree.*

Pilar woke with a start. Luisa came from the kitchen to look in at her.

"¿Te dehperté? Se me cayó un cuchillo de la mano." *Did I wake you up? A knife fell out of my hand,* Luisa said.

"Creo que me quedé dormida." *I think I fell asleep,* Pilar said, looking around her at Clara's neat room as if trying to find safe ground. Then her eyes came to rest on Luisa's face.

"Te voy a hacer un café." *I'm going to make you some coffee,* Luisa said, smoothing out the sheets.

The images of the dream began to fade. In their place Pilar saw Meli's face. She looked very serious. Pilar had found her sitting on her bed at La Serena looking out of the window. She didn't even turn to say hello.

"Meli ¿qué te pasa?" *Meli, what's the matter?* she asked.

Meli looked down at her hands without saying a word. Pilar sat on the bed next to her. This was not at all like Meli to act this way with her.

"¿Qué te pasó?" she asked again. *What happened to you?*

Meli was opening her hands and then closing them into fists, over and over again, and trying to hold back tears.

"Yo me voy a ir." *I'm going to go,* she said, looking at Pilar with bright eyes and with anger in her voice.

Pilar knew instantly that it was true. She recognized the determined look on Meli's mouth, the light in her eyes. For a moment she saw herself in Meli.

She reached for Meli's hand.

"Yo me voy a ir. Ya tú veráh. Aunque él no quiera. Yo me voy a ir," Meli said. *I'm going to go. You'll see. Even if he doesn't want me to. I'm going.*

Pilar nodded silently. Her whole body was raw with longing.

"Yo me voy," Meli kept repeating. "Yo me voy." *I'm leaving. I'm leaving.*

"Ehtá bien, niñita," Pilar said. *It's fine, little one.* She hadn't called Meli that since she was very small, when she used to tear her pajamas climbing trees.

Meli put her head on Pilar's shoulder and began to sob. Pilar held her shaking body as she used to when Meli had a fever. Just held her.

After that day it had been a constant worry to Pilar how Meli was going to get the money to leave. It was one of the few times she regretted not having money. She was so upset about it that one day she got distracted and singed one of Arturo's shirts with the iron. It was a good thing he had many shirts. Luisa noticed but didn't say anything.

Meli didn't seem to worry about not having the money. She just went ahead and wrote letters to art schools and got catalogues. Pilar could hear her typing away in the study on the old typewriter. Not when Arturo was around. She didn't talk much about it either.

Then one day, Pilar remembered, Meli came running to the back porch with a letter in her hand.

"¡Me aceptaron! ¡Me aceptaron!" *They accepted me! They accepted me!* she shouted.

Pilar and Luisa were having coffee. "¿Qué eh lo que pasa?" *What's going on!* Pilar asked.

Meli was breathless. "¡La ehcuela de arte en Nueva York! ¡Me aceptaron!" *The art school in New York! They accepted me!*

Pilar had felt as if someone had suddenly hit her right below the ribs. She had to tighten her throat to remain silent.

"¿De qué tú hablah?" *What are you talking about?* Luisa said with a frown.

"De la ehcuela de arte en Nueva York. Yo leh mandé una solicitud." *About the art school in New York. I sent them an application.*

Pilar could see that Luisa was beginning to understand.

"¿En loh Ehtadoh Unidoh?" *In the States?* Luisa asked.

"¡En Nueva York!" Meli said with a big smile on her face. *In New York!*

"Pero ¿y cómo te vah a ir?" *And how are you going to go?* Luisa asked.

"Por avión . . . . Me pone un poco nerviosa pensar en coger uno de esoh avioneh . . . ." *By plane . . . . It makes me a little nervous to think of going in one of those planes . . .* Meli answered.

"¿Y tu papá lo sabe?" *And your father knows?* Luisa asked.

"Todavía no." *Not yet.* Now it was Meli who was frowning.

A few months later Meli talked to Arturo about going to the U.S. He said he would think about it. But Meli knew he didn't want her to leave. Besides, he said there weren't any really good women artists.

On Meli's saint's day Luisa gave her an envelope. It had the money for the flight. Pilar knew it must have been hard for Luisa to get that money together. Luisa said to Meli, "Yo no sé porqué él quiere tenerte aquí." *I don't know why he wants to keep you here.*

Later that year Meli left. She never returned.

Luisa had brought flowers to Pilar. Pilar was not able to sit up very much anymore because of the discomfort in her belly. She didn't want to tell anyone that even with the pills she was in great pain. But the flowers made her calmer. They helped her pass the time.

The roses became paler and paler as they opened. Pilar had been watching them take on an other-worldly hue for the past day. They reminded her of Elena.

Pilar remembered that Elena had improved briefly after that time when she went to the hospital with pneumonia. But not for long. She died within six months. Juan was gone at the time of the funeral.

The wood coffin lay open at Marta's house. A neighbor had built it. Pilar had offered money to buy the wood but Pablo had refused. People brought food and flowers. Pilar remembered how quickly the flowers had wilted.

Pablo was uncomfortable in his good clothes and awkward talking with people. Marta looked very sad and old. Tía Micaela was always warm. She wanted to know everything about Pilar's children and asked polite questions about Juan's trips.

Pilar looked for a place to sit down. She brushed a chair with her handkerchief and sat next to the coffin. She felt she didn't belong there anymore.

Pilar tried to remember Elena, but mostly what she remembered was her own loneliness. She had decided not to bring the children. The young ones would just make trouble, and the oldest girls . . . well, they were young ladies already. Men got drunk and said things.

She felt a curious distance from everything. She thought she should have more feelings about Elena's death. She tried to make herself feel. For a moment Pilar felt jealous. Marta and Elena had always been together. Elena had never left home, because of her poor health. Pilar felt a tremendous weight on her chest. She had left. Elena had stayed. Marta said Elena was a saint, but Marta was angry at Pilar for leaving and, Pilar hated to admit it, for having money.

Marta and Pablo thought her life was easy. They didn't want to know how alone and responsible for the children she felt because Juan wasn't home very much. Pilar thought Marta should be thankful that Pablo was always there.

She sighed.

She remembered going to visit. She had returned many times looking for the mother she had loved. Sometimes Marta would hide behind the house, pretending she didn't hear Pilar come. Pilar had to go find her. She had been angry then.

She remembered Pablo turning away from her when she came. And one time, when Pilar brought the children, Manuelito saw Pablo standing by the bushes. He shouted where everybody could hear, "¡Miren, abuelo ehtá meando en lah matah!" *Look, abuelo is peeing in the bushes!*

Marta snapped at him, "¡Carájo! ¿Y tú no meah?" *Dammit! You don't pee!*

It was the only time Marta had been angry at one of Pilar's children. But Marta always cursed. Pilar knew Marta didn't even notice anymore. Pilar didn't want the children to be ashamed of their grandparents. Sometimes Pilar could understand why Juan didn't want Pablo and Marta at the house.

She had been ashamed of them. And there was very little they could say to each other.

The wake went on all night. Pilar wished she were home in her room talking to Seña Alba. But she knew she had to stay and visit with the neighbors who came para dar el pésame, *to give their condolences.* Some greeted Pilar shyly, some with curiosity. There were voices of children, sounds of dogs fighting for scraps of food, and a murmur of prayers. Late in the night everything quieted down and Pilar could hear someone playing a guitar near the front steps. She dozed and was awakened by loud voices outside. They died down before she could make out where they were coming from. She thought it must be men drinking.

Pilar got up from her chair quietly, trying not to stir Marta who was asleep with her mouth open. She crossed herself as she went past the coffin on the way out the back door to go to the letrina.

In the dark Pilar passed quickly a spot where it smelled as if someone had vomited. She held her breath when she went into the letrina. She realized this was also part of the reason she didn't bring the children to Marta's. Everything was too hard here, and too ugly.

Pilar was careful not to soil her clothes as she sat down, but it was pretty dark, even with the candle she had brought from the house. It was probably just as well; she knew that sometimes, as a joke, children or drunks would peek into latrines to embarrass women.

She was startled by some sounds in the bushes. She finished peeing quickly and went outside. She held the candle at arm's length and looked in all directions.

There was nothing there. She took a few steps on the path towards the house, then heard gasping and moaning. She was scared. She thought there was an animal in the bushes. She wanted to hurry back to the house and send her brother Tito out to look.

Pilar had taken a few more steps when she heard a loud groan to her right. It was a very frightening sound. Instinctively, she turned to face it, holding the candle out as if to protect herself with it.

In the candlelight she saw a bent figure throwing up.

It was Seña Alba.

Pilar couldn't get the image out of her head for a long time: Seña Alba in the candlelight, drunk and looking at her with wild eyes and vomit drooling out of her mouth. The night of Elena's wake.

They both stood there as if time had stopped.

Pilar didn't want to look, but she couldn't take her eyes away from Seña Alba. The smell of vomit hung in the humid night air.

"¡Vete!" *Go away!* Seña Alba ordered, suddenly looking at Pilar with anger.

Tears filled Pilar's eyes.

"¡Vete!" *Go away!* Seña Alba screamed.

"No me voy, negra." *I'm not going, negra,* Pilar said quietly.

Pilar saw the pain in Seña Alba's face.

Then Seña Alba turned as if she were going to run away, but instead she fell, swearing.

"¡Coño! ¡Carájo!" *Damn! Fuck!* she screamed while thrashing about in the bushes.

Pilar took a few steps and started to reach for Seña Alba, then she realized Seña Alba had fallen into her own vomit. Pilar froze.

Seña Alba scrambled to her feet again saying, "¡Vete!" *Go away!*

Pilar was suddenly filled with anger. She grabbed for Seña Alba's arm which felt wet and slippery.

"¡Quiero sacarte de' ehta mierda, negra borrachona!" *I want to get you out of this shit, you drunk nigger!*

Seña Alba jerked her arm away and screamed, "¡Me salió

blanquita la niña! ¡Blanquita! ¡Blanquita!" *The girl turn out white!*
White girl! White girl!

She tried again to run away but fell a second time.

"¡Coño! ¡Coño! ¡Puta negra!" *Damn! Damn! Son of a bitch*
nigger woman! Pilar screamed.

This time Pilar grabbed Seña Alba from behind, dragged her
up to her feet, and locked her arms around her. The stench of
vomit and rum nauseated her. Pilar had to keep herself from
throwing up too. Seña Alba retched again. Pilar could feel Seña
Alba's body twisting and bending, and the hot, sticky vomit falling
on Pilar's arm.

Seña Alba wrestled to push Pilar away. She was very strong.
Pilar couldn't hold her anymore. Seña Alba freed herself and disappeared into the night. Pilar could hear her stumbling in the
bushes.

Of the rest of that night Pilar only remembered that she had told
Marta she had stepped over a drunk and fallen. Marta helped her
wash herself. Gave her an old blouse of hers to wear. Marta
washed Pilar's blouse. It was dry by morning.

When the sun was already high, three or four women and the
family followed the cart with the coffin to the village cemetery. It
had been many years since she had walked on that road. Now they
all walked in silence.

It was dusty. The sugar cane on both sides of the road was
already taller than Pilar. Her shoes were uncomfortable when she
stepped on rocks and tree roots. The sun was hotter than she ever
remembered. Her blouse was drenched with sweat. She remembered holding Seña Alba the night before, and she felt faint.

Pilar went under the shade of a mango tree and rested her
forehead on the tree trunk. It felt cool. The funeral party stopped a
few steps ahead in the sun. No one moved.

Her brother Tito said, "¿Ehtáh bien, Pilar?" *Are you all right,*
Pilar?

"Me dió un vahido, pero ya se me pasa." *I got dizzy. But it's*
going away.

She started towards the others again. The party continued

down the road to the burial ground. Then Pilar found herself
humming under her breath.

The bus smelled of gasoline, but
at least it wasn't too crowded. Abuelita always let her take the
seat by the window. Meli didn't like to have people standing next
to her.

They had to wait for the bus drivers to change buses. The
men joked in their khaki clothes and caps. Meli thought of the
way mami used the word chofer, *chauffeur*, as an insult. Never to
someone's face, but to herself.

Meli looked at the drivers through the window of the bus.
They made her anxious. She never looked at them directly, but
always noticed what they were doing. She noticed they touched
themselves.

But she felt safe with abuelita. Abuelita was very serious. No
one would dare bother her, Meli thought.

Soon the bus started going up the steep hill towards the edge
of town. Meli thought the bus wasn't going to make it. That
happened a lot with the school bus. Sometimes she missed a
whole day of school because the bus had broken down somewhere
on this hill.

Meli tried to imagine she was travelling to a new place. She
wondered how somebody would look at the small cement houses
crowded against each other if she were seeing them for the first
time. Or the lagoon that was at the bottom of the hill on one side,
surrounded by palm trees. When she looked at things that way
they didn't seem poor and dirty anymore, and like they needed
fixing. They looked interesting, like when she looked at pictures
of other countries, or at the movies.

Meli got a glimpse of the big marble angel on one of the
tombs when they passed the cemetery. The angel looked like
something from an art book. It looked like it had just landed there
and hardly had a place to stand because the tombstone was so
crowded with virgins and little angels, urns, arches and azucenas,
the sweet-smelling *tuberoses*. It was like an apparition, with the
sun beating on the white marble.

Meli began to imagine herself walking up the steep hill from the gate of the cemetery. Leaving behind the crowded flower stands on the street. Going by a big shade tree. Stopping by a tomb behind a group of women in black mantillas. The afternoon sun made them stand out against the white marble. She didn't want to be there. She didn't know who had died. Nobody had asked her whether she wanted to come. Nobody ever asked her how she felt about things.

Abuelita crossed herself as they passed by the cemetery. Meli remembered Concha, a maid they once had, standing in the middle of the kitchen, looking at the ceiling for a long time and not moving or anything. A big cockroach landed on the edge of the white sink. Later, someone said that Concha was having a vision. Meli was scared.

The long bus ride made Meli tired. She wanted to get to Tía Clara's quickly. She didn't want to have to go to the caseríos, the *projects,* at the edge of town. One of abuelita's relatives lived there. All the buildings were the same. They were made of concrete and had writing on the walls. Looked bare and dark. There was packed dirt around them and bushes that looked like someone had been pulling their leaves off. Dark kids played in the dirt and fat women leaned over the railings.

Meli didn't like to go there. People looked at her. Because she wore nice clothes. They looked like they were angry. Meli thought they were envious of her even though they said, "¡Ay! ¡Qué linda eh la nena!" *Pretty little girl!*

Abuelita had taken Meli to the caseríos many times. Meli felt like nothing ever changed there.

"Siempre en lah mihmah." *Always the same,* the people at the caseríos often answered when abuelita asked how they were. As if there were nothing else in the world and time had stopped. Meli would begin to feel she was going to be there forever. It made her scared to think that way. She usually started imagining things when that happened. Imagining places where she would go when she was older.

The relative's apartment was dark and smelled different. Each house she visited had a different smell. There was one that smelled of pee. This one smelled of creso, a *disinfectant soap* people used to scrub floors, and alcoholado, perfumed *rubbing alcohol.* Abuelita put alcoholado on Meli's skin when she had a temperature. To cool her off.

The place smelled of lard too. She didn't like it when she could smell people's plates, their towels and their rooms. They gave their smell to everything around them. It was almost as if they were putting their hands on her. It made her a little sick to her stomach.

Abuelita brought clothes, food, or money. The relatives gave them coffee. Meli got restless after a while because she couldn't go out by herself and she got tired of listening to the same stories. They were always complaining about something.

"Tragediah, Doña Pilar. Muchah tragediah." *Misfortune, Doña Pilar. Too much misfortune.*

Abuelita nodded and put a couple of dollars in the woman's hand as they left.

Meli asked abuelita one time, "¿Quién es esa gente?" *Who are those people?*

Abuelita answered, "Son unoh sobrinoh." *They're nieces and nephews.* But she didn't say anything else.

Meli knew abuelita had a sister somewhere but nobody ever talked about her so Meli never asked.

Meli was glad they weren't going to the caserío that day.

The bus swung around and headed towards the center of town again. They passed small shops and dirty streets for a while, until they reached the part of town where the department stores were and the new movie houses with posters of the stars.

Clara's apartment reminded Pilar of Bocarío. It was open, with a terrace that went all around it. And there was always a breeze, although the sun beat fiercely because the apartment was on the top floor. There were no trees like there had been at Bocarío. It was almost too bright for her now. Her pain made her want to curl up inside herself. With her memories.

She remembered how Meli liked to visit Clara at the apartment because everything was new. New tiles, new furniture, new kitchen utensils. It seemed like it wasn't so long ago that Meli would come to stay overnight. Pilar could still hear Clara saying, "Dehpuéh de la comida te voy a dar dinero para ir abajo y comprarte una barquilla." *After dinner I'm going to give you money to go downstairs and get an ice cream cone.* There were stores on the ground floor of the building and a movie house next door. Pilar smiled, thinking how Meli liked to go to the soda fountain by herself.

She leaned back and closed her eyes. Her pain enveloped her. She kept having images of Meli. Of when they used to go places together. She remembered a time when Meli was staying overnight with her at Clara's. Pilar was sure now that Meli had heard everything that was being said that day while pretending to read her comic book. Clara was talking.

"Dijo el abogado que a cada una de lah mayoreh leh tocaba setenta cuerdah." *The lawyer said that there were seventy acres for each of the older ones,* Clara was saying.

"¿Ehtáh segura?" *Are you sure?* Pilar asked.

"Sí, sí. Yo mihma se lo pregunté." *Yes, yes. I asked him myself,* Clara answered.

"Pero ya hace demasiado de tiempo." *But it's too long ago,* Pilar said.

"No. Dice que todavía se puede." *No. He says it's still possible,* Clara insisted.

"Bueno, pero eso va a cohtar demasiado, tú sabeh lo que cobran loh abogadoh . . . no se puede." *Well, but it's going to be too expensive, you know how much lawyers charge . . . we can't do that.* Pilar felt discouraged.

"Él ehtá tan seguro de que vamoh a ganar el pleito que dice que le podemoh pagar cuando se resuelva." *He's so sure we're going to win the suit that he says we can pay him when it's all resolved,* Clara explained.

"Yo no sé m'ija . . . . ¿Qué dicen lah otrah muchachah?" *I don't know, honey . . . . What do the other girls say?* Pilar asked.

Clara didn't answer right away. Pilar was very aware that Meli was in the other room.

"Bueno, Mercedes ehtá de acuerdo que sería bueno hacer el pleito, pero Luisa . . . no quiere." *Well, Mercedes has agreed that it would be good to sue, but Luisa . . . doesn't want to.* Clara was speaking very slowly and carefully.

"¿Y por qué?" *Why?* Pilar wanted to know.

Clara was uncomfortable. "Bueno, eh que . . . ." *Well, it's that . . . .* She paused for a very long time. "Eh que, como no ehtabah casada . . . ." *It's that, since you weren't married . . . .*

Pilar put her index finger on her lips. She didn't want Meli to hear the conversation.

Clara continued in a lower voice. "Luisa dice que habría que hablar de eso en el juicio," she finally got out. *Luisa says that we would have to talk about that in court.* "A mí no me importa," she added. *I don't care.*

"Pero, uhtedeh ehtaban reconocidoh." *But your father accepted you as his,* Pilar said.

"Yo lo sé, yo lo sé. Pero, yo creo que ella no quiere que todo el mundo sepa que no te casahte." *I know, I know. But I don't think she wants everybody to know that you didn't get married,* Clara answered.

The images faded as Pilar turned to ease the pain in her belly. Movement became more of an effort each day. Some part of her wanted it to be over. She lay there looking at the line of sunlight on the window sill.

The sun was high like this at La Serena when she realized that Meli knew. Pilar remembered she was sweeping leaves on the walk right next to the house. Meli was helping her.

"Si Seña Alba estuviera aquí le echaría un fufú." *If Seña Alba were here, she would cast a spell on him,* Meli said.

"¿A quién, m'ijita?" *Who are you talking about, honey?* Pilar stopped to pull her handkerchief off her belt.

"A Aurelio," Meli said, looking very serious.

Meli had been angry at Aurelio ever since she heard, a few years before, that he had taken Pilar's money away. She wished she could have lived in Bocarío, where she could have gone to the beach without taking the bus.

Pilar put the broom on the ground, pretending it was Aurelio, and started waving the handkerchief over it. She rolled her eyes and swayed back and forth while calling out a spell she made up on the spot.

"Fufú macandá,
fufú macandá.
¡Ay, leilolé!
Ño Aurelio va caé,
pelo velde tiene é.
Fufú macandá,
n'uña va caé,
ni rascá pue' é.
¡Ay, leilolé!"

"¿Qué quiere decir eso?" *What does that mean?* Meli said, laughing.

"Que se le ponga el pelo verde a Aurelio y se le caigan lah uñah y que le dé un picor y que no se pueda rahcar," Pilar said with a grin. *That Aurelio's hair turn green and that his nails fall out and that he get an itch and can't scratch himself.*

All of a sudden Meli was looking at her intently. She wasn't laughing anymore. Pilar was afraid for a moment that she had scared her.

"Abuelita ¿por qué no te casahte?" *Abuelita, why didn't you get married?*

Pilar was startled. Meli had heard her conversation with Clara a few days before! Pilar wiped her face with her handkerchief. She didn't know what to say.

Then she noticed Luisa at the open window next to the walk. Her face was hard.

"No le hableh d'eso." *Don't talk to her about that,* Luisa said.

"Y ¿por qué no?" *And why not?* Meli wanted to know.

"Fué un rapto," Luisa answered, looking embarrassed. *She was kidnapped.*

On the plane I felt as if I were inside the hum of the engines. Under the spell of a mechanical monster that was devouring time and space.

I closed my eyes and let myself be transported to my destination. Through the miles and the years I called out, "¡Abuelita! ¡Abuelita!"

She was in Tía Clara's bed. Under the window that opened to the terrace. She turned slightly towards the door. She couldn't see me, her eyes were too dim. But she recognized my voice. Her mouth formed the word: Meli.

"Sí, abuelita, aquí ehtoy. Vine a verte." *Yes, abuelita, I'm here. I came to see you,* I said, reaching for her hand, which was bony and dry, but also cool. There was no strength left in it. She tried to smile but I could see that every effort brought pain. There was only a slight pressure on my hand. She wanted to say something. Her mouth was wet and trembling. I touched her handkerchief to the corners of her lips. Stroked her hair and her forehead.

Her arm moved towards the pills on the table. Then stopped before it went very far. For a moment I felt panic. I didn't know what to do. I just said, "Un momentito, abuelita. Tengo que preguntarle a mami si te puedo dar la medicina. Vengo enseguida." *Just a minute, abuelita. I have to ask mami if I can give you the medicine. I'll come right back.*

Tía Clara and mami were in the kitchen. They looked weary.

"Ha ehtado así por doh díah. Yo creo que ya se noh vá," Tía Clara said. *She's been like this for two days. I think she's going soon.*

My stomach tightened.

"Parece que quiere algo. ¿Eh hora de darle la medicina?" *It looks like she wants something. Is it time to give her the medicine?* I asked.

"Sí, ya eh hora, pero déjame ayudarte," mami said. *Yes, it's time, but let me help you.*

I put my arm around abuelita's shoulders and held her up in a sitting position. She felt small. Her body was almost lifeless. Mami opened abuelita's mouth and put a pill on her tongue, then brought the glass of water to her lips. She held a towel under abuelita's chin and tilted the glass very slowly. The water spilled out of the corners of abuelita's mouth onto the towel.

Abuelita coughed as if she were going to choke. Mami moved the glass away.

I held her for a long time. I wanted to put warmth into her body again.

The images faded back into the engine's hum. I looked in my purse for a handkerchief to dry my tears. Then my eyes fell on the photograph abuelita had sent me.

Pilar wished she could say something. She felt as if Meli were there. Visiting her. It was a comfort to her. But she was frightened too because she couldn't speak. She could only wait now.

After a while she felt that her body was away from her, at some distance. She couldn't get to it. She was left in a sea of images.

Pilar was scared to meet Juan.

She didn't bring Elena and didn't tell Seña Alba. Juan wanted to talk to Pilar alone. She was afraid he was going to be angry with her.

"Pilar, tu papá no quiere que te vea," Juan started out by saying. *Your father doesn't want me to see you.*

He was very angry.

Pilar didn't know what to say. She wished she could make her father understand that Juan loved her.

"Pilar, vente conmigo. Tengo una casa en la lomita afuera del pueblo. Si te vas conmigo ya no podrán hacer nada." *Pilar, come with me. I have a house on the hill outside the village. If you come with me, they won't be able to do anything,* Juan said.

It was scary to think of leaving with him. Pilar remembered Patria. But Pablo seemed so wrong, so stubborn. And what about Seña Alba?

Her heart jumped thinking about Seña Alba. Seña Alba wasn't going to like it either. She couldn't tell her. This time, Pilar thought, she was going to have to figure it all out by herself. She had to think about it, even if Juan got angry. She couldn't decide right now.

"Juan, tengo que pensalo." *Juan, I have to think about it,* she said.

His face darkened.

"No eh polque no lo quiera . . . pero eh que . . ." she began. *It's not because I don't love you . . . it's because . . . .*

How could she tell him about Patria, about her father's pride and her mother's burdens? And about Seña Alba? He wouldn't understand.

"¿Qué es entonces?" *What is it then?* Juan asked.

"Eh que . . . yo nunca he ehta'o con nadie." *It's that . . . I never been with anyone.*

His frown disappeared.

"Yo no te voy a hacer daño," he said gently. *I'm not going to hurt you.*

Pilar believed him. But she could still see Seña Alba's face questioning her.

"Tengo un poco de miedo." *I'm a little scared,* she said.

"Bueno, bueno, mujer, tómate unos días," Juan said. *Well, well, woman, take a few days then.* "Yo voy a arreglar la casa. Cuando estés lista mándame este pañuelo. Te lo traía hoy de regalo." *I'm going to fix the house. When you are ready, send me this handkerchief. I brought it today as a present for you.*

Pilar spread the handkerchief out in her hand. It was white with lace all around it. So thin she could see the lines of her hand through it. Juan folded it in her hand and closed her fingers over it.

"Mándamelo y yo te vengo a buscar la noche del día cuando lo reciba. Estaré debajo del flamboyán que queda cerca de tu casa. No quiero que vayas muy lejos sola en la noche." *Send it to me and I will come for you the night of the day I receive it. I will be under the flamboyán near your house. I don't want you to go very far alone in the night.*

For two days Pilar kept the handkerchief in the pocket of her dress with her hand closed over it. She didn't feel like going anywhere. She sat on the back steps of the house looking out towards the line of coconut palms by the ocean and listening to the far sound of the surf.

"¡Pilar!" Marta called out to her. "¿Qué haceh ahí to' el día? ¡Ehtáh en lah nubeh, muchacha!" *Pilar, what you doing there all day? You in the clouds, girl!*

Pilar came in.

"¿Te sienteh mala?" Marta asked, putting her hand on Pilar's forehead. "Yo creo que tieneh unah décimah, m'ija." *You feeling sick? I think you got some temperature, honey.*

"No, yo creo que eh el calol, mamá . . . . Deja que te ayude." *No, I think it's the heat, mamá . . . . Let me help you,* Pilar said.

Pilar went and got some red beans. She spread them on the table to pick out the bad ones and to see if there were any pebbles in them. Sometimes they sold them with pebbles, even at the store.

She felt like there was a big weight on her.

Pilar put the beans in an old black pan and poured water out of one of the cans from under the table. Marta kept the cans covered to keep out the flies.

"¿Quiereh que te haga el fuego?" *Do you want me to start the fire?* she asked her mother.

Her little brothers went outside with her. Pilar broke some pieces of wood. She sent the boys to get twigs and leaves. There was a small pile of coals next to the fire pit. After the fire was started she added the coals. The boys kept throwing twigs into the fire. She had to scold them to keep them from getting too close and burning themselves.

She was leaving. That was all she could think about.

Marta's face looked very, very tired. Like the ground. Like it had given everything it could give and now there was nothing left. And the last rain had left hard ruts.

Pilar took her mother's hand for a moment after Marta stopped peeling the calabaza, the *pumpkin,* and the potatoes. Her fingers were getting crooked from the reuma, *rheumatism.* Marta's hand felt cool after being in the water.

The next day Pilar wrapped the handkerchief in a piece of banana leaf. She gave it to Tito to take to Don Juan. At the store. She told him to give it to nobody else. If he ran the errand for her, she was going to give him a surprise.

Pilar was hoping Seña Alba wouldn't show up. But she did. That afternoon.

"¡Pilar!" Seña Alba called out to her.

"¡Ahí ehtá esa condená' negra!" Marta cursed. "No te voy a

dejal salil hoy, Pilar." *There's that damn nigger woman! I'm not gonna let you go out today, Pilar.*

Since they had found out about Pilar seeing Juan at the church, Pablo and Marta didn't want Seña Alba around.

"No voy a ningún sitio, mamá. Déjame habla'le a Seña Alba ahí afuerita un ratito," Pilar said. *I'm not going anywhere, mamá. Let me talk with Seña Alba right out there for a little bit.*

From within the dull, steady sound of the plane I could hear mami's voice whispering to abuelita, "Viejita, viejita. ¡No te vayas!" *Little old one, little old one. Don't leave!*

She told me once, "La madre eh lo mah grande que hay." *A mother is the most important thing there is.* She had only been happy as a child. Her mamá had been at the center of that happy time. After that there was no more innocence and too much suffering.

I imagined her sitting by abuelita's bedside. Or wandering around the house when it was Tía Clara's turn to sit with abuelita. Lost in an interminable time. Looking out at the city and not seeing anything. I knew that next to her mamá, time made sense. Away from her there was nothing.

I wondered which had been hardest for her: to watch someone fade day by day, as she had to do with abuelita, or to have them be gone suddenly, as with my father and her own father.

Sometimes Pilar would wake up at Clara's in the night when it was very quiet. She wished she could hear the ocean again.

Luisa would still be sitting there, asleep on the chair, in her clothes.

Pilar worried about Luisa. She could see the fear and pain in Luisa's eyes get deeper each day. Luisa sat for hours at Pilar's bedside saying nothing.

"¿Quién la va a cuidar cuando yo falte? ¿Y a quién va a cuidar ella?" Pilar whispered to herself. *Who's going to look after her after I'm gone! And who is she going to look after!*

Pilar remembered Marta. Marta had given Pilar up. She had sided with Pablo and didn't even fight for Pilar. She left Pilar to struggle alone.

Pilar hadn't wanted to do that. She had tried to take care of her children.

Lying in bed, Pilar remembered Aurelio bringing the papers. She had been very grateful. He said he was going to buy the property that Juan had left Pilar and make monthly payments to her in sums that would permit her and her children to live in comfort.

Pilar had signed the papers.

She said she trusted him and there was no need to read them. She didn't want him to know she still couldn't read very well. She didn't know anyone who could read the legal papers for her now that Don Ramiro was gone.

"Pilar ¿usted ha pensado mudarse? Aquí está usted muy sola." *Pilar, have you thought of moving? You're very alone here,* Aurelio said. He was very formal.

"Sí, he pensado mudarme a la capital para que loh muchachoh vayan a la ehcuela, pero, uhted sabe, yo no sé cómo voy a hacer eso. Yo no conohco a nadie allá." *Yes, I have thought of moving to the capital, so that the children can go to school, but I don't know how I'm going to do it. I don't know anyone there,* Pilar answered.

"Pues, mire, Pilar, deje ver si yo la puedo ayudar en eso. A ver si se le puede conseguir una casa en la capital." *Well, Pilar, let me see if I can help you. We'll see if we can get you a house in the capital,* Aurelio said.

Seña Alba came back the week after Juan died. Pilar had not seen her for five months.

Seña Alba stood at the door of Pilar's room.

Pilar's anger rose suddenly like the winds of a hurricane. She couldn't stop it.

"¿Y qué vieneh a hacer aquí ahora? ¿T'emborrachahte para venir? ¿Teníah qu'ehperar que Juan se muriera? Le teníah odio porque era blanco . . . pueh mira ¡yo también soy blanca!" *What are you doing here now? Did you have to get drunk to come here? Did you have to wait for Juan to die? You hated him because he was white . . . well, look, I'm white too!*

She pointed to the skin on her arms and on her face. "¡Mírame! ¡Soy blanquita! ¡Blanquita!" she screamed at Seña Alba. *Look at me! I'm white! White!* "Y negra . . . ." She began to sob. "Y negra también." *And black . . . and black too.*

Seña Alba stood quietly by the door looking at Pilar. She let the anger wash over her like a tidal wave.

When Pilar started sobbing Seña Alba moved towards her.

"¡No te me acerqueh! ¡Vete! ¡Sal de ehta casa de blancoh! ¡Vete a acohtarte en tu mierda!" Pilar shouted. *Don't come near! Get out of here! Get out of this house of white people! Go lie in your shit!*

"No te tieneh rehpeto ni me tieneh rehpeto a mí. Me dah ahco y láhtima," Pilar continued. *You don't have any respect for yourself and you don't have any respect for me! You disgust me. I feel sorry for you.*

Seña Alba stood frozen midway between the door and Pilar. She felt as if she were in the middle of a wave and was being thrown against the rocks again and again. But she just stood there.

Pilar went on. "Yo creía que erah la persona máh valiente y humana que conocía." *I thought you were the bravest and kindest person I had ever known.* Tears were streaming down her cheeks.

". . . pero ereh una cobarde. T'ehcondeh dentro de la caña para emborracharte. Ni siquiera tieneh la valentía de decírmelo. Pretendiendo ser algo que no erah . . . . ¡No me hableh de la hipocresía de loh curah! . . . Y yo que te tenía tanta admiración, que te veía caminar en la noche sola como un ser mágico, salvando vidah, ayudando a todoh, y lo que hacíah en la noche era emborracharte y arrahtrarte por la tierra como un animal . . . ." *. . . but you are a coward. You hide in the sugar cane to get drunk. You don't even have enough courage to tell me. Pretending you were something you were not . . . . Don't talk to me about the hypocrisy of the priests! . . . And I admired you so much! I saw you walking alone in the night like a magical being, saving lives, helping everyone, and what you were doing was getting drunk and dragging yourself on the ground like an animal . . . .*

Seña Alba stood there. Her life passing before her eyes like when you're going to die. Her mother on her deathbed. Pilar at the beach. The sugar cane stalks. The sand, hurricanes, deaths. The screams of newborns. Blood, blood everywhere. The gasping of people dying, babies with bloated bellies and staring eyes. The stench of vomit and shit. The stench of hate.

Each word from Pilar nailed a piece of her flesh. And her breath was drawing in blood.

Then out of somewhere in her, a place deep in the bowels of the earth, a place of the dead and dying, where nothing matters anymore, a place where the truth is all that's left because every shred of flesh and all the lies have been eaten by worms, out of that place a voice came.

"¡Cállate!" she said to Pilar. *Be quiet!*

Pilar had never heard that voice. She stood silent, listening.

"¡Cállate!" Seña Alba said again. "No sabeh lo que diceh. Cuando hayah pasa'o lah nocheh de tu juventu' llorando pol tu hijo que murió de hambre, llorando pol un hijo que vino de un ultraje, el ultraje de un cura blanco . . . cuando hayah vihto a tu mai vendel su cuelpo pa' dalte de comel . . . cuando t'ehcupan pol la calle polque ereh la víctima de abuso y te gritan: ¡puta! . . . o cuando la gente te llame bruja cuando loh ayudah . . . cuando nadie te quiere en su casa, na' máh que cuando te necesitan . . . cuando te tratan como un perro . . . cuando hayah pasa'o pol to' eso, niña, entonceh podráh pasal juicio pol mí." *Be quiet! You don't know what you say. When you spend the nights of your youth crying for your baby that starve to death, crying for a baby that come from rape, the rape by a white priest . . . when you see your ma sell her body to feed you . . . when they spit at you on the street and call you whore because you been abused. Or when people call you a witch after you help them . . . when nobody want you in their house, only when they want something from you . . . when they treat you like a dog . . . when you been through all that, then you can judge me, child.*

Pilar struggled with herself. She wanted to get up and run away from Seña Alba, but something else pulled her back. Something stronger, which spoke to her about where she belonged.

That was the day Seña Alba told Pilar her story.

"Nací en el pueblo de Saguey. Mi mai era prohtituta. Yo nunca supe quién fué mi pai. Ella noh mantenía con loh chavoh que hacía d'eso. Pero no quería que yo parara en lah mihmah. Quería gualdal unoh chavitoh pa' sacalnoh de ahí. Pelo ca' veh que tenía unoh chavitoh s'enfelmaba. Le había da'o sífilih." *I was born in* *Saguey. My ma was a prostitute. I never know who my pa is. She* *feed us with the money she make from that, but she don't want* *me to end up the same way. She want to save a little money to get* *us out of there, but each time she have money she get sick. She* *got syphilis.*

"La mujel del dueño del bal donde mi mai iba a buhcal hombreh noh dejó usal una casucha detráh del bal que había si'o un gallinero. Mi mai le ayudaba a limpial. Yo siempre ehtaba con mi mai, pero no cuando ella ehtaba con loh hombreh, pol la noche. Lo hacía en la caña. Y cuando ella ehtaba fuera m'ehcondía en un sitio diferente detráh de lah matah. Me decía que naide me iba a encontral, que ehtaba mejol afuera en la noche qu'en una casa. Cuando uno ehtá en una casa siempre te pue'n encontral pero si ehtáh ehcondí'a afuera naide te pue' encontral . . . . Bueno, cuando ella telminaba su trabajo, talde en la noche, me venía a buhcal." *The bar owner's woman where my ma go find men, she let us use* *a shack behind the bar. It's an old chicken coop. My ma help her* *clean. I'm always with my ma, but not when she's with men at* *night. She do it in the sugar cane. And when she's gone she hide* *me in a different place each time, behind the bushes. She say* *nobody's going to find me, that it's better to be outside at night* *than in a house. When you're inside people can find you, but* *nobody can find you if you're outside . . . . Then when she finish* *her work, late at night, she come find me.*

"Un día a la semana noh ibamoh caminando pol la carretera y pol loh campoh. Eso era lo único que noh hacía gozal. Ella m'enseñaba loh nombreh de lah matah. Me dijo que una tía suya había vení'o de una de lah otrah ihlah, que esa mujel era ehclava y curandera. Íbamoh caminando hahta que se sentía mala. Comíamoh lo que encontrábamoh pol ahí pol el camino: mangóh, papayah, cocoh . . . y lo que dejaba la gente del bal." *One day each* *week we go walking on the road and in the fields. That's the only* *good time we have. She tell me the names of plants. She tell me she* *have an aunt that come from another island that's a slave and a* *curandera, a healer. We keep walking until she feel sick. We eat* *what we find on our way: mangos, papayas, coconuts . . . and* *what the people at the bar leave.*

"Ya yo tenía dieh o once añoh, y un día mi mai se puso bien mala y la mujel del dueño, Doña Tulia, hahta llamó al cura . . . cosa suya, polque mi mai nunca iba a la iglesia. Yo me asuhté polque naide había entra'o nunca donde vivíamoh, así que me agaché en una ehquina, y el cura hizo suh cosah con el crucifijo y lah oracioneh, to' esah cosah que hacen. Bueno, al día siguiente mi mai se sintió mejol y en un pal de díah ya ehtaba bien. Ella ehtaba segura que fué el cura que la curó y dehde entonceh empezó a il a la iglesia conmigo, y el cura empezó a dalnoh limohna pa' que mi mai no tuviera que dolmil con hombreh. Mi mai empesó a ayudal en la iglesia y la casa parroquial y noh dieron un cualtito de silvientah allá. Mi mai ehtaba contenta y no se había enfelma'o pol un tiempo." *I'm ten or eleven and one day my ma get very sick and the bar owner's woman, Doña Tulia, even call the priest . . . that come from her because my ma never go to the church. I get scared because nobody ever come to where we live. I even squat in a corner. The priest do things with the cross and his prayers . . . all those things they do. Well, next day my ma feel better and in a couple of days she's fine. She's sure it's the priest that cure her and from that day on she start going to church and taking me with her. The priest start giving us money so my ma don't have to sleep with men. Ma start helping at the church and the parish house and they give us a little room they have for servants. My ma is very happy and she don't get sick for a while.*

"Ehtuvimoh ahí pol máh de un año. Ese fué el año que yo fuí señorita. Mi mai me habló d'eso. Me lo dijo to' y me dijo que ahora sí tenía que tenel cuida'o con loh hombreh polque podía salil encinta. . . . Bueno, yo ehtaba siempre con ella y le ayudaba en to'." *We are there for over a year. That's the year I'm a woman. My ma talk to me about that. She tell me everything and that I have to be real careful now with men because I can get pregnant. . . . Well, I'm always with her and I help her with everything.*

"Pero un día amanecí con una toh y fiebre y mi mai me dijo que me quedara en la cama y que ella iba ayudal en la iglesia y dehpuéh venía a traelme el almuelzo. Bueno, yo me quedé dolmí'a un rato y cuando me dehpelté ehtaba el cura allí. Dijo que había vení'o a rezal pol mí polque mi mai le había dicho que yo ehtaba enfelma." *But one day I wake up with a cough and a fever and ma say I better stay in bed and she go and help in the church and bring me lunch later. Well, I fall asleep for a while and when I wake up the priest is there. He say he come pray for me because my ma say I'm sick.*

"Me dijo que pa' curalme me tenía que ponel lah manoh encima, que el podel de Dioh pasaba pol suh manoh. Yo ehtaba bien nelviosa pero creía que si él podía cural a mi mai me podía cural a mí. Bueno, pueh me quitó la ropa y me empezó a tocal y a rezal al mihmo tiempo, y dehpuéh me dijo que se tenía que acohtal sobre mí pa' que to' el podel de Dioh pasara de él a mí . . . . Eso fué lo que hizo . . . y allí mihmo me ultrajó . . . ." *He say he have to put his hands on me to cure me, that God's power pass through his hands. I'm very nervous, but I think that if he can cure ma he can cure me. Well, he take off my clothes and he begin to touch me and to pray at the same time, and later he say he have to lie on me so that all God's power can go from him to me . . . . That's what he do . . . and right there he rape me . . . .*

She stopped.

Pilar didn't stir.

"Empezé a grital y él me cubrió la boca . . . me dolió mucho. Me dehtrozó. Cuando telminó me limpió la sangre con un pañuelo y se arrodilló a rezal . . . y me dijo que me arrodillara que yo tenía que rezal pol mi peca'o. Que lo que habíamoh hecho era un peca'o y solo le podíamoh hablal a Dioh d'eso y rezal. Y que Dioh me iba a peldonal si rezaba mucho y no le hablaba a naide d'eso." *I start screaming and he cover my mouth . . . I hurt a lot. He tear me up. When he finish he clean the blood with a handkerchief and he kneel to pray . . . and he tell me to kneel and pray for my sin. That what we do is a sin and we can only talk to God about that and pray. And that God is going to forgive me if I pray a lot and don't tell anybody about it.*

"Cuando vino mi mai se dió cuenta enseguí'a que yo no ehtaba bien. Yo no le iba a decil na' polque tenía miedo que Dioh me iba a cahtigal. Pelo dehpuéh, cuando mi mai se fué a acohtal, se dió cuenta que yo tenía sangre y yo le dije que era mi sangre mensual. Pelo ella se dió cuenta que yo ehtaba hinchá' y herida y me preguntó si algún hombre había entra'o y yo le dije qu'el cura vino y que yo tenía que rezal pol mi peca'o." *When ma come she*

*notice right away that I'm not feeling good. I'm not going to say
anything because I'm afraid God punish me. But later when she
get in bed she notice I have blood on me and I say it's my monthly
bleeding. But she notice I'm swollen and bruised and she ask if a
man come in and I say the priest come and that I have to pray for
my sin.*

"Bueno, se volvió loca. Salió de allí buhcando al cura. Lo
encontró en la iglesia y hizo un ehcándalo . . . le gritó insultoh y
hahta le dió puñoh. Vinieron lah monjah y entre to'h la ataron y
mandaron a buhcal a loh gualdiah polque se creían que ehtaba
loca . . . . Y la gente empezó a decil que yo había salí'o puta como
mi mai, y que mi mai se había enamora'o del cura y ehtaba con
coraje polque él no podía tenel sexo con ella. Y cuando pasabamoh
pol la calle noh llamaban putah y ehcupían en la tierra." *Well, she
go crazy. She go out looking for the priest. She find him in the
church and she make a big stink . . . she scream curses at him and
even punch him. The nuns come and between all of them they tie
her and they call the police because they think she's crazy . . . .
And people begin to say that I turn into a whore like my ma and
that ma fall in love with the priest and she's angry at him because
he can't have sex with her. And when we go on the street they call
us whores and they spit on the ground.*

"Querían folsahla a decil que el cura no había hecho na'.
Querían que confesara que se había inventa'o la hihtoria del
ultraje y como ella no me quería metel en to' eso, me tenía
ehcondí'a y la gente decía, 'y la muchachita ¿dónde'htá?' . . . 'esah
son mentirah' y 'si fuera velda la muchachita podría decil la velda.'
. . . Pelo mi mai era lihta . . . ella me dijo que nunca le iban a creel
a ella y mucho menoh a mí, que se iban a creel que ella se había
inventa'o el cuento y me lo había enseña'o a mí." *They want to
force her to say that the priest don't do anything. They want her
to confess that she make up the rape story, and because she don't
want me mixed up in the whole thing she hide me and people say,
'where's the girl?' . . . 'those are lies' and 'if it's true, the girl can tell
us.' . . . But ma is smart . . . she say they never going to believe her
and much less me, that they going to think she make up the story
and then teach it to me.*

"Así que mi mai decidió que noh ibamoh a il del pueblo a otro pueblo bien lejoh . . . ella siempre había querido vivil celca de la playa. Unoh díah dehpuéh del ultraje noh fuimoh temprano caminando pol la carretera." *So ma decide we going to leave town and go to another town very far away . . . she always want to live near the beach. A few days after the rape we leave early, walking on the road.*

"Yo to'avía no me sentía bien, así que ibamoh poco a poco, cantando bajito, como ella decía, y dehcansando pol el camino. Pedíamoh de comel cuando pasábamoh casah y dolmíamoh detráh de lah matah . . . caminamoh pol muchoh díah, polque mi mai quería ilse bien lejoh del pueblo donde ehtaba el cura. Así que un día llegamoh a Corona . . . ." *I don't feel well yet, so we go slow, singing softly, like she say, and resting on the way. We ask for food when we go by houses and we sleep behind bushes . . . we walk for many days because my ma want to go very far from the town where the priest is. So one day we get to Corona . . . .*

"Mi mai me dijo que ya no tenía máh chavoh y que noh ibamoh a moril de hambre si seguiamoh así y que iba a tenel que dolmil con hombreh pa' cogel unoh chavoh pa' mantenelnoh. Me dijo, 'Tú ehcóndete y yo voy a buhcal un hombre y yo te vengo a buhcal cuando telmine.' Bueno, noh quedamoh en Corona polque yo salí encinta del cura. Al principio, mi mai pensó que yo debía aboltal, pero dehpuéh cogió miedo . . . que me iba a pasal algo, así que no lo hicimoh. Ella siguió de prohtituta y encontramoh una casucha abandoná' celca de la playa, que la había tumba'o un huracán y allí vivimoh hahta qu'ella murió." *Ma say she don't have more money and we going to starve if we go on, so she have to sleep with men to support us. She say, 'You hide and I go find a man and I find you when I'm done.' So we stay in Corona because I get pregnant from the priest. At first ma think I should abort, but then she get scared, she think something happen to me, so we don't do it. She keep being a prostitute and we find an old shack by the beach that a hurricane knock down and we live there until she die.*

"Bueno, tuve el muchacho pero se murió. Nació ya enfelmo y como no comíamoh bien yo no tenía casi leche. Le dió una infección en el oído y se le fué a la cabeza . . . cogió una fiebre altísima.

La curandera no pu'o hacel na'. Ya el muchachito tenía unoh meseh. Yo me había acohtumbra'o a él . . . me conocía y to'. Cuando se murió yo me quería moril también. Yo lo que tenía eran doce añoh." *Well, I have the child but he die. He's born sick and I don't have much milk because we don't eat right. He get an infection in the ear and it go into his head . . . get a high fever too. The curandera can do nothing. The boy live for a few months. I get used to him . . . he know me and everything. When he die I want to die too. I am only twelve then.*

"Cuando mi mai to'avía vivía había empeza'o a buhcal yelbah pa' la curandera, que tenía máh de cien añoh y ya no podía caminal. Ella le hacía curah a mi mai y mi mai y yo le buhcabamoh yelbah. Dehpuéh yo empezé a ayudal a la curandera también y ella me enseñó to' lo que sabía. Era comadrona también. Dehpuéh de un tiempito yo empezé a haceleh remedioh a mi mai y a otra gente y me daban cosah cuando curaba a alguien. Cosah de comel, o ropa, o café . . . y yo se lo daba to' a mi mai. Yo le decía que yo podía trabajal ahora y ella no tenía que il a dolmil con loh hombreh. Así poco a poco dejó eso, pero ya su salu' ehtaba bien mala. Había cogi'o muchah infeccioneh. Así que un día se me murió . . . . Dehpuéh que la enterré detráh de la casa yo nunca volví allá. D'eso hace muchoh añoh, niña . . . me dijeron que la casa la tumbó un huracán de nuevo pero esa veh no quedó na'. Yo nunca volví a vivil en una casa dehpuéh que mi mai murió." *When ma is still living she begin to look for herbs for the curandera. That curandera is over a hundred years old and can't walk anymore. She make remedies for ma, and my ma and me find herbs for her. Afterwards I begin to help the curandera too and she teach me everything she know. She's a midwife too. After a while I start making remedies for ma and for other people too and they give me things when I fix somebody. Things to eat, clothes, or coffee . . . and I give everything to ma. I tell her I can work now and she don't have to sleep with men anymore. Little by little she stop it, but her health is real bad, she get too many infections. So one day she die . . . . After I bury her behind the house I don't ever go back there. That's many years ago, child . . . someone tell me the house get knocked down by a hurricane again but that time there's nothing left. I never live in a house again after ma die.*

Pilar cried quietly. Seña Alba sat Pilar on her lap and rocked her like a child.

Seña Alba smelled of herbs, coconuts, sand, the fabric of her life. Not what Pilar thought about, or saw, but the unspoken, what she reached for in the night when she was alone and despairing. The earliest silent presence of something that could be believed in. That didn't betray.

Images came and went. Like explosions of light and darkness. And in the midst of that a calmness rose that felt like love. Something warm and vast. Into that love everything could fall and not be lost: the sound of a horse, dust on a country road, an open door to the sea, angry words.

Here was something deeper. A gift found in the struggle to understand. Here was forgiveness, as if wings carried her above the waves. Here was something inside she could yield to, something true in herself she had forgotten.

She would need a lifetime to find that moment and lose it. Find it and lose it.

Pilar wandered through the rooms. Trying to figure out what she would take and what she would leave.

She couldn't do it. She had to go outside.

It was no use. No use. She couldn't take the sea with her. She couldn't take the coconut groves. The matted hills. Her childhood. The black faces. The bare feet, the mud. The green river. The sound of wind. The silence.

And Pilar was afraid of what she would find in the city. She was afraid of being alone. Of not knowing anyone who could teach her how she was supposed to be and what she was supposed to do. And of not having someone to share her fears with. She knew Seña Alba wouldn't come to visit.

She was afraid that she would find people like Juan's family who wouldn't like her because she had black blood and illegitimate children. And she couldn't protect the children from that knowledge anymore. Or from the shame.

"¿Por qué dijo mami que fué un rapto?" *Why did mami say it was a kidnapping?* Pilar heard Meli ask.

"Tú sabeh, en aquelloh tiempoh a veceh pasaba eso . . . que si lah familiah se oponían a loh novioh el hombre se llevaba a la muchacha y dehpuéh loh padreh tenían que darleh permiso para casarse," Pilar answered. *You know, in those days that happened sometimes . . . if the families were against the engagement, the man would take the girl away and then the parents would have to give permission for them to marry.*

"Pero no fué así. Yo me quise ir con él. Pero no le digah nada a tu mamá. Le da vergüenza," Pilar said. *But it wasn't like that. I wanted to go with him. But don't say anything to your mother. She's ashamed of it.*

Pilar could see from Meli's eyes that she was excited about Pilar's secret.

"La noche que me fuí con Juan . . . yo le había mandado un pañuelito que él me había dado para avisarle que me iba a encontrar con él. Se lo mandé con my hermanito." *The night I left with Juan . . . I had sent him a small handkerchief he had given to me to let him know I was going to meet him. I sent it with my little brother.*

Pilar continued. "Seña Alba había venido esa tarde y yo no le quería decir nada. Qué sé yo . . . por miedo de que no me dejara ir . . . ." Pilar was almost whispering. *Seña Alba had come that afternoon and I didn't want to say anything to her. I don't know . . . I guess I was scared that she might not let me go . . . .*

Meli sat closer to Pilar.

"Pero yo creo que ella lo sabía. Esa mujer se daba cuenta de todo . . . . Me dijo que me cuidara, que si yo necesitaba algo ella siempre me podía ayudar. Pero tenía que decidirlo yo mihma y hacerlo sola." *But I think she knew it. That woman noticed everything . . . . She said for me to take care of myself and that if I needed something she would always help me. But I had to decide for myself, and do it alone.*

Pilar knew she had to leave.

The rain came down on the window panes and the branches scraped the side of the house. She heard the wind. Footsteps inside. Pilar felt as if she were looking at the house from a distance. As if she were gone already.

Then she saw Seña Alba coming up the path from the beach. Barefooted. Wet.

She seemed smaller that day. Pilar didn't know why the wind didn't blow her away.

But her steps were steady. She didn't look in one direction or another but seemed to take everything in.

Black like a wet twig.

Pilar came to the kitchen door with a towel. Seña Alba asked for a bowl of water to rinse off her feet. She let Pilar dry them. Just that once.

"¿Quiereh algo de comer?" Pilar asked her. *Do you want something to eat?*

"No, graciah, m'ija." *No thanks, honey.*

Fernanda checked Seña Alba over, out of the corner of her eye, to make sure she didn't track any water on her clean floor.

Pilar's head became heavier and heavier. The pain took up all the space in her belly.

The wind blew hard and the trees sounded as if they were trying to get inside the house.

Pilar felt like crying. Because she was leaving.

She had to tear herself away from everything she had ever known. Her throat filled with tears.

Everything hurt. Everywhere she looked she saw something that she was about to lose.

That was the last time she saw Seña Alba.

"¡Un cuento, Seña Alba! ¡Un cuento, Seña Alba!" *A story, Seña Alba! A story, Seña Alba!*

The children flocked around her. Pilar couldn't put them off today. She was glad she didn't have to tell Seña Alba yet that she was leaving.

Seña Alba squatted in a corner of the dining room and the children sat on the floor around her.

"Había una vez una mujel pol la cohta que podía miralte loh ojoh y decilte to' lo que te había pasa'o y to' lo que te iba pasal . . . ." *Once upon a time there's a woman on the coast that can look in your eyes and tell you everything you done and everything you going to do . . . .*

Could Seña Alba really know what I was thinking by looking into my eyes? I had always wondered.

I let my thoughts return to her as I looked through the window of the plane at the clouds below and the ocean becoming indeterminate at the horizon. What would she say now of my life? Of mami's and abuelita's life? Could she see how I had wanted to escape?

An answer began to form in me as if Seña Alba had curled herself in my heart and her voice were coming through me.

Escape was not enough. I had to return to the island to give something back; to say what lay so deep in me that words had not reached it yet. And to call back to myself what was mine: memory, song, sound, the voice of my mother. My own. The lives that were hidden by fear, locked in rooms, avoiding the street, the public place, ashamed and suffering daily the doubt of having only imagined hurts.

Could I begin now?

I saw the light streaming through the milk glass panels at La Serena, as if at a place of worship; the mango tree witnessing the chiaroscuro of the driveway; the metal gate, guardian to secrets; and the flamboyán crowning the yard in its red glow. Meli's world, where in order to believe the truth of her life she had to make it into a story.

"Abuelita, termina el cuento." *Abuelita, finish the story,* I asked.

Abuelita lay next to me in the dark. I knew I would not be scared if I fell asleep listening to a story.

Abuelita began again, "Esa noche, dehpuéh que todoh se acohtaron ... tú sabeh, yo, imagínate, no pude dormir ... lah muchachah, lah hermanah míah, haciendo cuentoh y papá roncando en el otro cuarto ... y yo muerta del miedo pensando en lo que iba a hacer." *That night after everyone went to bed ... you know, I ... you can imagine, I couldn't go to sleep ... the girls, my sisters, telling stories and papá snoring in the next room ... and me scared to death thinking about what I was going to do.*

"Pensando en qué iba a hacer si no se dormían ... si papá se dehpertaba y me cogía saliendo de la casa .... Si iba a haber una dehgracia si papá se me iba detráh y me encontraba con Juan .... ¡Imagínate!" *I was thinking about what was going to happen if they didn't go to sleep ... if papá woke up and caught me going out of the house .... Or whether there was going to be a tragedy if papá followed me and he found me with Juan ... can you imagine?*

I did. I saw the house on stilts in the middle of the sugar cane field. The rooms without doors. I felt the breeze and heard the sound of the ocean at a distance. It was a very dark night, without a moon.

Everything was very quiet. I saw Pilar getting up. Taking nothing with her. Standing at the doorway for a moment to look back, then walking quietly down the stairs and slipping into the darkness.

At a distance, if I listened very carefully, I could hear a horse galloping.

Seña Alba squatted in the dark in the tall sugar cane, not far from the flamboyán. She saw Juan approaching. Walking his horse. She could hardly make him out because it was a very dark night. He wore black.

He tied his horse to a low branch of the tree and stood leaning against the trunk.

The stars moved. The wind died down.

She knew Pilar was coming.

The horse lifted its head as if to listen. Then Juan moved away from the tree.

A figure appeared suddenly from behind the bushes. It was Pilar. Juan moved towards her and they embraced. Seña Alba felt something tearing inside her.

Juan helped Pilar up on the horse and then climbed on it himself. They disappeared into the night.

Pilar remembered that night, as the time got close for her to leave. Being wrapped in a warm darkness. Flying away. Free again like that day she found Seña Alba at the beach. She had wanted that moment to last forever.

Holding on to Juan as if nothing could ever tear them apart. Not knowing where she was going or what she would find. Trusting herself to the night, to his breathing, to the violent forward movement of this animal carrying them. Trusting the ground to hold them. Leaving behind a small house lost in the sugar cane field. Leaving behind a world.

A long time went by. Was she sleeping? Was she remembering? What time was it? Pilar wondered.

The pain was gone.

"Abuelita ¿qué horas son?" *Abuelita, what time is it?*

Pilar saw Meli there.

She tried to answer, but no words came. Only sounds came out with her breath. Like the ocean inside a cave.

It was time to leave.

She had done it like in a dream. Days and nights had gone. Cartloads of furniture and clothing had been sent to the city. Fernanda would stay behind for a few days to do the final cleaning.

Two carriages had been hired by Aurelio to take them into the city. Fernanda had prepared baskets of food for the trip, which would take all day. She would follow in a couple of days with the last load of furniture.

The sound of surf had kept Pilar awake all night. Washing over her, bringing up images of her life. Finally, at daybreak, she got up and walked alone to the ocean.

There she said goodbye.

"¿Qué horas son?" The sound of my voice woke me from slumber. When I looked out the window I could see, at a great distance, the outline of an island.

My whole body reached out. I felt for a moment as if I were holding abuelita again. Then I heard a sound. A faint humming. Blending, yet distinct from the steady drone of the engine. I thought I heard abuelita call my name: Meli.

Then she was gone.

The plane was frightening the first time. Now I have become used to it.

I feel outside of time. Suspended between sky and sea, between past and future. Between worlds.

For a while this is neutral ground. There are no fights here. No ghosts, no ugliness. This is what I had hoped to find when I left home: a place where things were not deteriorating, or dying.

On my lap there's the photograph I always have near me. Of abuelita smiling. Her house dress hanging loose from her shoulders.

I close my eyes and see us walking together.

"Vamoh cantando bajito y así no te cansah," she said. *Let's go singing softly and you won't get tired.*

On our way home.

1. The word *negra* or *negro* has been translated in this book as "black" when used descriptively, and as "nigger" when used as an insult. When used affectionately, there is no equivalent word in English, so the Spanish word has been retained.

2. Santería is a form of the African religion of Yoruba tribes as practiced in the Caribbean islands.

Born near San Juan, Puerto Rico in 1933, Carmen de Monteflores came to the United States at age sixteen to study art at Wellesley College, where she received a B.A. in 1953. She studied sculpture in Paris and painting in New York City, and continued her work as an artist while living at a cattle ranch in Montana and raising five children. After the family moved to California in the late sixties, Carmen stopped painting, began writing, entered graduate school and came out as a lesbian. In 1978 she completed her Ph.D. in Clinical Psychology and is currently a practicing psychotherapist. She has published a book of poems and has written two plays (one in progress). She lives in Berkeley with her partner, their child, a dog, a cat, two birds and a recently planted apple tree. In this first novel she brings her skills as a poet, playwright and painter to the sensual re-creation of the island of her childhood.

▩spinsters | *aunt lute* ▩

Spinsters/Aunt Lute Book Company was founded in 1986 through the merger of two successful feminist publishing businesses, Aunt Lute Book Company, formerly of Iowa City (founded 1982) and Spinsters Ink of San Francisco (founded 1978). This consolidation of skills and vision has strengthened our ability to produce vital books for diverse women's communities.

We are committed to publishing works outside the scope of mainstream commercial publishers: books that not only name crucial issues in women's lives, but more importantly encourage change and growth; books that help to make the best in our lives more possible.

Though Spinsters/Aunt Lute is a growing, energetic company, there is little margin in publishing to meet overhead and production expenses. We survive only through the generosity of our readers. So, we want to thank those of you who have further supported Spinsters/Aunt Lute— with donations, with subscriber monies, or low interest loans. It is that additional economic support that helps us bring out exciting new books.

Please write to us for information about our unique investment and contribution opportunities.

If you would like to know about other books we produce, write or phone for a free catalogue. You can buy books directly from us. Our efficient fulfillment department welcomes your order and will turn it around quickly. We can also supply you with the name of the bookstore closest to you that stocks our books.

We accept phone orders with Visa or Mastercard.

Spinsters/Aunt Lute
P.O. Box 410687
San Francisco, CA 94141
415-558-9655